Heard it
Through the
Grapevine

Heard it Through the Grapevine

Lizbeth Lipperman

MIDNIGHT INK
WOODBURY, MINNESOTA

First Edition
First Printing, 2013

Book design by Donna Burch
Cover design by Adrienne Zimiga
Cover illustration: Linda Holt-Ayriss/Susan and Co.
Editing by Connie Hill

Midnight Ink, an imprint of Llewellyn Worldwide Ltd.

This is a work of fiction. Names, characters, places, and incidents are either the product of the author's imagination or are used fictitiously, and any resemblance to actual persons (living or dead), business establishments, events, or locales is entirely coincidental.

Library of Congress Cataloging-in-Publication Data

Lipperman, Lizbeth, 1947–
  Heard it through the grapevine / Lizbeth Lipperman. — First edition.
     pages cm — (A dead sister talking mystery ; 1)
  ISBN 978-0-7387-3602-0
1. Sisters—Fiction. 2. Television talk show hosts—Fiction. 3. Murder—Investigation—Fiction. 4. Murder victims—Fiction. 5. Domestic fiction. I. Title.
  PS3612.I645H43 2013
  813'.6—dc23   2012049081

Midnight Ink
Llewellyn Worldwide Ltd.
2143 Wooddale Drive
Woodbury, MN 55125-2989
www.midnightinkbooks.com

Printed in the United States of America

ACKNOWLEDGMENTS

I would be remiss if I didn't mention my other sisters who were the inspiration for this story. We grew up best friends and still are. Take a bow Mary Ann Nedved, Dorothy Bennett, and Lillian Magistro. I love you all so much.

And to my agent extraordinaire, Christine Witthohn, I can only say thank you for your untiring efforts to see this book in print. I could never walk this journey without you.

To Terri Bischoff, my amazing editor, I knew from the first moment I spoke to you in Chicago at the bar that you and I would work well together. Thanks for being so enthusiastic about me and my story. And I have to give kudos to the wonderful people at Midnight Ink who worked behind the scene to make this book a reality. Donna Burch, who did an awesome job designing the book; Adrienne Zimiga who designed the fantastic cover; and Connie Hill who made this book so much better with her editing.

To the Bunko Babes, Tami, Judy, Linda, Marilyn, Nancy, Barbara, Jane, Anna, and Vaneesa—thanks for all the good lines in this book. Keep them coming for book two.

To John Alexander, owner of Colibri Ridge Winery and Vineyard for showing me how a winery is run and for introducing me to Viognier.

And lastly, to Dan and my wonderful kids, Nicole, Dennis, Abby, and Brody. Thanks for my adorable grandchildren, Grayson, Caden, Ellie, and Alice and for giving me a reason to smile every day. I love you.

PROLOGUE

Vineyard, Texas

THE FIRST WAVE OF light-headedness hit like an out-of-control hangover when she leaned forward to put the half-empty glass on the coffee table.

How much wine had she drunk?

Then she smelled it. Struggling to get up, her knees buckled, and she slid to the floor, inhaling the acrid odor that grew stronger with each labored breath.

Trying not to panic, she turned to the front door, but everything was a blur. She had to get out of the house, get some fresh air to clear her head.

She clawed at the carpet, not caring about the forty-dollar nail job from that afternoon.

Damn it! Why can't I catch my breath?

Her eyes caught a flicker of movement at the patio window, but she was too woozy to focus.

Help! She mouthed the words, but her breathing was so rapid, no sound came out. She glanced at the window again. No one was there. Had she imagined it?

Now gasping for air, she dug her nails deeper into the rug and pulled her body inch by agonizing inch across the living room. Panic set in seconds before she heard the light on the end table click on, followed by a thunderous explosion that tossed her like a rag doll into the black of the night.

ONE

Savannah, Georgia

"You're a skeptic, Miss Garcia?"

Lainey Garcia closed her mouth before she said something she'd regret. She'd prided herself on staying neutral no matter who she interviewed. Even when it involved something as ridiculous as Extrasensory Perception.

"I'm trying not to be, Clarisa. You say you see the future, talk to spirits. Personally, I've always believed in scientific evidence. There's no way to prove you didn't have prior knowledge of your earlier predictions that came true." She bit back a sarcastic smile. "Nor have your spirit friends verified any of your information."

Lainey glanced at her producer and rolled her eyes. She had fought Dan tooth and nail when he'd informed her Clarisa Hogan, self-proclaimed psychic and "spirit whisperer," as the media called her, was appearing on the show. But nothing swayed Dan, not even when she'd turned up the heat under the sheets.

Clarisa had been the talk of Savannah for the past three weeks after leading police investigators to the shallow grave of an eight-year-old child who had been abducted and murdered. Getting her on the show was a major coup since she rarely gave interviews.

"Can you prove I had prior knowledge?" Clarisa's eyes flashed in anger, then softened. "I understand your doubts, Lainey, I really do, but even I can't explain it. I just know when a strong feeling hits me."

Strong feeling, my ass! Lainey stole another glance toward Dan.

Suddenly, Clarisa took a sharp breath and fell back in the chair, her eyelids fluttering. The 250 surprised people in the audience sat up and watched.

An eerie silence engulfed the studio when the psychic hummed in a yoga-like monotone. As quickly as Clarisa fell into the trance, she came out of it. She turned to Lainey, her eyes first questioning, then concerned. "Someone is trying to reach you."

The collective gasp of the audience echoed through the room.

"Hopefully, to give me the winning numbers of tonight's Power-ball," Lainey joked, ignoring Clarisa's pointed remark. This voodoo stuff freaked her out, even when it was so obviously staged for effect. The woman was a charlatan who preyed on people's emotions, and it annoyed the hell out of Lainey that she had been chosen as bait.

It was criminal the way this woman scammed a fee out of griev-ing human beings. The same way the guaranteed-to-speak-to-your-loved-one phony had bilked her own mother out of most of her father's life insurance.

The psychic attempted a smile. "There's that skepticism again."

The audience was on the edge of their seats, some even holding their breath waiting for Lainey's response. This made for great television and even better reviews. Dan wanted her to milk it for all it was worth.

"If you can tell me who wants to talk to me and what they want, I might be more inclined to believe you." *Yeah, right!*

Clarisa shook her head, the smile gone. "I don't know. But whoever it is wants to tell you something important."

"I'm sure," Lainey said, more sarcastically than she intended. She felt Dan's disapproving glare.

The flashing lights on the overhead board reminded her to wrap it up. She faced the camera, turning on the charm with a practiced ease. "Unfortunately, we're out of time. I would have loved to continue this conversation with Clarisa Hogan, renowned psychic and author of *Talk Dead to Me*."

Lainey held up the book. "Clarisa will be signing copies of her new book at Franklin's Book Store in downtown Savannah today from one to four. Go out and say hello. In the meantime, from all of us at *Good Morning, Savannah*, I'm Lainey Garcia. Join us tomorrow with Joe Wellington and all his friends from the Savannah Zoo. And you won't want to miss Friday's show when our special guest will be the ever-popular Paula DeMarco, queen of Southern cuisine."

When Dan yelled, *Cut*, Lainey's smile faded. "Thank you, Ms. Hogan. Good luck with your book sales."

The psychic stared at Lainey for a full minute before speaking. "There's usually a good reason when a spirit reaches out."

"I'm sure there is." Lainey turned toward her dressing room, freezing in place when the studio went dark.

Seconds later, the lights flickered on again.

Lainey scanned the room and found Dan next to Clarisa, his eyebrows raised in question. *What in the hell was that?* she mouthed.

As Dan shrugged, Clarisa glanced up and met Lainey's eyes, rubbing her forehead with fingers tipped with fire-engine red polish. The hint of concern on the psychic's face was unmistakable.

Finally behind closed doors in her dressing room, Lainey shivered. She'd never liked scary movies, hated it when Dan watched reruns of the *Twilight Zone*, the "do-do-do-do" ditty playing in the background. It gave her the creeps.

She shook her head to clear the image. Why get so uptight about this? Clarisa Hogan was an imposter. You could predict anything about anybody, and sooner or later, part of it would come true. She knew that. Dan knew that, and it was a given, Clarisa knew it, too.

The lights went out, for godsakes! Happens all the time when it rains.

Lainey glanced out the window of the cramped dressing room. They were in the middle of a Savannah early spring heat wave. A little rain would be a welcome event.

I am not buying into this crap.

She blew out a breath, sat down in front of the mirror, reaching for the cold cream to remove her makeup. The psychic and the blackout were still on her mind when the door flew open and banged against the wall. She jumped, sending the jar clattering to the dressing table.

Dan stormed in and slammed the door behind him. "What were you doing out there, Lainey?"

"You didn't think that was bullshit?"

He moved closer. "That's not the point. It was obvious you were mocking her. You've never done that before, not to anyone during an interview." He paused. "Hell, you didn't even do it to that idiot who claimed he saw aliens in his back yard."

Lainey sighed. "Okay already. I'll send her an apology and something from Flower Boutique."

"That would be the smart thing to do if you expect to get other controversial guests to come on the show." He moved up behind her and massaged her shoulders. "Is everything okay?"

"Why wouldn't it be?" She leaned her head to the right so he could reach the burning spot in her neck, moaning softly when he did.

"I don't know. You tell me. For the past few weeks, you've been acting weird. Even the crew has noticed."

She whirled around and glared. "You're talking to the crew about me?"

Dan's fingers dropped and he met her stare, the concern evident in his eyes. "Relax. Larry mentioned you seemed preoccupied, that's all." He put his hands back on her shoulders and kneaded, moving slowly down to her breasts.

"Oh, yeah, your hands all over my boobs are just what I want the crew talking about after they're done analyzing my moods." She pulled away and turned back to face the mirror, grabbing a tissue to scrub off the cold cream.

She knew that sounded snippy. Dan didn't deserve her sarcasm. Sooner or later she would have to tell him her feelings had changed. That she felt more alone with him than when she was by herself.

And she still hadn't told him about Florida.

"I have been a little tired," she said. "Maybe it's time I took that vacation you're always harping about."

Dan's face brightened. "You're finally talking sense. We could fly to New York. Stay in that hotel across from Central Park and live on room service and—"

"Dan," she whispered.

He grinned, ignoring the interruption. "Maybe this time we can see more of the city than the inside of our hotel room."

Lainey lowered her eyes. "New York's too cold right now. I was thinking more along the lines of Florida."

He looked confused. "Florida? I thought you said your mother and stepdad were in Colorado visiting friends?"

It was now or never. She plunged ahead. "Walk with me to my office. There's something I need to tell you." She stood up and grabbed his arm. This would be harder than she thought.

When the door to her office closed behind them, she pointed to the chair across from her desk. "Sit. You're not going to like this."

Dan lowered his body into the chair, his eyes questioning. "I knew something was bothering you. Even in bed, you've been distracted."

Lainey let the comment slide and walked behind her desk. Instead of sitting, she moved to the window and looked out at the city. Downtown Savannah was beautiful, still small enough to be quaint. She'd miss it.

"Lainey?"

She turned back to Dan and smiled, pacing to collect her thoughts. She had to do this. She'd put it off too long already. "You know as much as I love the show, as much as I love working with you…" She paused and exhaled slowly. There was no way to say it except straight out. She met his gaze. "Henry got a call from the CBS News affiliate in Tampa. They're looking at me for their six o'clock anchor slot."

There was silence while Dan chewed his lower lip. In the two years she'd been intimate with him, she'd come to recognize this as his way of gaining control before he spoke.

"When did your agent get the call?"

She sat down at her desk. "Two weeks ago."

Surprise, then anger flashed in his eyes. "Jesus, Lainey! When were you going to tell me?"

"I was waiting for the right moment."

"And all those nights I was at your house? In your bed? Not the right moment?"

She lifted her chin, meeting his anger head on. "It's a decision I had to make on my own. I needed time to think it through. It's not like we're married or anything."

His face registered the hurt. "For the record, it's not because I haven't asked. You always manage to hedge. Maybe I should have listened to what you weren't saying."

"I'm sorry. I wanted to tell you sooner." She walked around the desk and stood in front of him.

How could she explain the emptiness she felt without making him feel guilty? Dan Maguire was an extraordinary man. She'd be damn lucky to have him at her side for the rest of her life. But something was missing. She couldn't explain it, but she knew they would both be miserable in the end because of what she didn't feel.

"When are you leaving?"

The sadness in his voice squeezed her heart. "The interview is this Friday. Henry and I are going down on Thursday after the show. I'm scheduled to interview all day, then we're booked on the seven o'clock home." She paused when the cell phone vibrated in her pocket. Pulling it out, she glanced at caller ID.

"Sorry. I have to take this." She flipped the receiver, grateful for the interruption. "Hey, Maddy. What's up?"

"Tessa's dead." Maddy's voice cracked, and she began to cry. "Oh, Lainey! Tessa's really dead."

"Ohmygod! How?" Lainey backed into the desk for support.

Dark brows furrowed, Dan leaned closer.

When Maddy's sobs slowed, she continued. "There was an explosion at her house last night. A gas leak or something. They found her body in the front yard and called me after midnight with the news. I waited until this morning to call you." Maddy's voice broke. "They're doing an autopsy and should be finished sometime today. The viewing is from six to eight tomorrow night, and the funeral is Friday."

Lainey swallowed the lump in her throat. "You know I can't come, Maddy."

"Your sister's dead, Lainey. You can and you will."

Lainey sighed, running her fingers through her hair. Madelyn rarely played the older sister card, but when she did, there was no use arguing. "I'll call with the flight information," she said, resigned.

"Do you want someone to pick you up at DFW?"

"No," Lainey answered quickly. "It's easier to rent a car." Safer, she should have said. She could split whenever she wanted. Whenever she had to. "I'll call later."

A rush of emotions pulsed through Lainey's body as she held the receiver long after Madelyn had disconnected. She kept her back to Dan, unwilling to let him see the tears flowing unchecked down her cheeks.

Her sister was dead. Why did she suddenly feel as if someone had plunged a knife into her heart? When she left Texas years ago, she'd vowed never to return. As far as she was concerned, Tessa had been dead since then.

She felt Dan's hand on her shoulder, unaware he had gotten up and now stood beside her.

"What's the matter, honey?" His voice was soft, worried, the anger gone.

Lainey took a deep breath and swiped at the tears, hoping he wouldn't notice.

He touched her cheek and turned her to face him. "In the four years I've known you, I don't think I've ever seen you cry. What is it?"

She bit her lip, shaking her head. How could she explain her broken relationship with Tessa? He didn't even know she existed. She'd told him she only had three sisters.

He pulled her to him, his hands moving up and down her back, as if comforting a child. "Lainey, honey, tell me."

She wanted to stay in the warmth of his arms longer, but she forced herself to draw back and meet his eyes. "My sister was killed in an explosion last night."

"Oh, no!" He drew her closer to his body. "Which one?"

"Tessa."

She held her breath as she felt his body stiffen.

"Tessa?"

Hearing her name brought a fresh stream of tears. "She was two years older than me. We hated each other growing up. When I left Texas, I cut all ties with her. I haven't seen or spoken to her in nine years." Lainey's voice caught.

"Why didn't you tell me about her?"

She heard the sadness in his voice. She'd been sleeping with him all this time and hadn't mentioned something as personal as a long-lost sister. He must be wondering what else she'd kept from him.

"Is that why you've never gone back to Texas? Why you meet your sisters in Florida at your mom's?"

"Yes." Lainey was numb, like somehow Tessa's death was her fault.

That was absurd! How could she be responsible for an explosion?

She pulled from his embrace and pushed the intercom. "Shelly, can you book me a flight to Dallas tonight, please?" An inner voice screamed that was too soon. "No, make that tomorrow."

"Sure, Lainey," the receptionist replied. "Any specific time?"

Lainey glanced at her watch, realizing how ridiculous that was. "Mid-afternoon. Let me know when you get that confirmed. Thanks, Shel."

She stroked her forehead like she was rubbing away a migraine, still fighting her emotions. "Can you get Angie to do the show for the next two days, Dan?" She glanced at the calendar on her desk. "Dammit! I really wanted to interview Paula DeMarco."

The minute the words left her mouth, she realized how cold they sounded. A quick glance at Dan confirmed he agreed.

"I'm sure there'll be another opportunity," he said, barely able to conceal the disapproval in his voice. "Do you want me to go to Dallas with you?" he asked, softening.

She couldn't meet his eyes, knowing she was about to hurt him again, knowing he wanted her to say yes. "I'll be fine." She saw the disappointment on his face. "The funeral's Friday morning. I'll be on a flight to Savannah by dinner. No sense in both of us missing Paula."

Vineyard, Texas

Lainey shifted uncomfortably on the couch in the far right corner of the funeral parlor. She scanned the crowded room while her aunt droned on about the changes in Vineyard since she'd left. Tessa's popularity hadn't diminished one bit over the years. All her life people had gravitated to her. It baffled Lainey, especially since Tessa was rarely nice to anyone unless she wanted something.

"Have you seen her?"

Lainey glanced up at her sister Kate and smiled. "No."

She and Kate had grown up best friends. Despite their busy schedules, they still were. With Kate working ungodly hours at the hospital, it had been way too long since they'd had one of their two-hour phone conversations.

Kate had shown up an hour after Lainey settled in at the DFW Conquistador, and it was like all the years apart had never happened. Two years younger, Kate was an obstetrics resident at County General, the biggest teaching hospital in Dallas, and had little time for anything else.

"Come on. I'll walk up with you."

Lainey shook her head. "You go."

Kate leaned down. "Can't you forgive her even now?" she asked, her voice barely a whisper.

"I'm trying, but just because she went and died, it doesn't mean the slate is wiped clean."

"I'm not thinking about Tessa, Lainey. You'll never forgive yourself if you don't deal with this before it's too late."

"I'd say it's already too late."

Kate reached for Lainey's hand and pulled her up from the couch. "I'll be right beside you. It won't be as bad as you think. Promise."

Lainey knew her younger sister was right. It was too late to heal the relationship, not that she wanted to, but she had to say good-bye. No matter what Tessa had done, she was family. When she'd left Vineyard for good, Lainey swore she would never cry again, but she'd been unable to stop the tears when Maddy called. She had to get closure.

As the two sisters drew closer to the casket, the mounting volcano in Lainey's gut threatened to explode. She exhaled slowly and prayed for strength, all the while cursing the scent of the damn gladiolas with their crosses and bright-colored ribbons. She wanted nothing to do with this kind of circus when she died.

Close enough to see Tessa's face, Lainey gasped, raising her hand to her mouth to stifle the cry. Tessa was as beautiful as she remembered. She exhaled slowly, praying she'd get through this as Kate squeezed her arm in support.

After a few seconds, the initial shock wore off, and Lainey leaned in to study Tessa's face, noticing the bruising despite the thick makeup. Up this close, she saw the fine lines around her mouth and eyes, the only visible sign her sister had aged. Gone were her famous long black curls that had boys from three counties flocking to their house on weekends, replaced by a short, stylish bob. She wondered how long ago Tessa had cut off those curls.

I hate this whole fucking funeral thing.

Lainey turned to Kate, surprised at her outburst. "I was just thinking the same thing."

Kate stared at her, a puzzled look covering her face. "What did you say?"

You know, for being the smart one, Lainey, sometimes you act like you're not the sharpest knife in the drawer.

Lainey opened her mouth to respond, confused. Kate's mouth hadn't moved when she spoke.

Most of these idiots only showed up to make an appearance.

Lainey glanced again at Kate, but she had already turned away and was reading the condolence notes on the flower arrangements. Lainey shook her head to clear her mind then felt a light tap on her shoulder. Turning to her left, she looked directly into the eyes of her dead sister.

Hello, Lainey. Long time no see.

TWO

When Lainey's scream pierced the low-keyed chatter in the room, Kate rushed to her, a horrified look on her face.

With tears brimming, Kate grasped her sister's hands in hers and pulled her close. "Lainey, it's okay. Tessa knew you loved her."

That's a big-ass lie. You never took my calls and returned my letters unopened even after I'd divorced him.

Lainey turned in the direction of the voice, then back to Kate. "Can you see her?" she whispered, her lips brushing Kate's ear.

Kate tightened her hold, massaging the back of Lainey's neck. "See who, honey?"

Lainey pulled back far enough to look into Kate's eyes. "Tessa."

A sob escaped the younger woman's lips. "Oh, Lainey, I had no idea bringing you up here would affect you like this. I'm so sorry."

"No," Lainey said, louder than intended, creating an awkward silence as the crowd watched the exchange between the two sisters in front of the coffin. She glanced over her shoulder, her eyes finding Tessa again, now examining her body in the casket.

16

You'd think for what this asshole charges, he could get my hair halfway decent.

Lainey jerked her head toward the body. "Can't you see her?"

Kate sighed. "Of course I can." She smiled through her tears. "They did a great job despite all her injuries."

Lainey leaned closer. "Not *in* the coffin, Kate, *in front* of it." She nodded in the direction where Tessa stood, sporting a half grin, obviously enjoying the unfolding drama.

She can't see me, Lainey. Tessa walked up to Kate and touched her shoulder. *See. You're the only lucky one.* Then she disappeared.

Lainey pulled away from Kate's embrace and did a 180, scanning the room. A hand on the small of her back nudged her toward the sofa in the far corner of the room, and she whirled around, expecting to see the dead woman again. Relief pulsed through her as she realized it was Kate.

"Let's sit for a minute." Kate guided her through the crowd, now staring at them like they each had three heads. "You need a cup of coffee."

Lainey exhaled noisily, searching the room again. Still no sign of Tessa. She shook her head and smiled, cursing her mind for playing tricks on her, convinced it was payback for her behavior with the psychic yesterday. "Trust me. Coffee isn't strong enough."

———

"Your sister was an asset to Vineyard," Joseph Rogers said, munching on a chicken wing. "Throughout my term as mayor, she was generous with her time and money. I wouldn't have been reelected without her support."

Lainey nodded, pretending to care. The funeral service had been filled with testimonials like this about how wonderful Tessa had been. The stories contradicted her own memories of her sister, yet without exception, everyone agreed she'd been a pillar of the community. She couldn't believe Tessa would do anything nice unless there was an ulterior motive.

The church had been standing room only, with local politicians and Chamber of Commerce big wigs all decked out in their Sunday best. Most of them had gathered in her sister Deena's living room after the service, visiting like it was a social event. She didn't get it. The Tessa she knew hadn't earned this kind of sendoff.

It was the first time Lainey had set foot in a Catholic church since she'd left Vineyard. Not that she was a heathen; she had simply slipped away from anything having to do with her past.

"Are you planning to stay long, Elaina?"

"What?" Lainey asked, embarrassed to be caught day-dreaming. "Oh, no. My flight back to Savannah leaves this evening."

"That's too bad," the mayor said between bites of Madelyn's chocolate cake. "You would have enjoyed seeing all the changes we've made with your sister's help."

Lainey's eyes drifted around the room as the mayor rambled on about how he and Tessa had elevated the small town northwest of Dallas to great things. Every other word was Tessa this, Tessa that. If she didn't know better, she'd think the woman had been St. Theresa.

Lainey's gaze rested on Tessa's daughter, Gracie. The child was beautiful, a spitting image of her mother. Her big dark eyes would drive the boys crazy one day, just as Tessa's had done. Only eight, she stood away from the crowd, clinging to her father, even when her Aunt Maddy tried to coax her into eating a piece of cake. The shy gene hadn't come from her mother.

Lainey forced herself to look at Gracie's father, something she'd avoided all afternoon. Colton Winslow was chatting with someone Lainey didn't recognize, his hand moving protectively up and down his daughter's back. Other than a touch of gray at his temples, Colt looked exactly like he did when he was scoring the winning touchdowns at Vineyard High. Exactly as Lainey had pictured in her dreams for so many years after she'd left the small town.

His thick sandy-blond hair still curled at the ends, giving him a just-got-out-of-the-shower appeal. Even from across the room, she could see his eyes crinkling as he laughed at something that was said. Lainey had tried not to keep up with his life, but it hadn't worked. Besides Tessa, Kate was the only one who'd known she'd been in love with Colt since she was fourteen, and she managed to slip in some tidbit of information about him every time they talked.

Lainey knew he'd bought the old Keating ranch on the north side of town when the courts awarded him sole custody of Gracie. Knew he'd worked his way up the ladder on the Vineyard police force and was now the chief. Knew he'd never remarried.

At that moment Colt glanced her way, a slight smile spreading over his face when he caught her looking. A surge of heat crawled up Lainey's neck. Try as she might, she couldn't stop her heart from racing while she watched him from across the room. She smiled back.

With one simple smile, she was transformed into the scrawny teenager with braces who used to peek down the steps whenever he'd shown up at their house with David Rivera, Tessa's boyfriend.

But the star senior running back had no idea Tessa's shy, bookworm sister had a crush so bad, sometimes she thought she would die watching him with her sister's best friend.

Dressed in a navy suit with a light blue shirt and matching tie, he took her breath away, even now. She closed her eyes, picturing him in his uniform, a gun strapped to his hip, and the image nearly sent her over the edge.

Lainey caught her breath when a man she didn't recognize tapped his glass with a spoon, startling her. When the room was quiet, he walked to the corner by the bar.

"For those of you who don't know me, I'm Charles Prescott, Tessa's lawyer. This may seem like an inappropriate time to talk about Tessa's will, but she left me explicit instructions. In the event of her demise, she asked that the entire family be present when I read her last testament on the day of her funeral." He paused to sip from his glass. "Deena has graciously allowed us to use her office. If y'all will follow me there, we can proceed."

When no one reacted, he continued, "Colt, you need to be there." He pointed to Tessa's second ex-husband. "And Jerry, I'll need you and your lovely wife to come, too." He paused to glance around the room. "Where's Carrie? This concerns her as well."

Plastered to the spot, Lainey watched while her family and the others followed the lawyer into Deena's office off the living room. Impatiently, she glanced at her watch. Six hours before her flight. She'd hoped to spend the time catching up with her family. It had been a year since their annual Florida girl trip.

"Come on, Lainey. The faster we get in there, the quicker this will be over," Kate said, appearing at her sister's side and taking her arm. "I'm curious why Tessa wanted us to be there."

Lainey jerked her hand away. "Tessa didn't consider me family. I'm going to sneak out and head back to the hotel to catch a nap. Call when you're finished. Maybe the four of us and Mom can meet for a drink before my flight."

Kate pursed her lips. "You can't leave. The guy wants us all in there." She reached for Lainey's arm again.

"Are you Elaina?"

Both Kate and Lainey turned to face Tessa's lawyer.

"Yes," Lainey said, hesitantly.

"Tessa specifically requested your presence in the room."

"Why?"

He shrugged. "I think it'll be clear after you hear her wishes." He pointed to the study. "Everyone's waiting."

Lainey's pulse raced. Why had Tessa included her? Was her sister going to take one last shot from the grave?

"Come on. It won't take long, I hope," Kate said with a resigned sigh. "Then we'll go in search of something to make your flight to Savannah more relaxing."

Lainey allowed her younger sister to push her toward the crowded office where everyone was already seated on chairs brought in from the other room. Her older sisters, Madelyn and Deena, were on the far side of the room and motioned for them to come over. After Lainey and Kate were seated, there was a brief pause while Prescott shuffled a stack of papers. Lainey used the time to scan the room.

Her mom and stepfather sat in the back of the room with Colt, who looked like he wanted to be here as much as Lainey did. She couldn't help wondering what had gone wrong with his marriage to her sister.

Her eyes darted to the front of the room where Tessa's other ex, Jerry Moretti, and his new wife were sitting in silence, anxiety apparent on their faces. Tall and good-looking in a rough sort of way, Jerry kept glancing at his wife as if they shared a secret. When the woman caught Lainey staring, she wrapped her arm protectively through Jerry's.

Lainey remembered Jerry from high school. He'd been the rich kid driving a T-Bird convertible, always with a girl huddled next to him. Since Tessa only went for jocks, she hadn't given Jerry the time of day, although it was obvious he had the hots for her. Apparently, after she and Colt divorced, her tastes changed when she found out Jerry had inherited the family winery.

Lainey focused on Jerry's new wife, Roxy, with her big blond hair and enough makeup to keep the cosmetic companies profitable. Roxy's micro-mini skirt showed off long tanned legs, and the tight sweater left no doubt her oversized girls were store-bought. Kate had mentioned the latest Mrs. Moretti was an actress who had done a few X-rated movies before marrying Jerry less than a month after his divorce from Tessa was finalized.

Lainey smiled, wishing she had been there when Jerry brought his porn star wife to Vineyard, expecting the small community nestled in the middle of the Bible Belt to embrace her in their social circles. At least Roxy had enough sense to know if you're going to wear slutty clothes to a funeral, they should be black.

As the lawyer began reading Tessa's will, Lainey's eyes moved from Roxy to Carrie Phillips, Tessa's best friend since high school. Carrie, Tessa's personal assistant for the past few years, sat off to the side, occasionally dabbing at her eyes while the boring legal document was read.

Lainey stole a peek at her wrist again, wishing she was anyplace but here. She was anxious to get back to Savannah and get on with her life. She was more than a little excited about the interview in Florida that had been rescheduled for the following week and she needed time to prepare. Henry said it looked promising, but even if that fell through, she had a few major decisions to make. It was time to go after her dreams, to get out from under the security blanket Dan's love had provided for the past few years. It was time to move on. Dan deserved that much, and so did she.

Look at that gold digger up there next to Jerry with her fake tits. Bet she's thinking about how rich she'll be now that I'm dead and gone. Someone needs to tell her whatever look she was going for, she missed.

Lainey gasped and everyone in the room turned to her.

Go ahead, tell them. They'll think you're nuts. They might even have Doctor Kate here give you a sedative. Tessa frowned. *I could use one of those myself right about now.*

Lainey coughed, knowing there wasn't a person in the room who would believe her if she told them Tessa was talking to her. Not even Kate, who knew her better than any of them. Whatever was happening in her mind was best kept secret. The last thing she wanted was to become the latest gossip tidbit in Vineyard.

She envisioned the headlines. *Batty sister talks to ghost.*

She closed her eyes, wishing away the image of her sister now standing beside her chair. When she reopened them, Tessa was still there, but the smile was gone.

Seriously, Lainey, I'm not going anywhere soon. Get used to it. Tessa glanced at the lawyer. *Listen up. Chuck's just getting to the good part.*

23

Lainey turned her attention to the front of the room.

Wait for it, Tessa prompted.

"I bequeath to Elaina Nicole Garcia a share, not to exceed fifty percent, of my interest in Spirits of Texas, provided she maintains and oversees its daily operations, and with the stipulation that when my daughter, Graciella Elaina Winslow, reaches twenty-one years of age, Elaina Nicole Garcia will transfer forty percent of the company to Graciella Elaina Winslow, with Elaina Nicole Garcia retaining the final ten percent. In the event Elaina Nicole Garcia is unable to make the transfer to Graciella Elaina Winslow, my interest in Spirits of Texas will transfer to Jerald Michael Moretti as provided in the bylaws of the company, with a one-time payout to Graciella Elaina Winslow of half the current appraised value."

"That's bullshit," Jerry shouted, jumping from his chair and turning toward Lainey. "There's no way I'll let you run my winery. I'll see you in court first." His face was red enough to explode.

"Sit down, Jerry," Colt commanded from the back of the room. "This is Charlie's show. Anything you have to say will have to wait."

Jerry stood unmoving for a good two minutes, glaring at Lainey until he finally sat down.

"Continue, Charlie," Colt said, walking toward the door. "I have to take this call."

"Basically, that's it. Tessa left her house and personal effects to her mother and her other three sisters. Although the house is destroyed, the reimbursement money from the insurance company will be divided equally four ways. She left her prized Jaguar to you, Carrie." Prescott paused before gathering the papers into a stack.

Kate poked her sister's arm. "Say something. Everyone's staring."

"There's no way," Lainey managed to whisper despite her shock. She glanced first at Tessa, now sitting in the chair beside her, then back to Kate.

"That's the first thing I've heard today that makes sense," Jerry bellowed from the front of the room. "I have no idea what Tessa was trying to pull, but believe you me, I'm not about to get screwed by that woman a second time."

In your dreams, big boy. Tessa turned to Lainey, a mischievous grin crinkling her eyes. *Eight thousand nerve endings in the clitoris, and that idiot couldn't find a single one with a flashlight and a road map.*

Lainey coughed to cover up the laugh. How bad was this? She was actually laughing at something a ghost had said. They'd lock her up in a New York minute if they knew.

When she found her voice, she stood. "It seems my sister wasn't thinking clearly when she drafted this will."

Yes, I was. It's probably the smartest thing I've ever done in my life.

Lainey ignored the voice in her head. "Regretfully, I must decline. I have a life in Georgia and have neither the desire nor the expertise to run a winery."

Look at him, Lainey, Tessa said, pointing to Jerry. *See that shitty grin on his face? He's already thinking about how he'll bribe somebody to appraise the company for a fraction of what it's worth. Hell, this year alone, sales increased over thirty percent, but he'll find a way to hide that. Gracie will lose most of her inheritance.*

"I can't," Lainey said aloud.

The door opened and Colt walked through, his expression dark with unreadable emotion. "That was the coroner," he said, his eyes darting around the room. "Tessa didn't die in the explosion. Someone poisoned her."

THREE

COLT SURVEYED THE ROOM after his announcement, searching for anything out of the ordinary. He relied on his police instincts to pick up on a look, a gesture, an emotional outburst. Even a lack of reaction spoke volumes in a homicide investigation.

According to the medical examiner, despite the fact Tessa's injuries from the blast were enough to kill her, his ex-wife was dead before her body landed beside the tree in her front yard. There was no doubt she had been murdered.

Unable to stop the rush of emotions, he lowered his eyes. Although they'd been divorced for over seven years, he still loved her in his own way. A wave of helplessness washed over him as memories of his own father popped into his mind. He hadn't been able to protect him, either, but at least he'd found the man responsible for his death.

"Who'd want to kill her, Colt?" Sylvia Garcia Lopez asked as she approached, her eyes filled with sorrow. "Who'd want to kill Tessa?"

Taking his ex-mother-in-law in his arms, Colt kissed the top of her head, massaging her back in a soothing circle when her tears escalated to sobs.

Sylvia's daughters rushed to her side, visibly fighting their own tears as they comforted their mother. It was one thing to think Tessa was killed in a freak accident, but to find out her death was deliberate was a whole different ballgame.

Madelyn gently pulled her mother from Colt's arms and led her to a nearby chair. Colt used the time to study the Garcia family. He'd always been crazy about them, especially the two oldest sisters who still treated him like part of the family. He'd even hired Madelyn to man the phones at the station after her husband died several years earlier. He barely knew Lainey, remembering her only as a teenager.

He stole a glance her way, wondering what could have torn the two sisters apart, especially since the others were so close. Although Tessa never talked much about the relationship, she'd always said Lainey was the smart one of the bunch, that one day she would be the next Barbara Walters.

Lainey sat beside her sisters bonding with their mother, but she looked disconnected, like she wasn't really part of the family dynamics. One thing was for sure, she'd grown up since the last time he'd seen her. No longer the skinny kid with her nose constantly in a book—her curves were evident despite the bulky sweater she wore over the black dress. The long, jet-black hair she'd worn in a ponytail now fell to her shoulders, highlighting her matching eyes. Of all the sisters, Lainey looked the most like Tessa. Maybe that's why they'd fought so much.

"Colt, Tessa really was poisoned?"

He turned sharply to see Lainey approach. He'd been so deep into his reverie, he hadn't noticed her getting up from the chair and walking toward him. "We won't know for sure until the tox screen comes back, but Tommy's fairly certain it was cyanide."

"Tommy?"

"The Medical Examiner. You remember Tommy Arrington, don't you? His parents owned the skating rink."

Lainey squinted in deep thought. "Janet's older brother?"

"Yeah. He runs the show at the morgue now. Janet sold the rink to some rich guy from Chicago and moved to California about five years ago. I haven't seen her since."

Lainey stepped close enough for him to catch a faint whiff of her perfume. "You said cyanide? Isn't that what they found in the Tylenol capsules back when all those people died in Chicago?"

"Yeah."

"My God! How is it possible to get cyanide? I thought they banned it."

"Unfortunately, anyone can order it off the Internet, no questions asked."

She lowered her head for a moment before meeting his eyes straight on. "Why does Tommy think it was cyanide?"

He debated whether she could handle the gory details, then decided she had a right to know. Lowering his voice so the others couldn't hear, he recited what the ME had told him just a few minutes earlier. "Cyanide leaves a very distinct almond odor. Fortunately, Tessa was thrown clear and didn't burn in the fire. Tommy noticed the smell right off." He paused to make sure he hadn't confused her. "Plus, her blood was cherry red, another indicator. Preliminary tissue samples showed the presence of some kind of poison, but only the tox screen can prove it was cyanide."

She gulped hard, her eyes bordered with tears. He cursed himself for thinking she could handle this. Tessa was her sister, for godsakes.

He caught an escaping tear and tilted her chin. "Death by cyanide is quick, Lainey. She probably never even knew she was dying." He watched her swallow hard, biting back more tears.

"Who would want Tessa dead, Colt?"

He looked away. He wasn't about to tell her half the people in the room qualified. Tessa hadn't been the easiest person to live with.

"I don't know, but I promise, I'll find out." Colt hoped his eyes didn't betray him. Of all the people in the room, he probably had the strongest motive to kill his ex-wife.

———

Lainey helped her sisters clean up after everyone finally went home, making small talk as they bagged and labeled the leftovers. Tessa's death was carefully avoided, the cause of death too horrific to consider.

She'd rebooked her flight to Savannah on Monday night after Colt suggested she stay around long enough to answer questions about Tessa. The look on Jerry Moretti's face when she'd agreed had been priceless. It was obvious the sooner he got her out of town, the better he would like it. Maybe Tessa was right on about him screwing Gracie out of her inheritance. She made a mental note to have a conversation with the probate lawyer before she left to make sure that didn't happen.

"Let's go into the living room," Deena said when the last of the dishes was loaded in the dishwasher. "There's a fresh pot of coffee."

"Please tell me you have something stronger," Madelyn wailed.

For the first time since everyone left, Deena smiled. "Why didn't I think of that? I might still have a tub of Cool Whip left over from my book club luncheon last week." She opened the refrigerator and pulled out the container. "If there is a God, it won't have green stuff on it."

"Ew!" Kate cried, scrunching her face. "If you only knew how much that reminds me of gangrene."

"Thanks for sharing." Deena laughed, pointing to the overhead cabinet. "Lainey, you're the tallest. Can you reach the Kahlua?"

Lainey pushed a chair against the counter. "I can now." She stepped on the chair and stretched to reach the nearly-full bottle. "The Garcia girls have definitely earned a shot or two of this with our coffee." She giggled as she jumped down.

You always were a sissy drinker.

Lainey jerked her head around, knocking her body off-balance and falling back into the chair, nearly breaking the bottle. Tessa stood next to the sink, shaking her head.

I forgot how klutzy you were.

"Lainey, what's wrong?" Deena asked, rushing to her side.

Lainey ignored her sister's question and took a step toward the sink, toward Tessa. "Can any of them see you?"

Kate gasped. "Oh, Lainey, not again."

"What?" Madelyn demanded.

"She thinks she can see Tessa."

Deena turned sharply to face Kate. "What do you mean, see Tessa?"

"See her, like in the flesh. Like not dead anymore," Kate replied, her voice dripping with sadness.

"Oh, God, Lainey, you really do need this alcohol," Maddy said, moving up behind her. "I had no idea forcing you to come back to Vineyard would get to you like this." She tugged at Lainey's sleeve. "Come on, let's make one last toast to Tessa, and thank the Lord we still have each other."

Lainey looked past her sisters to the sink. "Why are you here?" She felt Maddy's arm tighten on her own.

Your guess is as good as mine.

Lainey whirled around to face her sisters. "Did you hear her?" The look in their eyes told her not only had they not heard Tessa, but they were convinced she was losing it. Kate began to weep, and Deena's mouth hung open. She didn't have to look any farther than Madelyn's eyes to see the horror.

Madelyn reacted first, pushing Lainey toward the living room. "Oh, honey, this has been a really bad day for you. Come on. Let's get wasted and put it behind us."

Lainey wanted to do just that, but she couldn't. She pressed her hand against the door frame, effectively stopping the march into the other room. "No, Maddy, I have to deal with this."

She turned back to the sink to see if Tessa was still there. She was. She heard Kate's sobs, but couldn't stop. "Who killed you?"

Tessa shrugged. *Not a clue.*

"Why am I the only one who can see you?"

Don't know that, either.

Lainey spun around to her three sisters and saw the fear covering their faces. They thought she was delusional. She turned back to Tessa. "You have to let them know you're here. I can't deal with this by myself."

Tessa shook her head. *It doesn't work that way.*

"Dammit, Tessa, even dead, you're still a pain in the ass."

Tessa smiled. *Don't you think if I had a choice about this, I'd be talking to Madelyn instead of you? She never passed judgment on me the way you did.*

"Passed judgment?" Lainey screamed. "Let me tell you something, Tessa. I idolized you growing up. You with your dynamite looks, your unbelievable popularity at school. I wanted to be like you so much, I sometimes cried at night because I wasn't."

"Stop it, Lainey," Kate screamed. "I can't bear to watch you do this." She rushed to Lainey's side and enveloped her in her arms.

Ask her about the day she came to me to borrow money for her last year in medical school.

Lainey pushed Kate away from her and met her eyes, now slightly red and swollen. "Tessa wants me to ask you about the day you borrowed money from her."

Kate gasped. "Nobody knows about that."

Ask Deena about the time I had a talk with the nursing home administrator when the Director of Nurses was on her case about every little thing.

She faced her second oldest sister. "What about when Tessa intervened with the head honcho at the nursing home when your boss was giving you grief?"

Deena had the same reaction as Kate.

Now ask Maddy about her cancer scare a few years back.

"Maddy?" Lainey released Kate and walked toward her oldest sister. "Why didn't you tell anyone you thought you had cancer?"

"Oh, God!" Maddy groaned.

"You thought you had cancer and didn't tell me?" Deena's voice jumped an octave.

"I didn't tell anyone. I wanted to wait until we were sure. The breast biopsy came back as a fibrocystic growth."

"Why did you tell Tessa and not me?" The hurt was evident in Deena's eyes. She and Maddy had been best friends since childhood just as Lainey and Kate had been.

"I didn't tell her. I ran into her at the hospital the morning of the biopsy. Just my luck, Jerry was getting his knee scoped the same day." She moved closer to Deena. "You know I can't lie. When she asked why I was there so early, I gave it up. She promised not to ever tell anyone." Maddy paused, shaking her head. "Apparently, she lied."

"You really are talking to her!" Kate exclaimed. "Where is she?"

"By the sink."

All three sisters turned in that direction.

Happy now?

"Can she hear us?" Deena asked, cautiously leaning her head closer to the sink.

"Yes."

"Can we talk to her?"

"Yes. Obviously, you can't hear her responses, though."

An awkward silence followed as the women edged closer. Lainey knew they wanted desperately to believe there was a reason—other than the obvious one—how she knew their secrets.

Maddy inched slowly in the direction of the sink. "Here?"

She poked her finger in the air.

Tessa smiled. *As much as I love Maddy, she was never the rocket scientist of this family.*

"No, Maddy, over there." Lainey pointed to the end of the sink by the dishwasher.

Maddy's eyes squinted, and she huffed. "Okay, hot shot, if it's really you, tell your sister about the time I hauled your drunken ass out of that bar in Dallas when that irate woman caught you making out with her fiancé and was ready to skin you alive."

Deena threw her hands in the air. "How many more things have you kept from me, Maddy?"

Maddy turned. "She made me swear not to tell. Didn't want the uppity ups in Vineyard to hear about it."

Obviously, Maddy sucks at keeping secrets. Tessa pursed her lips. *Tell her it was Jason Martin's latest floozy.*

"Who's Jason Martin?" Lainey asked.

Maddy's eyes widened. "Oh my God! It's really her."

Bingo!

"Is she okay?" Deena asked, a slow tear making its way down her cheek.

No, Deena, I'm freakin' dead.

Lainey smiled. "She looks good."

"Why is she here?" Maddy asked.

"Why don't you ask her yourself?"

"Me?" Maddy gulped. "You ask her. You're the one she talks to."

Lainey crossed the room stopping directly in front of her dead sister. "What do you want from us?"

Tessa lowered her eyes momentarily before meeting Lainey's stare. *Find my killer.*

FOUR

"WHAT DID SHE SAY?" Kate asked before she sprinted to her sister's side. "You're as pale as a ghost, Lainey." She slapped her hand to her mouth and giggled. "Sorry, Tessa."

And that's so damn funny, why?

Lainey bit her lower lip to hide her amusement. At least now she wasn't the only one who talked to dead people. "She wants us to find her killer."

"What?" Maddy put both hands on her hips. "How the hell does she expect us to do that? I answer phones at the police station for a living, Deena runs the bingo game at the nursing home, Kate delivers babies, and you look pretty for the cameras. Not great resumes for finding a killer."

"I beg your pardon, Madelyn. I do more than run bingo at the nursing home. I'm the activities director, for godsakes." Deena huffed. "You can be such an ass sometimes."

"That's for sure," Kate chimed in. "I can't believe you think I went to school all those years just so I could deliver babies." She frowned at her older sister. "And Lainey worked hard to land that position looking pretty in front of the cameras." She clamped her hand over her mouth a second time. "Oh, sorry, Lainey. That didn't come out the way it was supposed to."

Can we cut the crap and get on with finding the son-of-a-bitch who poisoned me?

"Tessa's right for once," Lainey said, shaking her head. Hard to believe she actually agreed with her sister.

"What do you mean she's right?" Deena asked.

Lainey shrugged. "Forgot you can't hear her. She said to cut the chatter and find out who killed her."

Not exactly what I said, Lainey, but close enough.

All three sisters turned to the sink.

"She doesn't know?" Deena finally asked, verbalizing the question on everyone's face.

Lainey raised her brow. "Doesn't have a clue."

"She's a ghost," Madelyn shouted. "Aren't they supposed to know everything? Walk through walls?"

The others nodded.

For Christ's sake, Maddy. I'm not fucking Casper.

"So now what'd she say?" Deena asked when Lainey snorted.

"She has no idea who killed her. As for walking through walls, I don't think so."

Again, not exactly what I said. Tessa shook her head. *I'm beginning to get why you were chosen by the powers that be as the lucky sister I talk to.*

Lainey stepped closer to the sink. "Can you help us at all, Tessa?"

Tessa licked her lips. *I would if I could, but I have no idea how someone managed to poison me.*

"Think." Lainey moved closer until she stood directly in front of her dead sister. The others leaned in. "Colt said cyanide works fast. It had to have been something you breathed or ate right before you died."

Hmm. I'd just had this huge argument with Jerry, and he'd stormed out of the house.

"About what?"

About Quinton Porter.

"Who?" Lainey asked as the other sisters leaned closer.

Just some asshole who wants to buy the vineyard and turn it into a bloody oil field.

"What's she saying?" Kate asked, moving so close behind that Lainey caught a whiff of her day-old perfume.

"Shh," Lainey commanded before nodding to Tessa. "Go on."

I ordered take-out from that new Chinese place off the freeway by Target, but by the time it arrived, I wasn't feeling very hungry. I only picked at it.

"According to Colt, it only takes a little," Lainey said, mostly to herself. She glanced up at Tessa. "Anybody you know work at the restaurant?"

Not that I know of. Tessa pursed her lips. *Besides, who'd want to kill me? Everybody loved me.*

Lainey laughed out loud, and before long, even Tessa was grinning.

Okay, maybe not everyone, but who hated me enough to do this?

"You tell me." Lainey put her finger to her lips to silence Maddy who had joined Kate behind her and was now whispering something in her ear.

Tessa put her hand on her forehead and sighed. *If I was being honest, I'd have to say there are probably a lot of people I've run off over the years.*

"Ya think?"

For the record, Lainey, I never meant to hurt you.

"That's bullshit, and you know it. You deliberately went after Colt to spite me."

"Jeez, Lainey! Now's not the time to bring that up," Kate scolded. "Find out what she ate that night."

"Chinese food," Lainey replied, glad for the detour from memory lane. "Apparently, there's a new place in town, and she had it delivered."

"That's it," Deena shouted. "Carolyn Winters' son is the delivery boy for East Meets West." She stepped closer to the sink, visibly excited. "Remember how outraged Carolyn was when she found out you slept with her husband who, by the way, is a jackass. It nearly broke up their marriage, not that I can figure out why she stayed married to that jerk after that."

"You slept with a married man?" Lainey asked, incredulous that anything Tessa did surprised her.

I did no such thing. Tessa's eyes turned defiant before she frowned. *Okay, maybe once. But his son Joey was only nine or ten at the time. Besides, Carolyn stayed married to him for another year or two after that.*

"Yeah, but she never forgave you, even after the jerk left her for a girl not much older than Joey. She still calls you the Whore of Vineyard," Kate commented after Lainey repeated Tessa's words.

"A married man, Tessa?" Lainey scolded. "Even for you, that's a new low."

What can I say? I've always been a sucker for a guy who could do the Electric Slide better than me.

Lainey crossed the room to the built-in desk in Maddy's kitchen, shaking her head. She searched until she came up with a notebook and pencil, then walked back to the sink. "Okay, enough about how easy you were. What about Joey? How old is he now?"

Both Deena and Kate answered. "Sixteen."

"He's pretty screwed up, from what I hear," Maddy added. "I've seen him down at the police station several times. He's never been charged with anything except criminal mischief. He set old man DeLuca's garbage on fire the night before Halloween, and it got out of hand. Burned down that old shed in the back yard."

"So he's got a record." Deena shook her head. "I knew that kid was a bad seed."

"Actually, he doesn't. The charges were dropped when his mother paid off DeLuca. The gossip hot line reported she took casseroles to his house every day for a week after," Maddy said.

Rumor has it she offered the old fart super sex, and he said, "just soup, please." Tessa slapped her thigh and doubled over with laughter.

"You always did like your own jokes." Lainey turned back to her other sisters. "Okay, we've established Joey was not the model child, but jumping from criminal mischief to murder is hardly a plausible leap."

God! I hate that word. I can't believe anyone would do this to me.

Lainey turned back to Tessa, noticing the sadness crinkling her nearly flawless face. Could she have been totally unaware of her penchant for pissing people off?

"Okay. I'll do a little snooping around Joey. He was too young to know who I am, and he might tell me something he wouldn't tell you guys." She turned to Tessa. "Who else wanted you dead?"

"If you're making a list, Lainey, I can promise, you don't have enough paper," Maddy interrupted. "It might take less time listing people who didn't have a motive."

Both Deena and Kate laughed out loud. "Tessa knew just what to say to get under someone's skin. It was an art," Deena finally said when she could.

"People at the hospital can't believe you and I were sisters, Tessa," Kate said. "You made them pay out of the nose for every last cent you donated."

A bit pissy today, Katie? Anyway, most of the yahoos at County General eat a bowl of stupid every morning. Someone had to keep them on their toes.

"Okay, enough about Tessa. We are all in agreement the list will be long," Lainey interjected.

Tessa huffed and crossed her arms.

"Make sure both Jerry and Roxy are at the top of the list."

"Other than the obvious reason, why do you say that, Deena?"

"Because that porno whore isn't satisfied with half of Jerry's money. She wants it all."

"One might have said the same thing about Tessa," Kate said.

Aren't you just a ray of fucking sunshine?

Kate smiled. "I know you probably said something evil, Sis, but you have to know I love you. I'm just trying to stay real."

If I could, I'd kick your ass like I used to.

"Okay, moving right along," Lainey said. "Who else needs to be on our potential killer list?"

"PKL. I like that. Makes it sound dangerous," Maddy said. "What about Carrie Phillips?"

Are you freakin' kidding me? Tessa asked. *Carrie's my best friend. Besides, she isn't smart enough to pull it off.*

"She said no way to Carrie," Lainey explained to her sisters. "Then who, Tessa?"

Hmm! For starters, I'd check out Quinton Porter.

"You've mentioned Porter before," Lainey said, scratching her forehead with the eraser.

Kate moved closer to Lainey and peeked over her shoulder to see what she had written. "Who's that?"

"An oilman from Houston who wants to turn the winery into a drilling mess," Lainey responded, remembering her earlier conversation with Tessa.

"No kidding. You think he'd kill to get what he wants?" Maddy asked, taking a step closer to Lainey and Kate.

He probably already has.

"Tessa thinks it's a possibility. We definitely need to check him out." She turned to her dead sister. "Anyone else you can think of?"

Let me toss it around in my head for a while.

Lainey slammed the notebook closed. "Okay, let's get back to Joey Winters. Maddy, can you get a look at his file without Colt knowing?"

"Oh, hell yes." Maddy straightened up. "When Colt hired me, he made sure I had access to all the files. Said I needed to pull things from them when he asked." She turned to the sink. "He said I was the total opposite of you, Tessa."

Never believe anyone who slept with your sister, Maddy, Tessa blurted.

And don't forget, I'm the one who walked out. That doesn't make for cozy warm feelings. She made a face. *Total opposites, my ass!*

"What'd she say to that?" Maddy asked, the smirk still covering her face.

"She was the one who walked, so naturally, Colt would be a little ticked still," Lainey explained.

"Yeah, you're the one who walked out, all right," Kate said. "But only after he caught you screwing around with about three different guys."

Tessa glared at her youngest sister, who was now high-fiving with Maddy. Despite the frown, she couldn't hide the twinkle in her eyes. *Whatever!*

The last thing Lainey wanted to hear about was Colt and Tessa's marriage. "Okay, let's move on. We've got a lot to do in a short time. My agent rescheduled my interview in Florida for next Friday. No way I'm missing it again."

"You're not still thinking about that, are you, Lainey?" Kate asked. "I was hoping you'd hang around for a while to keep Jerry from putting the screws to Gracie."

Lainey sighed. "I can't. This job is too important to me."

And the fact that some dickhead poisoned me isn't?

Lainey ignored the sarcasm. "You have me for four days. Five, max. Then I'm gone. I have a life of my own, you know. So, let's quit wasting time and get on with this." She re-opened the notebook. "Tessa, do you remember who delivered the Chinese food that night?"

A full minute passed before Tessa finally spoke, her eyes wide. *Son of a—*

"Was it Joey Winters?" Lainey interrupted.

Tessa pursed her lips, her eyes now narrowed. *I tipped that little bastard ten bucks.*

———

The sun was just setting out the back window of the car as it rolled to a stop in front of the Shady City Motel. A glance at the neon sign, way overdue for a makeover, flashed SH   ITY MOTEL.

No shit, Sherlock! God only knows how many different specimens of body fluids still lingered in the sheets.

But none of that mattered. Tessa was dead, although she hadn't exited without her usual drama queen performance.

Damn it! She'd screwed everything up, like always.

The good news was Colt and the rest of the Barney Fifes under him assumed the explosion was an accident. Setting the timer on the living room lamp had been brilliant, but after counting on there not being enough of Tessa to autopsy, finding her in her front yard against the tree was a real shocker. Still, even that wouldn't give the police much to go on.

And now, with Tessa out of the way for good, there was only one reason for the trip to this shitty motel.

Someone is about to get screwed, and it's not gonna be me!

———

Colt opened the car door for his mother and watched as she drove off. He had no idea how he would have been able to make it the past couple of years without her help. After he and Tessa divorced and he was awarded full custody of Gracie, his mother had stepped in and taken over until he'd gotten the hang of taking care of a two-year-old on his own.

Had it really been six years since he and Tessa went their separate ways?

Thinking about his ex-wife, Colt blew out a slow breath. Tessa was really dead. A sadness washed over him at the thought of Gracie growing up without her. Despite the fact Tessa would never be mistaken for mother of the year, she'd loved Gracie in her own way. She'd had no idea how to actually mother her daughter and instead, tried to be a friend. That hadn't worked.

"Daddy?" a small voice from the bedroom called out.

"In a minute, sugar," he answered. "Let me make sure the horses are settled, then I'll tuck you in."

He strolled to the barn, his mind still on Tessa. Their marriage had been the biggest mistake of his life, but he had no choice when she'd turned up pregnant. He and Tessa had always been friends in high school, and he and Carrie had even double-dated several times a week with Tessa and David Rivera.

David! What kind of man screws around with his best friend's girl?

Colt shook his head to clear the image. That was so long ago, but his broken relationship with David had never been mended, even after the divorce. Who could blame him? David had been in College Station thinking his girl was waiting back at home only to discover the person he'd trusted the most had betrayed him.

"Take care of Tessa," David had begged when Colt dropped out of school his senior year.

He'd taken care of her, all right. His first night in town and a drunken pity party was all he'd needed to end up in bed with her.

Not only had he betrayed his best friend, but he'd hurt Carrie in the process. He'd screwed up big time, but not even in his wildest dreams had he imagined the consequences.

He opened the door to the barn. "Whoa, girl," he said softly to the horse when she jumped up. "Take it easy, Shiloh."

Tessa had given the pony to Gracie on her seventh birthday. In a way, it was all Gracie had left of her mother.

He rubbed the filly's head now nudged against his hand, then walked farther into the barn to check on the other two horses. Sure everything was in order, he headed back to the house.

By the time he made it up the stairs to Gracie's room, she'd fallen asleep, clutching the floppy-eared rabbit she'd slept with since she was a baby. He reached down, pulled the covers up, and kissed her forehead.

Colt loved his little girl more than life itself. He'd do anything for her. There was no way he'd let anyone take her away from him. Not now, not ever.

Tessa's death had guaranteed that.

FIVE

THE RAY OF LIGHT peeking in through the half-opened curtain cast a yellow and black pattern across the animal-skin comforter. Making exaggerated circles with his neck to work out the kinks, Jerry Moretti sat up and yawned, nearly causing a tidal wave. His back ached as if he'd slept on a concrete floor instead of the king-sized waterbed Roxy had insisted on.

He glanced at the clock radio on the nightstand. Seven fifteen. He'd had a grand total of three hours sleep last night, not nearly enough to focus on the day ahead. He and Colt were supposed to meet at the winery at nine to filter through Tessa's desk, looking for anything that might shed some light on her death.

Closing his eyes, his thoughts drifted to his ex-wife and life without her. Since yesterday's funeral, it was all he could think about.

Truth be told, he'd never really stopped loving her, not even when she'd made life so miserable those last few years before the divorce. Something about that woman had gotten under his skin in junior high when she was the prettiest girl in Vineyard.

Still is, he thought.

Still was. He groaned, blinking his eyes open.

Rolling to his left, he glanced at his sleeping wife snoring gently beside him. His eyes traveled to her heaving chest where her double D's kept perfect time with her slow breathing.

Damn, he'd loved Roxy's incredible tits the second he'd laid eyes on her. A buddy had brought her latest video to cheer him up after the divorce was final, and he'd been hooked, intrigued that a woman that small and top-heavy could stay upright without falling on her face. To his amazement, she'd mastered that, staying on her feet even as the young stud in the porno flick banged away, shoving her against the wall with each nine-inch thrust.

Jerry was getting hard just thinking about it.

He'd watched that video more times than he could count. When he'd heard she was coming to Fort Worth for the stock show with her rodeo boyfriend, he'd finagled an introduction.

Yes siree, money does talk.

He remembered the way her eyes had lit up when she discovered he owned a multimillion-dollar vineyard. Dropping that tidbit of information never failed to get him laid, and it had worked that day, too. He'd conveniently forgotten to tell Roxy he had a partner until they'd slept together.

A smile curved his lips, thinking of wallowing between those massive mounds of flesh. Sucking enormous nipples was at the top of every man's wish list since the day he was weaned from his mother's breasts. Jerry was no different.

When Roxy discovered Jerry had signed over half the vineyard to Tessa when he married her, she'd nearly bolted.

Tessa wouldn't sleep with him until he did. Said not signing the deed over was like telling the world he was only in it for the short haul. He'd wanted the woman so badly he would have given his left nut. Which is basically what he did, along with his right one.

How stupid was he to lose half his inheritance? His lawyer had warned him not to sign it over, but Tessa had sweet-talked him one night during a hot and heavy make out session that left him crazy when she pulled away. She'd warned their love would never last forever if she wasn't an equal.

As far as he knew, four years didn't qualify as forever in any book he'd ever read, and they weren't even together that long. He didn't count the last eighteen months before the divorce as a marriage. More like hell.

Soon after the wedding, Tessa had convinced him to build an apartment behind the office so she could sleep there on the nights when she worked late.

Another mistake.

After a year of marriage, she'd worked late so many nights that finally, she had moved all her things to the small apartment. That forced him to seek female companionship wherever he could get it. A man has needs, and Tessa certainly hadn't offered to take care of his.

When she'd discovered his little liaisons, she'd used it as leverage in the divorce. Then she made sure to align herself so tightly with all their buyers that no one wanted to deal with him anymore.

But that wasn't all bad. In the two years since their divorce, sales had increased almost forty-five percent. Spirits of Texas was poised for a record-breaking year, and it was only March. Any idiot could see that was the direct result of Tessa's creative ways of enticing new buyers to stock their products. Their wines were now available at most of the exclusive restaurants in the Dallas-Fort Worth area, and the international demand was growing.

Despite it all, he'd somehow talked Roxy into marrying him, promising to buy Tessa out within two years. He'd convinced his new wife if she signed a pre-nup, he'd promote her to Vice President of Marketing, giving her access to their day-to-day operations.

Yeah, like that was ever gonna happen.

Number one, Roxy was a high-school drop-out. Number two, half the men in the country had seen her doing what she did best, making it look like every dick she sucked was some god-damn cherry popsicle.

Shit!

He shoved his hand under the blanket and grabbed himself, moving to a rhythm that increased with every thought of what was to come. When he'd nearly reached the edge, he slid over, causing another tsunami, and pulled the remaining covers off Roxy, thanking the gods his wife slept in the buff. The woman was built like a freakin' brick house. A faint scent of the high-dollar perfume she'd insisted he buy her tickled his nostrils, turning him on even more.

With one swift movement, he positioned himself over her face as she opened her sleepy eyes. "Show daddy how much you love him, sweet thing."

When she didn't respond, he added, "Come on, baby. Today's a big day for me. I'm gonna make you very rich before you climb back into this bed tonight."

Her lips parted as the smile spread. "Bananas are my favorite fruit," she cooed as her mouth swallowed the length of him.

All thoughts of meeting Colt vanished as the woman worked her magic on him. Silently, Jerry applauded himself for using Tessa's death to his full advantage. As he exploded into Roxy's mouth, he knew his life was definitely going to get better now with Tessa out of the way forever.

———

Lainey stood beside the rental car for several minutes staring at the small rundown house, trying to decide what she would say. She nearly jumped out of her skin when her cell phone suddenly blared.

"Hello," she answered, grateful for the delay.

"Lainey, are you okay?"

She'd meant to call Dan when she'd returned to the hotel last night after spending the day with her sisters and her mom, but it had been too late. She sighed. That wasn't entirely true. Although it was late, she'd purposely put it off. He wouldn't be happy that she intended to stay in Vineyard an extra week.

"I'm fine. I would have called last night, but I got back to the hotel way late."

"You don't sound fine."

Dan Maguire knew her too well. Since the day he'd hired her as an intern on the morning show, he'd been able to see right through her. Tall, handsome Dan with his warm brown eyes and curly hair, now graying at the temples. Ten years older than her, he had been her mentor long before he became her lover.

"I am, really. The funeral was worse than I imagined, but I got through it."

"How about your mom and your sisters?"

Good ole Dan. Always worrying about everyone. He was a keeper, definitely. A sudden sadness washed over her. Then why didn't she want to keep him?

"Last night was hard on everyone, especially when Colt…" she paused. "When the sheriff told us Tessa had been poisoned before the explosion."

"What?"

"They think it was cyanide. They're checking through the rubbish for clues, but they're saying the gas explosion was only a cover-up."

"Any suspects?"

"Not so far." Lainey clamped her mouth shut before adding that even Tessa didn't know.

"Honey, I'm so sorry."

If she closed her eyes, she could see his face, caring, comforting. "There's more," she said, bracing herself for his reaction. "Tessa left me her half of the winery. She was afraid her partner who, by the way, is her second ex-husband, would try to screw her daughter out of her inheritance."

"Why you?"

"I don't know, but I have to stay in town a few more days to work things out with her lawyer. I need to make sure her ex plays fair." When Dan didn't respond, she continued, "Can Angie run the show a while longer?"

"Of course she can. She did a good job Friday with Paula DeMarco."

Lainey frowned. "I'll bet she did." Angie Summers had been waiting in the wings for the past nine months like a cat ready to pounce, not only on Lainey's job but on Dan as well.

"What do you think you can do there that you can't do from Savannah?"

"Things will go a lot faster if I don't have to depend on phone conversations." Dan would think she had lost touch with reality if she tried to explain about Tessa, but he'd really flip out if he knew she and her sisters planned to launch their own investigation into Tessa's murder. "I'll wrap things up and head to Florida on Thursday. I'll see you Friday night."

Again, he was quiet. "You're really serious about the Florida job?"

She heard the sadness in his voice. "If I don't check it out, Dan, I'll always regret it. It's something I have to do."

"I know," he admitted. "I guess I'll have to wait till then to find out how you really are. You've become too good at hiding things from me."

Despite the softness of his voice, Lainey heard the thinly veiled sarcasm. "I'll see you Friday night," she repeated.

She closed the receiver and changed the ringer to vibrate. Then she sucked in a deep breath and walked to the front porch, knocking quickly before she lost her courage.

In less than a minute, the door flung open, and Lainey got her first glimpse of Carolyn Winters since leaving Vineyard so many years ago. In Carolyn's younger years, she'd clerked at Servalli's Grocery Store before old man Servalli closed the doors, but nine years had taken its toll on the once-pretty woman. Now she looked "rode hard and put up wet."

"Can I help you?" Standing in the doorway in a sleazy robe, Carolyn's half-smile quickly faded when her eyes widened in recognition.

"Carolyn, I'm Elaina Garcia, Tessa's—"

"I know who you are. You look just like her."

Lainey wrinkled her nose. What was this woman smoking? Tessa had been beautiful her entire life. "I was wondering if I could talk to you and Joey for a minute."

Carolyn's eyes narrowed, lines now creasing her forehead. "What for?"

Lainey shifted uncomfortably. How do you ask a woman if her son had anything to do with killing someone? "I'm only in town for a few days, and I'm trying to get some answers about my sister's death."

"Thought it was a gas leak or something." Carolyn positioned her body in front of the door, effectively blocking the view as Lainey leaned forward for a look into the house.

No sign of Joey.

"It was," Lainey explained, moving to the left slightly so she could see around the woman into the living room. From this angle, there wasn't much that wasn't cluttered. Everything from discarded take-out boxes to rumpled clothing strewn around the room, resembling the aftermath of a recent strip tease party.

Lainey's gaze returned to Carolyn. "Tessa was poisoned before the explosion. It's on the front page of today's paper."

"Poisoned?"

Do you honestly believe this skank reads the paper?

Lainey swung her head around as Tessa walked up behind her, a smirk on her face.

54

Seriously, Lainey.

Lainey covered her surprise with a cough and focused her attention back on Carolyn, who now looked puzzled and more than a little annoyed.

"What makes you think I know anything about that?" She locked her eyes on Lainey in a challenge.

The last thing Lainey wanted was to put this woman on the defensive. "I'm sure you don't, but I'd still be really appreciative of any help you can give me. May I come in?"

Lainey's mouth tilted at the corners as she held Carolyn's stare.

Good one, Lainey. I had forgotten about your condescending smile. That 'I'll let you think you're important if that's what it takes to get what I want' smile. I hated when you used it on me.

Lainey glanced sternly over her shoulder at Tessa before turning back to Carolyn with another convincing smile. "I'll only keep you a minute."

Reluctantly, Carolyn pulled the door open and stepped aside. "I have to be at work in an hour, and Joey isn't home." She gestured for Lainey to sit on the rundown gold couch which had definitely seen better days.

A dingy gray bra peeked out from between the cushions. Lainey wondered if Carolyn had gotten lucky the night before, but the belly protruding from the gaping robe as it opened when she walked quickly dispelled that notion. Plainly, life had not been good to this woman. Did she blame Tessa for that?

Before Lainey could speak, Carolyn plopped down on the chair opposite the couch, spilling the half full glass of liquid on the end table. She made no attempt to clean it up, glancing instead at the big clock above the TV. "What do you want to know?"

Lainey swept the empty bag of Cheetos aside before sitting down.

Tessa plunked down beside her, rubbing her hands together. *This is gonna be good.*

"Tessa was poisoned with cyanide," Lainey began. "Since we know cyanide works quickly, it had to have been in something she ate or drank that night."

"And you're telling me this, why?"

Lainey ran her hand through her hair and then pushed a palm against her forehead. Dan called this her moving-in-for-the-kill technique, but she had to be careful. One wrong word would piss this woman off, and she'd end up with nothing. She took a deep breath, hoping that four years of guest interviews at KSAV would pay off now.

"It seems your son was the last person to see Tessa alive." When Carolyn looked confused, Lainey added, "He delivered her dinner to her a few hours before the explosion."

Carolyn leapt from the chair, her eyes blazing. "Wait just a minute, sister. Are you saying my Joey had something to do with that slut's death?"

Takes one to know one.

If Lainey had learned anything from Dan, it was that angry people speak before they think. She moved quickly. "He certainly had a reason to, don't ya think?"

Carolyn's face flamed into the color of a plump strawberry. "Yes, he did, as a matter of fact. Your sister screwed around with his father. Did you know that?"

"Yes," Lainey answered truthfully. "I also know she wasn't the first person your husband cheated with, nor was she the cause of your divorce. Correct?"

Carolyn's chin dropped to her chest, her lips pursed. When she looked up at Lainey, a lone tear puddled in the corner of her eye.

Quickly, Lainey reverted to a different tactic. "That really must have been a hard time for you and Joey, Carolyn. I apologize for my sister."

Carolyn sighed, glancing once again at the clock. "How would you like to find out your husband was sleeping with the town whore?"

Lainey reached with her right arm to halt Tessa when she reared up to confront Carolyn.

Bullshit! I did her a favor.

When Carolyn's eyes darted nervously at the sudden move, Lainey thought fast. "Sorry. When my bad shoulder freezes up, I have to jerk it loose."

Besides, it was only one time. Off the dance floor, the man was worthless. His little pistol ran out of ammo long before the big bang. Tessa lowered her voice and leaned closer to Lainey. ***Come to think of it, there was no big bang. I was left to fend for myself. I—***

"Tessa."

Tessa's mouth turned down in the little pout that used to get her anything she wanted.

Aware that Carolyn was looking at her like she had lost her marbles, Lainey continued. "Tessa did a lot of things she regretted. I would probably be as mad as you are," Lainey continued, hoping Carolyn bought into this.

I can't believe you're gonna let that woman get away with calling me a whore. Where's your family loyalty?

"It must have been especially tough on Joey, watching his parents go through all that and then the divorce," Lainey continued, ignoring her sister.

Carolyn laughed. "Not hardly."

Lainey straightened. "Not hardly?"

"As far as Joey was concerned, it was the best thing that ever happened."

Told you.

Lainey bit her lower lip. This conversation had suddenly taken a twist. "That seems strange, considering the circumstances."

Carolyn jumped up, giving Lainey another look at her belly straining against the black spandex, hip-hugger panties. "You gotta go. I have to get ready for work now."

Lainey settled farther back into the sofa cushion. She'd come for information, and she wouldn't leave without it now that Carolyn had dropped that little "not hardly" bomb. "Why would Joey be glad about that?" she probed.

Carolyn sniffed, pulling the robe tighter across her body. "The day Joe Senior walked out, Joey celebrated. He called it the best day of his life."

Lainey leaned forward again and got right up in Carolyn's face. "Why would he say that?"

Carolyn defiantly met Lainey's stare. Lainey knew immediately this woman had never stopped loving her ex, no matter how much he'd hurt her.

"Because the SOB used to beat the hell out of him at least once or twice a week."

SIX

COLT STARED AT THE pictures on his desk before glancing up at Danny Landers. "These came from Tessa's computer?"

"Yeah, boss. They were in a file hidden among some old correspondence. If it wasn't for Sean, we wouldn't have found them."

"Sean?"

The young deputy's grin faded. "Don't go getting mad. Sean is Flanagan's computer-geek nephew who's home on spring break. Just for fun, we had him take a look at the laptop in case we missed something."

"You thought I'd be okay allowing a civilian access to evidence in a homicide investigation?" Colt slumped into his chair and reached for the picture again. He didn't know if he was more pissed because his guys missed a crucial piece of evidence or because some techno nerd hadn't.

A sheepish grin spread across Danny's face. "Who needs to know we didn't find it?"

Colt glared. Danny Landers was his youngest officer, joining the Vineyard Police Department straight out of the academy with a long list of recommendations. He was turning out to be a good officer, but every now and then his age showed.

Colt backed off, realizing the pictures were more important than who discovered them. "So do we have any idea about the guy in the photos?"

Danny shook his head. "Not so far. Flanagan and Rogers are on their way to the motel now to talk to the desk clerk. Maybe we'll get lucky and find out the guy was stupid enough to use his real name."

Colt chuckled. "And when we catch him, he'll have an empty bottle of cyanide with Tessa's name on it stuck in his coat pocket," Colt retorted. "That motel is cash only, Danny. Nobody uses their real name." His expression turned serious. "Where's Tessa's laptop now?"

Danny lowered his eyes and mumbled, "Sean's still checking it out."

Colt shook his head, then glanced once again at the pictures. There was no mistaking those gigantic boobs or that kinky, bleached-blond hair. Like every other red-blooded male in Vineyard, he'd taken a look at one of Roxy Moretti's videos to see what all the fuss was about when Jerry brought his new wife to town. The woman definitely knew her way around the bedroom.

What was she doing in a fleabag hotel with a strange man?

Colt grinned. Okay, it was obvious what she was doing. The camera had caught Roxy with her hand on the guy's crotch and his hands all over her fake boobs right before they entered the room.

Apparently, they couldn't wait until the door closed behind them to go after each other.

For a split second, Colt felt a pang of envy pulse through his body. He couldn't remember the last time he was in that big of a hurry with a woman. Hell, he couldn't even remember the last time he had sex, enthusiastic or not. Unless solitary sex counted.

He concentrated on the images, searching for something that might tell them the man's identity and get his mind off his own lack of a social life. The big guy was wearing a nondescript shirt and jeans, but his face was hidden by an expensive-looking cowboy hat, probably a Stetson. No big clue there. Half the men in the county paid more for their boots and hat than they did for the rest of their wardrobe combined. Unless some miracle happened, and this dude was dumb enough to use his real name, Colt would have to confront Roxy about her afternoon tryst with the cowboy.

But something nagged at him. Why were the pictures on Tessa's laptop? Was his ex-wife blackmailing Jerry's new wife? And if so, was that a strong-enough motive to want her dead?

That thought disappeared when he noticed Lainey Garcia walking toward Madelyn's desk. Bending to whisper something in her older sister's ear, her silky blouse ballooned out, revealing a scallop of lace outlining her cleavage.

Danny whistled. "Now that's one helluva looker. Wonder if she goes for younger men."

Colt laughed out loud. "You call her older? She can't be much past twenty-eight or so."

"Hey, remember I'm not ancient like you. I still get turned on by a pretty girl." Danny licked his lips. "Let's see. Twenty-three goes into twenty-eight with a little to spare," he said, gawking at

Lainey. "Come on, Maddy, sink down in that chair, so she'll have to bend over more."

"Get out of here," Colt commanded, his voice barely able to conceal his amusement. "And tell Sean thanks for the catch." He waved Danny out the door, then settled back in his chair to watch Tessa's sisters in an animated conversation. He wouldn't mind seeing a little more skin himself.

He studied Lainey for several minutes, trying hard not to stare at the gaping blouse. She'd left Vineyard before graduating from college, which would put her in her late twenties. From this angle, her dark black hair looked like silk as it fell across her face when she giggled, the soft curve of her mouth inviting as she ran her tongue across her lips. With her short black skirt, cinched tightly at the waist by a wide belt, she could still be a girl on campus somewhere.

The only time Colt noticed details like that on a woman was when he interrogated her.

Jesus! She's your ex-sister-in-law, fool.

He stood and walked around his desk, hesitating only momentarily before pushing through the door. Lainey glanced up as he approached, unable to hide the surprised, almost guilty look that flashed in her eyes. Had he caught her telling Maddy something she didn't want him to know?

Quickly, she recovered and straightened up, a half-smile now replacing the guilty look. "Hey, Colt. I just stopped by to con Madelyn into buying me lunch."

Colt noticed the look that passed between them before Lainey continued. "Anything new with the murder investigation?"

He shook his head and shrugged. In a precinct as small as this one, it was a given Madelyn had heard about the pictures of the ex-porn star. Hell, she probably knew about it before he did. "We found a few pictures on Tessa's computer that suggest she may have been blackmailing—"

"You think my sister was blackmailing Roxy Moretti?" Madelyn interrupted.

So much for the police chief being the first to know. "We aren't sure, Maddy. Like I said, it's only a couple of pictures, and Flanagan and Rogers are checking it out."

The phone rang suddenly, and Madelyn reached for it. "Vineyard Police Department." After a few seconds, she held it out to Colt. "Speak of the devil. It's Flanagan. They're still down at the Shady City Motel asking about the guy in the pictures. He needs to talk to you."

Colt grabbed the receiver, annoyed that everyone seemed to know more about the case than he did. "What'd you find?" After a few minutes, he handed the phone back to Maddy.

"Well, who was he?"

If he didn't love Tessa's family so much, he would have reminded Maddy she was paid to answer the phones and keep up with the paperwork. Period. But she had always been his favorite, and she adored Gracie. That bought her a little leeway.

"Know anyone named Kate Forney?" he asked, biting his lip to suppress the smile as both sisters caught the play on words.

Lainey threw back her head and laughed. "Can't say that I do, but I'll bet she's related to Ima Slut."

Maddy jumped up and high-fived her sister. "And I know she was reading *Hole in the Mattress* by Mister Completely."

"Cut it out, you two," Colt commanded, unable to pull off a serious look.

Still grinning, Lainey glanced at her watch. "So, are you going to take your starving sister to lunch or what? I have to be at the lawyer's office at two."

Maddy wrinkled her nose. "Can't. I promised Father McElroy I'd stop by the rectory. In a weak moment, I let him talk me into heading up the renovations committee for the elementary school. I really have to be there for our first meeting."

Lainey's face dropped. "No problem. I'll just grab a bite on the run." She reached for her purse. "We're still on for tonight at the hotel, right?"

Maddy smiled. "Oh yeah. Even Kate's coming. We're all dying to hear what you found out from Carolyn this morning." She slammed her hand to her mouth. "You remember Mom's friend Carolyn from San Antonio?"

Colt watched silently as the unspoken conversation played out on the two sisters' faces. Between Maddy's, Oh-my-God!-What-have-I-done? look and Lainey's meant-to-kill glare at her sister, it was obvious something was going on. His instincts told him it couldn't be good.

Without thinking, he grabbed Lainey's arm. "Do you remember that great country café down on Main Street?"

"Ruby's?"

"That's the one. They still serve the best damn chicken-fried steak in the state of Texas." Colt paused. "I was just thinking about going there and could use some company. Otherwise, Ruby will talk my ear off the entire time I'm trying to eat."

Lainey looked away, patches of red appearing on her cheeks. "I don't think so, Colt. That would blow a whole day's calories." She pulled her arm away, a pensive look on her face. "I haven't eaten chicken-fried steak since I left Vineyard."

"All the more reason to indulge yourself." He let his eyes wander over her body. "Trust me, Lainey, you don't need to worry about calories." He grinned as the red splotches on her cheeks spread. "Come on. Say yes. My treat."

"Go, Lainey," Maddy urged. "Colt doesn't spring for lunch very often." She reached into her desk for her purse and waved as she walked to the door. "See you tonight," she said over her shoulder.

Colt caught Lainey's elbow and gently guided her toward the door, acutely aware that everyone had stopped to stare. He stole a glance at Danny, who grinned and gave him a thumbs up.

He increased his stride. The faster he got her out of there the better. "Come on. We'll go in my police cruiser. I'll even wager you can't make a dent in Ruby's lunch portion."

A faint light twinkled in her jet-black eyes. "What if I do?"

"Then I'll run the siren all the way back to the station," he teased, seeing the smile return to Lainey's face. This woman definitely loved a challenge. He mentally filed that away for future reference.

"You're on."

He held the cruiser door open for her to slide in. Instinct told him Lainey knew something about the investigation she wasn't telling, and he was damn well going to find out what it was before she popped the last bite of gravy-covered, chicken-fried steak into that pretty little mouth.

———

"Ohmygod! I forgot how unbelievable this was." Lainey shoved another chunk of steak into her mouth. When she looked up and caught Colt staring, she rolled her eyes and laughed. "You must think I'm a glutton," she said, glancing at her nearly empty plate.

"The only thing I'm thinking is how I'll explain the siren to the guys at the station."

Lainey's eyebrow hitched. When Colt pointed to the plate, the sudden memory made her grin. "Oh, the bet."

"I love a woman who isn't afraid to eat like a lumberjack."

She sighed out loud. "Now I'm really embarrassed." She shoved the plate aside. "I don't think I can eat another bite."

"Liar," Colt challenged.

She looked up, eyes narrowed, before reaching for the plate and moving it back in front of her again. "Thanks to you, I'll need an extra hour in the workout room today." She cut another piece of meat.

"Want dessert?"

Colt turned to the waitress, who suddenly materialized holding the dessert menu. "Who eats dessert after your chicken-fried steak, Ruby?"

The woman's broad smile almost matched her hips. "Who's your lady friend, Colt?"

"Oh, sorry. Ruby, this is Elaina Garcia, Tessa's sister. Lainey, Ruby Dalton, the best damn cook in the entire state of Texas."

Her smile spread. "You're such a bull-shitter, Colt." She looked at Lainey. "I was sorry to hear about your sister, Elaina. She did a lot of good things for the community."

"Thanks. I'll bet she loved this place."

Ruby shifted from one foot to the other. "Actually, she rarely came in here."

Oh, here we go. Now's when she tells you what a worthless human being I was.

Lainey jerked her body to the left just as Tessa waved, then slid into the empty seat. Quickly, she turned back to Ruby, hoping no one had noticed the sudden body shift. "Guess she watched her figure, like I should be doing." Lainey pushed the plate toward Tessa and sipped her sweet tea.

Ruby stepped back and squinted. "Honey, I saw you walk in here. The only one who's watching your figure is Colt." She waved her hand around the restaurant. "Not to mention every other cowboy in here."

Much as I hate to admit it, Lainey, your ass does look amazing in that skirt. Tessa winked. *You still have a way to go to beat mine, though.*

"Maybe I will have some of that dessert, Ruby," Colt said, effectively changing the subject as if he didn't like where the conversation was headed.

"Your sister didn't care much for me," Ruby said, folding her arms across her chest.

I never got any warm and fuzzies from you, either. I learned a long time ago to think like a dog. Tessa waved her arm in the air. *If I couldn't eat it or screw it, I'd piss on it and walk away.*

Lainey wiped her mouth with the napkin, biting her lip to hide the smile. "I've been told Tessa didn't get along with a lot of people."

Ruby shook her head. "Everyone in Vineyard loves Colt. After what Tessa did to him, she lost a lot of friends."

Oh, please. Why don't you run back to the kitchen where you belong? I heard there were a couple pans of cobbler you forgot to eat.

"Yeah, your sister was a piece of work, all right." Ruby continued. She glanced over her shoulder at the cashier who was hollering her name and waving frantically. "Gotta go. My granddaughter can screw up a one-man roll call."

Her gene pool could use a little chlorine.

Ruby turned back and smiled, unaware that Lainey had shot Tessa a look meant to kill.

What? Tessa asked, her eyebrows arched, her face scrunched.

"It was a pleasure meeting you, Elaina," Ruby said. "I'll have Jenna bring coffee with the desserts."

"Oh no, there's no way I can do dessert," Lainey protested, but Ruby was already on her way to the front of the restaurant.

"Guess you'll have to take one for the team. Ruby hates people leaving any of her bread pudding in the bowl."

Lainey groaned. "You'll have to carry me to the car."

"That can be arranged," Colt said, successfully bewitching her with a huge smile.

Uh oh! Brace yourself, Lainey. When that man flashes those pearly whites, panties drop all over Vineyard.

Damn! He was flirting. He thought he had forgotten how to do that. He took a deep breath, noticing the way Lainey was staring at him. "Do I have food stuck in my teeth?"

She glanced away, the adorable blush returning to her face. "Sorry. I was curious about what Ruby said about Tessa." She shrugged. "Never mind. It's none of my business."

Colt studied Lainey's face, wondering how much she knew about him and her sister. "Tessa and I made a lot of mistakes. We were much better at being friends than being married."

"I know how that goes," Lainey said, making Colt wonder about her own relationships. "I'm sorry, Colt. I know the last thing you want is to dredge up old memories."

"How much do you know about our marriage?"

Lainey squirmed in the seat. "Well, I know—" she paused, shaking her head. "Nothing, really. Only that one day you were just friends and the next you were married. Seven months later, Gracie arrived. What else should I know?"

He met her gaze. "That's another whole conversation."

The waitress interrupted with the dessert and coffee, giving Colt an opportunity to sit back and observe Lainey as she laughed with the girl about calories. He knew nothing about Tessa's sister, and for his own sanity, he wanted to keep it that way. Something about this woman got under his skin, and it wasn't a good idea to find out why.

"We did get something right, though. Gracie is the best thing that ever happened to either of us, despite all the bad stuff." He lowered his head, remembering his argument with Tessa the week before she died. Quickly he pushed that to the back of his mind.

"Gracie's a doll." Lainey stirred cream into her coffee and sipped, then glanced at her watch.

"Do you need to go?" He wasn't ready to end this, not without getting a handle on what she was hiding. He plunged ahead. "How long has your mom been friends with Carolyn?" He had no idea who Carolyn was, but the shared look between Lainey and her sister at the mention of her name told him Carolyn was someone he needed to know about.

Lainey's eyes widened in surprise. "A long time," she blurted.

He decided to go fishing, remembering Madelyn had asked what she'd found out that morning? "Flanagan said he saw your rental car parked in front of Carolyn's house this morning." He held his breath, hoping she took the bait.

She inhaled sharply. "I only stopped by for a minute."

Colt leaned across the table. "Lainey, if you know something you're not telling me, I'd suggest you do so now."

"I just stopped by to chat. That's all." She took her first bite of the bread pudding, licking her lips as the vanilla pecan sauce dribbled. "Wow, this is fantastic!"

Despite the many images that sight conjured up, most of them X-rated, he didn't want to lose his edge while he was making progress. "You chatted with Carolyn?"

"Yes." She met his stare then shook her head. "You didn't already know that, did you?"

Colt smiled. "That's why I'm the cop, and you're the reporter." He rubbed his forehead. "Who's Carolyn?"

The corners of her mouth tipped in a smile, and she shook her finger at him. "That wasn't nice." She paused as the waitress took away the empty dessert bowl and refilled her cup. "Carolyn Winters," she said, almost inaudibly.

"Carolyn Winters?" he repeated. "Why would you talk to her? Everyone knows she hated Tessa, but that was years ago."

"Her son delivered take-out to my sister a few hours before she died."

Colt's jaw dropped. "How could you possibly know that? The little bit of evidence we retrieved after the fire is still being processed in Dallas. Even I won't know anything for another day or so."

Her luminous eyes flashed with mischief. "Because I'm the reporter, and you're the cop."

Colt threw his head back and laughed out loud. "Boy, did I deserve that one." Leaning forward, he reached for her hand, the smile fading from his face. "Seriously, Lainey, this isn't some weirdo you're interviewing. Tessa was murdered in cold blood. Whoever did it will not look kindly on your questions." He released her hand but held her stare. "Especially if you're getting close."

She shook her head. "I'm not. It was a wasted trip. When I first found out Joey Winters delivered the food, I thought he or his mother might open up to me since I'm virtually a stranger."

"You still didn't tell me how you knew Joey delivered the food."

She wrinkled her forward, as if pondering whether to tell or not. "Deena knew. Tessa had mentioned it to her earlier."

Colt watched the way she lowered her eyes. In his experience, that was a sure sign someone was lying, but it wasn't proof. He moved on. "What did you find out from Carolyn?"

"Nothing," she answered quickly. Maybe too quickly. "We thought Joey might be mad at Tessa because she had a thing with his dad, and we wondered if he blamed her for the broken relationship between his—"

"And did he?" Colt interrupted.

Lainey pushed a strand of black hair behind her ear, exposing a pale pink earring that matched her silk blouse. And her lips.

Since when did you start noticing lip gloss, Winslow? He forced himself to refocus.

"According to Carolyn, Joey would have thanked Tessa if he could have. Seems his father roughed him up on a regular basis."

Colt scowled. "Do you have any idea how dangerous it was for you to go to their house and ask questions about this investigation? What if Joey did poison her food? Do you honestly think they would let you walk away, knowing you would go straight to the cops?" When she didn't respond, his voice softened. "I'm just saying you need to leave the police work to me." His ringing phone interrupted. "Excuse me." He pulled it out of his pocket and pushed the button. "Winslow."

"Boss, you better get back to the station. Flanagan's nephew found something," Tom Rogers said, his voice rising an octave and about three speeds faster.

"Slow down, Rogers. Tell me."

"He found out where the cyanide came from."

Colt straightened and glanced at Lainey, drumming his fingertips impatiently on the table as he waited. "Are you going to tell me, or do you want me to guess?"

"Sorry, Chief. Flanagan just dropped the invoice on my desk. We found an online order for cyanide salts from a place in Indiana."

"Whose computer?"

"Tessa's laptop."

Colt gasped. "You're sure about this?"

"Yeah, boss. It was ordered two weeks ago and paid for with a company credit card."

Colt blew out a breath. Why would Tessa order cyanide? "Did Sean find anything else on her laptop?"

A cold knot formed in his gut as he waited for Rogers to answer. Jerry had mentioned only this morning that Tessa used her laptop exclusively for business trips and at the office. He had been praying her last e-mail to him had come from her home computer, the one that was totally destroyed in the explosion. Otherwise, he would have a lot of explaining to do.

"He's still looking, but so far, nothing else," Rogers replied. "Do you have something specific in mind?"

Colt bit his lower lip. "Anything that looks out of place." He motioned for the waitress to bring the check. "I'm leaving Ruby's now. Don't let Sean out of your sight until I get back." He disconnected, aware of Lainey's intense stare.

"I have to get back. Is your car at the station, or do I need to drop you off somewhere?"

"The station." Her eyes held his. "Are you going to tell me what that was about?"

"Can't. It's part of the investigation."

Lainey was already more involved than he wanted, and this information would only fuel her fire to nose around.

"Is it about Tessa?"

When he nodded, she grabbed his hand. "Come on, Colt. I have a right to know."

Against his better judgment, he leaned closer to make sure no one else heard, breathing in the slight scent of lavender from her hair. "They found an invoice for cyanide on Tessa's computer."

"What?" Lainey's voice echoed through the noisy diner, causing customers to turn and look.

Colt threw a twenty on the table and grabbed her arm. "Come on. I'll tell you in the car."

SEVEN

As Lainey drove the rental car out of the parking lot into traffic, the new information whirled in her mind. How did the invoice for cyanide end up on Tessa's computer? Could Tessa have ordered it for something else and then used it on herself? But why else would you use cyanide?

Lainey shook her head, tapping the steering wheel as she waited for the light to change. She would have liked to bounce this off Maddy, but her sister hadn't returned from her meeting at the church.

Checking her watch, she remembered her two o'clock appointment with Charles Prescott, Tessa's lawyer. If she hurried, she would only be a few minutes late. Kicking off her pumps, she floored it when the light changed, glad the cops were all back at the station poring over the new evidence.

I know what you're thinking, Lainey. You're wrong. I didn't off myself.

Lainey screamed and nearly ran her car off the road. "Dammit, Tessa. Don't scare me like that. I almost wrecked this car," she scolded, glancing to her right to scowl at her dead sister's ghost.

Tessa reached for the seat belt and draped it around her body. *You never were a good driver, Lainey, always daydreaming about stuff.* She sniffed. *Did you ever write that book about the Cuban immigrant's family? You know, the one you always talked about?*

"Don't change the subject. If you didn't order the cyanide, then who did?"

Tessa shook her head. *Your guess is as good as mine.*

"You say that a lot," Lainey responded. "How could you not know?"

Tessa huffed. *Not all of us are as smart as you, Lainey.* Her voice dripped with sarcasm.

Lainey stiffened. "Where did that come from? Nobody ever said I was smarter than you."

Mom did.

"What?" Lainey cocked her head toward Tessa, then jerked the steering wheel back to the left when the tires hit the gravel on the side of the road. "Shit!"

That's all I ever heard. Lainey this and Lainey that. Did you know Lainey made the Dean's list? Again! She tsked the way their mother did when she told a story. *Oh, and did you hear? Tessa's on academic probation. Again!* She tsked a second time. *She was Miss Wine Country for the second year in a row, though.* Tessa exhaled noisily. *Just forget it, Lainey. I got over that a long time ago.*

Lainey slipped into a parking spot at the lawyer's office in downtown Vineyard and turned off the ignition. For a moment, neither spoke before Lainey turned toward her sister. "I didn't realize that bothered you so much." She forced a laugh. "The irony of this is that while you wished for better grades, I would have traded every single 'A' I made to have guys look at me the way they did you."

Their eyes locked. *Yeah, that's overrated if you ask me.* Her mouth tipped with amusement. *So, you're just as screwed up as I am.*

Lainey shook her head. "Nobody's that messed up." She pulled the key from the ignition. "You really don't know who ordered the cyanide?" she asked again, uncomfortable with the conversation. When Tessa was alive, the two had never talked about feelings, and Lainey wasn't about to go down that road now.

Tessa pursed her lips, shaking her head. *The computer sat on my desk for anyone to mess with when I wasn't there. Most of the time, Carrie went with me to sales meetings, and the office was empty. Any of the vineyard employees could have walked in and used it.*

Lainey frowned, creasing her forehead. "Back to square one." She turned one last time to Tessa before she got out of the car. "You're absolutely, one hundred percent sure you didn't order the cyanide?"

Give it a break, Lainey. There's no way I would have killed myself. My life was about to change big time.

"What did Carolyn say?" Kate asked, sliding into the booth with her sisters. "Sorry I'm late, by the way."

"We're just on our first drink," Deena said. "We ordered you a Cosmo exactly the way you like it."

"Sounds wonderful. Today was a long day at the hospital." Kate sipped the pink drink. "Umm! Sure beats the hell out of hospital coffee."

"Talk about a long day," Deena said in between drinks. "Our little nursing home has become a reality show—*The Real Seniors of Vineyard Continuous Care*. I had to shift into damage control mode when old man Jessup's family went at it with Myrtle Fuller's daughter and son-in-law."

"Why on earth were they fighting?" Maddy asked, leaning across the table to hear Deena's story.

"The night nurse caught the old fart nearly sitting on her face last night, his joy stick raring to go."

"No way," Kate said. "What did she do?"

"She freaked out," Deena continued. "Said he kept saying 'Take your teeth out, Myrtle. Here I come.'"

Lainey snorted, spitting her drink across the table. "You're kidding, right?" she asked as Deena shook her head, wiping her arm with a napkin.

"So, what happened?" Kate asked, tears rolling down her cheeks.

"After several hours I was able to convince both families to chill out. I promised to have the nurses keep their eye on the horny old devil."

"Ohmygod! Even at that age, they still think we like that. You can't make up stuff like that," Maddy said, still laughing. "But why you, Deena? You're just the activities director. Why not the administrator or the nursing director?"

Deena shook her head. "Because everyone hates the director, and the administrator is out of town. She called and asked me to do it since both families adore me." She winked. "What's not to love about me?"

Lainey smiled as Kate hugged Deena.

"You are adorable, Deena, but I'm pissed your bad day topped mine." Kate drained her drink and summoned the waitress for a refill. "All I had were two emergency C-sections, one because of a twin that was presenting breech. It got a little hairy for a while on the OB floor but nothing like your story." Kate turned to Lainey. "You never finished telling me about Carolyn."

"Joey didn't do it," Maddy said. "He probably threw a party when Joe Sr. left to celebrate no more beatings."

"Jeez!" Kate exclaimed, grabbing a pretzel from the bowl on the table. "Tessa sure could pick 'em."

Let's not start pointing fingers, little sis. What about that biker you brought home from spring break your last year at UT?

Lainey looked up as Tessa slid in beside her.

Tell them about the cyanide.

"I was getting to that," Lainey said, annoyed by the reminder.

"She's here again?" Maddy asked.

"Yep, and she wants me to remind Kate about the biker boy she once brought home."

Kate scrunched her face. "Touché." She turned to her older sister. "Now what, Lainey? Are we through chasing killers for a while?"

"They found out the cyanide was ordered two weeks ago from Tessa's computer," Maddy said.

"What the hell does that mean?" Deena tossed back her head and drained her margarita. "I need another one of these." She waved to get the waitress' attention.

"Someone with access to Tessa's computer and the company credit card ordered it," Maddy explained. "At least, that's what Colt said. He's looking at everyone who works at the winery. Seems Tessa never locked her office or the drawer where she kept her credit card.

So, sue me.

"Where is she?" Deena looked around as the waitress arrived with a new round of drinks.

Lainey patted the seat next to her.

"Wasn't that kind of stupid, Tessa?" Maddy asked.

Give it a rest, Maddy. Don't get me started on some of the dumb things you've done. I know it was stupid. I don't need any more reminders.

"What'd she say?" Maddy asked.

"She knows it wasn't the smartest thing in the world, but it's past history. We have to find out who ordered the poison."

"Are we sure it wasn't her?" Deena asked in a hushed voice, turning her head away from the empty seat.

I can hear you, Deena. Of course I didn't order it.

"It wasn't her," Lainey said, omitting Tessa's statement that she was about to make a radical change in her life. Tessa had clammed up when she'd asked about it, and Lainey still hadn't figured out what she'd meant.

"Okay, should we add all the freakin' Spirits of Texas employees to our list?" Maddy asked.

"Shoot!" Lainey exclaimed, a hint of mischief in her voice. "We'll be investigating the whole damn city before long."

Stick to interviewing, Lainey. Humor has never been your strong suit.

"Okay, I say we forget all this for now and concentrate on celebrating being together," Kate said. "Lainey will be leaving for Florida before you know it." She raised her glass. "To the best sisters in the world."

The others reached for their drinks to toast their special bond. Lainey held up her glass again to send Tessa a mock salute, but she had already vanished.

———

Lainey stared at the building, unable to shake the weird feeling that Tessa's killer had been in the room she was about to enter. Built in the late eighteen hundreds, the winery had become a tourist attraction, its office at the entrance proudly displaying the historical landmark placard attached to the old Chicago brick exterior. Jerry's great-grandfather had immigrated from Italy, planting the first vines out back from cuttings he'd carried with him on the boat from his own father's vineyard in Palermo.

Lainey took a deep breath and walked in. A pungent orange smell greeted her.

"Hello, Lainey. I wondered when you'd stop by, now that you own half this place."

Lainey was surprised to see Carrie Phillips, Tessa's personal assistant, sitting in her sister's office with what looked like the company books spread across the desk. In front of her was a bowl filled with potpourri. Tessa must have loved the orange fragrance as much as she did. "Hey, Carrie. It's been a long time."

Tessa's best friend stood up and walked around the desk to hug Lainey. "Last time I saw you, you were just finishing up your freshman year at that fancy Georgia college." She stiff-armed Lainey away from her body. "You've gotten prettier. I'll bet you keep those East Coast boys on their toes."

Lainey snorted. She'd been called a lot of things, but pretty wasn't one of them. That had always been Tessa's department. She pulled away from Carrie's embrace and flopped into a chair. "Thought I'd better come down and see how everything worked if I'm going to be involved now."

Carrie didn't even try to hide her surprise. "You're not serious. You're really going to stay in Vineyard to run the winery?"

Lainey lowered her eyes, hoping she could pull this off. At the consultation with Tessa's lawyer yesterday, he'd advised her to pretend as if that was her plan. He said if she could make Jerry Moretti believe it, he might be more anxious to strike a deal to buy her shares at current market value if only to get rid of her. The more money she could get for Gracie, the better.

"I've missed being around my sisters. This gives me the perfect opportunity to be near them again." She took a deep breath and blew it out slowly before glancing up.

The initial surprise on Carrie's face was replaced with a smile. "That's great news. Having family close is important."

Lainey was only half-listening, instead making a visual sweep of her sister's office, her eyes halting on the wide ornate desk that nearly filled the room. The size of the room seemed out of character for Tessa. She'd always been about big. Nothing she ever did was on a small scale.

She finally tore her eyes away and continued scanning the room. In the corner behind the desk was a full-blown beverage center, the kind you see at car dealerships. The kind that kept you hydrated and happy while you waited for the service manager to tell you your car was ready. It seemed especially out of place in the small space, but it was so Tessa. She'd always had a flair for anything over the top.

"Have you given any thought to where you'll stay?" Carrie asked, interrupting Lainey's visual tour of the room.

"Not really." She reached into her purse for her checkbook and fanned her face. The room had suddenly turned stifling, as if the heat index had elevated several notches. She whirled around to see if her sister had popped in once again before remembering she'd read somewhere the room got chilly, not warm when a ghost was present. Other than Carrie, who was now looking at Lainey like she was on drugs, there were no other females in the room.

"For now, I'm fine at the Conquistador," Lainey said. "It got a little hot in here. Must be hormones," she added, continuing to fan herself.

Carrie walked to the door and turned on the overhead fan. "You could always move in here."

Lainey's eyes circled the tiny office once again before settling on Carrie. "A little small for a bed."

Carrie laughed. "Don't you know your sister hated this small office. That woman did like wide open spaces." She pointed to a door in the corner opposite the beverage bar. "Tessa split this room and turned the other side into an apartment. She spent many nights here after she married Jerry."

"I'm not surprised," Lainey said. "From what the locals all said about her, she was a big hit in the wine industry. It stands to reason she'd have to put in a lot of hours here to maintain that success."

Carrie laughed out loud. "Your sister used to say any time away from Jerry was quality time."

Lainey laughed, too. That made sense. According to her sisters, Tessa had only been married to Jerry for a short time. It hadn't exactly been a marriage made in heaven.

Carrie stood up and walked to the beverage bar. After pouring two coffees, she handed one to Lainey and sat down beside her. "So, catch me up on your life. Other than you landing that great job in Savannah after you graduated, I really don't know much about you. Are you married?"

"No," Lainey answered quickly then forced a laugh. "I'm way too busy for a social life." She took a sip of the coffee before continuing. "What about you? Last I heard you were talking marriage with Colt."

A shadow of annoyance crossed Carrie's face before her eyes crinkled in a half-smile. "That was a long time ago, Lainey. Colt and I were just teenagers, too young for commitments. Too stupid to know any better."

Lainey knew her questions were out of line, but she couldn't stop herself. Your best friend stealing your boyfriend and having his baby was a strong reason to hate someone, but was it enough to kill?

She pressed on. "I remember you two were pretty serious your senior year. When you went off to A & M with him, I thought for sure you'd stay together."

Carrie bit her lower lip as if considering her answer before she blurted it out. "Yeah, I thought so, too, but it didn't happen that way. Colt and I grew further and further apart instead of getting closer the way it should have been. After our junior year at College Station, we both knew it was over."

"Is that when Colt's father was killed and he came home?"

Carrie lowered her eyes and nodded. "It was around that time."

Carrie's body language left no doubt this was a painful subject, and Lainey scolded herself for being so insensitive. After a brief argument with her conscience, she plunged ahead, her investigative instincts winning out. "Wasn't that about the same time Tessa left Southwestern Community and came home?"

Carrie walked back around the desk and shuffled some papers before glancing back up. "We were talking about you. How'd this conversation switch to me and stuff that happened so long ago I'd already forgotten about it."

Oh, really. You might want to tell that to your heart.

Carrie held up her left hand and flashed a huge diamond ring. "Do you remember David Rivera?"

"Tessa's old boyfriend?"

Her eyes narrowed as she leveled a momentary look at Lainey. "One and the same. We hooked up a couple of years ago. The wedding is scheduled for late September. He's the city manager now."

"Congratulations. I remember David always made me laugh when he was at our house."

"That's what I fell in love with." Carrie turned when the desk phone rang. "Excuse me for a sec, Lainey. I hope this is the call I've been waiting on."

Lainey walked to the beverage center for a sweetener packet. Above the granite counter, there was a wall of pictures, mostly of Gracie and her horses. Among the pictures was an old black and white photo of Tessa and Lainey as little girls. Tessa was holding her hand protectively in a big sister sort of way.

Surprised, Lainey glanced at the other photos. Other than one of the other three sisters at Tessa's wedding, the rest were of Gracie.

Why would Tessa keep this picture of her and Lainey in the office? They had fought nearly every day of their lives growing up and had been dead to each other for years.

Lainey's attention was diverted when Carrie said goodbye and hung up the phone. As she watched her sister's best friend making notes on an invoice, she noticed how much older Carrie looked than Tessa, even though she knew they were exactly the same age. Obviously, Carrie didn't have the great genes Tessa had inherited. Shorter than Lainey's five-eight, with blond highlights in her stylish brown hair, Carrie had maintained her great figure, but her face had not escaped the curse of getting older. The beginnings of deep wrinkles were visible around her eyes and her lips. Lainey automatically touched her lips and vowed to get aggressive with her own moisturizing routine.

"Sorry. I had to take that call. They're one of our biggest clients."

"No problem." Lainey walked back around the desk and was about to sit down.

"Sit here." Carrie held out Tessa's chair, "This is your office now."

Lainey smiled. "Yeah. I'd better get used to it. I hope you'll hang around to show me the ropes."

Surprise crept across Carrie's face a second time. "I hope so. I've agreed to stay on as Jerry's assistant, though. We—he—thought you'd be anxious to sell your half of the business and get back to your career in Savannah."

"He was wrong."

Carrie bit her top lip before her mouth tipped in a slight smile. "I'm glad. Having another woman around will be nice." She paused. "So, when do you want to get started?"

Lainey fought back the panic. All she wanted was to give the impression she was staying. She had no desire to get into the boring details of running a business. "Do you have any thoughts on who might have killed my sister?" she asked, hoping to steer the conversation in a new direction.

Carrie rubbed her finger over her upper lip. "I've thought about it a lot since Colt came by and asked the same question." She met Lainey's eyes. "Did you know the cyanide was ordered on Tessa's computer?"

Lainey nodded. "I was with Colt at Ruby's when he got the call telling him that."

"You were with Colt at Ruby's?"

"We had lunch yesterday to discuss a possible lead in the case."

Carrie started to say something, then stopped. "Why would he talk to you about the investigation?"

"My sisters and I are trying to help out any way we can," Lainey explained. "There might be things we can find out that he can't. That's all."

"Like what?"

Lainey rubbed her jaw, not comfortable talking about this with Carrie.

"You might want to have a chat with Quinton Porter." Carrie said when Lainey didn't elaborate.

"Who's he?" Lainey asked, remembering Tessa mentioning the oilman from Houston. Mentally, she placed him in the number one spot on the list.

"He wanted to buy Spirits of Texas and turn it into a natural gas reserve. He offered Tessa and Jerry a ton of money to drill under the vineyard, but they turned him down. He's the kind of guy who doesn't like no for an answer."

"Where can I find Porter?"

"In Houston." Carrie's eyes widened. "Oh, wait. I almost forgot." She walked around the desk and pointed to the calendar under the glass. "Normally, he comes to Dallas the last week of every month to check up on all his accounts, but he called this morning. He must have heard about Tessa's death, said he was in town and wanted to talk to Jerry." She rolled her eyes. "Jerry was going over the books with Colt and said he would return the call. I'm not sure if he ever did."

"Do you have his number?"

"No, but he always stays at the airport Conquistador. Isn't that where you're staying?" When Lainey nodded, she continued, "The bartenders all know him by name." Carrie chugged an imaginary drink. "Know what I mean?"

Lainey rolled her eyes before glancing at her watch. "Gotta run. I'm picking Maddy up after work, and I'm late." She stood and turned toward the door. "It was good seeing you again, Carrie. I'm looking forward to your tutoring me in the wine business."

Before Lainey even made it to her car, she was already thinking about what she would wear to the Conquistador bar that night.

EIGHT

Lainey sauntered into the bar, praying her fake bravado looked believable, hoping she didn't break her neck in Kate's black heels. She had only packed short black pumps, and the sisters had decided this escapade demanded sexier shoes.

Tessa hadn't shown up at Deena's tonight when the four of them discussed the latest tip. Since Deena was married, Maddy had to work early the next morning, and Kate was pulling a double at the hospital, Lainey was elected to check out the oilman. After dinner, they'd piled into Lainey's car and driven to Kate's apartment to pick out an outfit designed to attract Porter's attention. The plan was to get him liquored up and then pump him for info.

How hard could it be? It's what she did for a living. Well, maybe not the liquored-up part, but pumping for information was definitely her thing.

Dressed in a blue jersey number belted at the waist, she felt naked. Kate was three inches shorter than her, so the dress ended thigh high and revealed her legs, long and brown, thanks to a quick stop at a spray-on tan place.

She took a calming breath before glancing around the darkened room. Tuesday nights were slow at the Conquistador, judging by the handful of businessmen still in suits huddled around the bar. The waitress was the only other female.

She grabbed an end stool and feigned interest in the hockey game blaring on the overhead television. She stole a quick glance at the four guys sitting at the bar, wondering if any of them was Porter. Two other men in a booth in the opposite corner acted like they were really into each other. If either of them turned out to be the oilman, hers wasn't the right equipment to attract his attention.

"What's the lady drinking?"

Lainey looked up as the bartender placed a bowl of peanuts in front of her. "A Baileys on the rocks, please." She would have preferred a frozen margarita, but she had always been a cheap drunk. Two of those tequila drinks made her giggly, and she needed to be on top of things. Baileys, on the other hand, was so expensive, the servings were small. She could nurse two or three all night and still not stagger in the "F" me shoes.

After the bartender walked away, she resumed her scrutiny of the men at the bar. She watched the one at the far end guzzle a beer, still wearing his cowboy hat. He was her pick for Porter. The two suits near the middle seemed too stiff for the Houston oilman, but the guy closest, already eyeing her up, was her second choice.

The bartender placed the drink in front of her. When she handed him a twenty, he shook his head. "This one's on him." He pointed to the man closest to her who smiled when she looked.

Oh crap! She had no idea how to do this. She had never been much of a bar-hopper in college, always at the library or studying alone in her room.

She picked up the glass and flashed him a smile.

I can't believe you drink that stuff. It's like chocolate milk.

"Thank God!" Lainey exhaled noisily when she turned to see Tessa on the stool beside her. "Where in the hell have you been?"

I can't control when I show up. It just happens.

"Yeah, well, good thing you did. I was about to haul ass out of here. Carrie told me to check out Quinton Porter, and I have no clue if he's even in here."

The guy at the end of the bar all alone. I swear, that jerk couldn't score in a monkey whorehouse with a bagful of bananas.

Lainey turned in time to catch the cowboy staring at her, probably wondering who she was talking to. "The one in the hat?" she asked, trying not to move her mouth as she smiled at Porter.

Yep. That's one dude I'd like to see well hung.

Lainey's eyebrows hitched. "Well hung? You said he was an asshole."

He is. In his case when I say well hung, it means I can barely slip my finger between his neck and the freakin' noose.

Lainey nearly choked as she forced herself to hold Porter's stare. When he lifted his glass in a salute, she raised hers back to him.

Take a deep breath, Lainey. You'll never squeeze anything out of him sitting this far away. Get up and go over there, Tessa prodded. *And shake your booty.*

Cautiously, Lainey rose from the barstool, thankful her bare thighs didn't stick to the leather. Out of the corner of her eye, she noticed the man who had bought her drink, his smile indicating he thought his eight-dollar investment was about to pay off. It killed her not to glance at his face as she walked to the other end of the bar, just as Garth Brooks belted out "Friends in Low Places" from the jukebox in the corner.

Taking a deep breath, she stopped in front of the empty stool on Porter's left. "Mind if I join you?"

Quinton Porter hadn't taken his eyes off her the entire trek across the bar. Standing here now, suddenly feeling vulnerable, Lainey met his stare as she offered him a bird's eye view of herself. When she glanced back up, she discovered his leering appraisal had stopped at her thighs.

You always did have great legs, Lainey. Tessa nudged her forward. *Make me proud, girl.*

Tessa plopped down on his right side and rested her head on the bar. Quickly, she straightened up. *Ew! I could see his nose hairs from that angle. Not a pretty sight.*

After Porter's eyes moved from her lower body, he smiled as he patted the empty seat. "What's the pretty lady drinking?"

"I'm good." Lainey pointed to her full glass as she slid onto the barstool.

"Suit yourself." He raised his hand to signal for another beer. After the bartender placed the frosted mug in front of him, he turned back to Lainey. "What'd you have in mind?"

Despite telling herself to stay calm, Lainey blushed. "Can't a girl share a drink in a bar without an agenda?"

Christ, Lainey. That's so lame. Like Porter has a clue what having an agenda means.

Porter's eyes crinkled as he took a long swallow of his beer. "Not one who looks like you. What are we talking here—a couple hundred bucks?"

Her color deepened. "I'm not... You misunderstood," she stammered.

"Really? Then tell me what I can do for a beautiful woman like you?"

Give me a freakin' break.

Lainey extended her hand. "I'm Elaina Garcia. I'd like to talk to you about selling Spirits of Texas."

Porter nearly spit the swig of beer across the bar as he swiveled closer to her, eyes narrowed. "Who'd you say you were?"

"Elaina Garcia, Tessa Moretti's sister."

His eyes lit up with recognition before he turned back and glanced at the hockey game on the flat-screen TV at the end of the bar. "Should have known. You look like her."

Lainey moved closer, her nose twitching at the overwhelming scent of musk. The man must have taken a bath in the stuff. "Are you still interested in buying the vineyard?"

"Who wants to know?" he asked, keeping his eyes on the TV.

"Tessa willed her half to me when she died."

He twisted around until his knees touched the side of her bare thigh, a gesture that didn't go unnoticed by either of them. "Is that right? And you're looking to sell, why?"

"I'm a reporter, Quinton." She paused and smiled at him. "Can I call you that?" When he nodded, she continued. "I have a career waiting for me in Florida. The faster I sell, the faster I can get back to it."

He flexed his shoulders and leaned forward, his eyes holding hers. "I might be in the market. What'd you have in mind, Miss Garcia?"

Despite the nausea threatening to bubble up in her esophagus, she leaned closer. "Call me Elaina."

Tessa slapped the bar. *Thatagirl, Lainey. I was beginning to think all those smarts had suffocated your sense of adventure.*

Porter's eyes held hers in a cold stare for a moment before his mouth tipped at the corners.

Right now he's thinking he's gonna get a look at your lacy undies before the night's over. He can't keep his eyes off your legs. Probably pitching a trouser tent as we speak. Tessa grinned. *You're on a roll, Lainey. Bring him in for the kill. Just like I saw you do in Savannah.*

Lainey's back straightened as she shot up in the chair, peering around Porter to stare at her sister's ghost. When did Tessa ever see her in Savannah?

Tessa lowered her eyes. *No big deal. I saw you once when I landed at the Savannah airport on my way to Hilton Head.* She waved her hand. *Now get back to Porter before you lose your momentum.*

Lainey mentally filed away the remark for a future conversation when she and Tessa were alone. Tessa in Savannah was something that needed explaining. She raised her head and returned Porter's gaze, determined to find out if he knew anything about her sister's death. "Like I was saying, I'm looking for a quick sale and wondered if you were still interested in the real estate."

"Hell, yes!" he bellowed. "But the price has dropped a notch since your sister's death. With her gone, Moretti has about as much chance of making the kind of money she generated as a one-legged cowboy doing the Cotton-Eyed Joe."

Now that's the first intelligent thing that man has said all night. All this time I thought he passed up his opportunity to drink from the fountain of knowledge, and now I find out he may have stopped to gargle.

Lainey grinned broadly at Tessa's sharp wit, but she was immediately sorry. Porter took it as a good sign and leaned closer, letting his hand rest on her bare knee.

The nausea rose higher, but she resisted the voice in her head screaming for her to slap the loser's hand away. Instead, she studied his face. He wasn't half bad, if arrogant cowboy was what she was looking for. Standing at least six feet tall without his boots, his broad shoulders filled the Western shirt while his tailored jeans hugged his slim waist. She found herself thinking it was incredulous that Tessa hadn't slept with him. He was exactly her type. Or had she? Maybe that's why she hated the guy so much.

She shook off the image of her sister in bed with this joker. "I think we can work out a deal here, Quinton, if we put our heads together."

His hand moved an inch or two up her leg. "I'm sure anything's possible when my head gets together with yours."

Christ! Can you imagine him with a personality?

Lainey glanced at her watch, thinking that she'd already wasted enough time, and his hand up her leg was getting dangerously close to being whacked. "I hadn't seen my sister in over nine years," she said, feeling his fingers inch higher. "I was more surprised than anyone when she left me her share of Spirits of Texas, but to tell you the truth, her death was a godsend." When he looked confused, she added, "I need a sizeable chunk of change to set myself up in Florida."

"Yeah, I hear you. I never got along with your sister myself. Thought she was too good for me." He snorted. "She had no idea what was going on behind her back. She was about to get the surprise of her life."

Hello! Tessa said, jumping off her stool and racing around behind Porter to stand by Lainey. *You sorry bastard. Start talking.*

"Really? Why do you say that?" Lainey asked, hoping her eyes didn't reveal her elevated interest. She tried to look nonchalant, but he had just dropped a bomb.

For the first time, Porter acted less confident, probably pissed off at himself for telling her that. He took his hand off Lainey's leg and swiveled his stool toward the TV again. After draining the remainder of his beer, he blew out a breath. "Let's just say her world was about to change big time."

"I think dying qualifies as world changing, wouldn't you agree?"

"I wasn't talking about that. I'm just saying she was surrounded by people who would have loved to see her crash and burn." He raised his hand for another beer.

Lainey's investigative instincts kicked in. "That's kinda what happened to her. Who wanted that badly enough to see her dead?"

Porter threw back his head and laughed, an unmistakable hint of hatred and anger blending with the chuckle. "Easier to ask who didn't. Your sister was a class 'A' bitch."

Bite me!

"What about you, Porter? You stand to make one helluva profit because she's dead." Lainey stared him down, unable to explain her sudden anger.

He grabbed her arm and jerked her toward him. "Now wait just a minute, sweet cheeks. Are you accusing me of something?"

"You're hurting me."

"That's just too damn bad, isn't it, missy? I wanna know who sent you here to question me. Was it Moretti? He's the only one who knew I was in town."

Lainey attempted to break free, but he had her arm in a death grip. She could already picture the nasty bruise she'd have by morning.

"No one sent me. Now let me go before I scream bloody murder."

"Oh, no you don't. Not until I find—" He yelped as a hand reached around Lainey and pried his fingers from her wrist.

"I believe the lady asked you nicely to let go of her arm."

Both Lainey and Porter did a 180 and came face to face with Colton Winslow, standing so close to Lainey, she could pinpoint a slight hint of garlic on his breath along with a pepperminty smell.

Colt loomed over Porter, his eyes threatening, almost daring the oilman to react. "Is someone going to tell me what the hell is going on?"

NINE

Colt stared down the oilman, still gripping his arm before he turned his glare on Lainey. "I repeat. What the hell is going on here?"

Porter rubbed his wrist after Colt released it, then pointed to Lainey. "You might oughta ask her. I was minding my own damn business, enjoying a brew or two, and she comes on to me."

"Bullshit!" Lainey exclaimed. "I was only attempting to have a conversation with you."

For the first time since he'd entered the bar, Colt took a good look at the woman seated on the barstool. This one was a far cry from the woman he'd had lunch with the day before. Her hair was pulled back with only little ringlets of curls on her cheeks that bounced every time her head moved. The dress was tight enough to show every curve in her body, and dammit, she had a lot of them! But the legs were what stopped him cold. Where in the hell had she been hiding those?

Lainey pulled at the hem of the blue dress when she noticed him staring. A hint of mischief flashed in her eyes before they turned defiant. "I was on the way to my room, and I decided to stop by for a drink before I crashed."

"Dressed like that?" Colt's eyes hardened, wondering if the innocent persona Lainey had displayed earlier was merely a disguise for a darker side. Maybe looks weren't the only thing she had in common with her older sister.

Her cheeks colored, and she jerked at her dress, trying unsuccessfully to cover a little more of her thighs. "What's wrong with the way I'm dressed?"

"Nothing, honey. I always say if you got it, flaunt it."

Both Lainey and Colt turned to Porter. "Nobody was talking to you. Sit there and shut up until I'm ready for you."

The oilman's smile faded as fast as it had materialized.

Colt turned back to Lainey, his eyebrow raised in question. "Well?" He watched as she took a deep breath, unable to look away from the swell of her chest when she inhaled.

"I wanted to talk to Mr. Porter to see if he knew anything about Tessa's death."

"So now it's Mr. Porter? A few minutes ago, it was Quinton."

Colt shot him another shut-the-hell-up look, and without a word, Porter lifted his half-empty drink and chugged it, before signaling the bartender. "Scotch rocks this time, Mac, and make it a double."

Colt was ready to pull Lainey out of the bar and make her tell him everything, but he hadn't come for that. He'd labeled Porter a person of interest ever since Jerry mentioned he had been making a play for the vineyard before Tessa's death.

During his four-hour interrogation of Tessa's ex, he'd discovered Porter was in town until the following morning, and he'd stopped by the bar to ask him a few questions. He hoped the man might be able to shed some light on the investigation, but the minute he'd walked through the door and had his first look at the Houston man, he knew he was on to something.

He'd get to him in a minute, but first, he had to deal with his ex-sister-in-law. "Lainey, how did you find out about Porter?"

"Tessa." Lainey blurted then covered her mouth. "I can't believe I said that. I meant Carrie Phillips. I stopped by the winery today, and she mentioned Porter was in town to talk to Jerry about buying Spirits of Texas. Since I'm now half owner, I thought I'd just have a talk with him over a drink."

Colt squinted. "And you needed a dress like that to loosen him up?" What the hell was the matter with him? He was acting like a jealous boyfriend. Without waiting for her response, he turned back to Porter. "Did you and Jerry make a deal this morning?"

The oilman's lips tipped in a smile, as if the liquor had suddenly grown him a set of balls. "Frankly, Sheriff, I don't see how that's any of your business."

Colt leaned in, lips pursed.

Porter's smile faded. "I never got the chance to talk to Moretti. Seems he was tied up with you all morning, and he wasn't available the rest of the day."

Something about this man grated on Colt's last nerve. He studied his face, searching for any telltale sign of guilt or anything that indicated he was lying. Porter was rich and arrogant, but did he have it in him to commit a murder?

"What were you doing at the Shady City Motel with Jerry's wife?"

Lainey gasped. "That was him?"

Porter's face turned ashen, and he gulped the rest of his drink. "I have no idea what you're talking about." His confidence seemed to build back up with each sip of the double shot of scotch.

"Really? Then maybe you can explain why I have an eight by ten that says you're a liar."

Porter drew a sharp breath. "Who took the picture?"

"You tell me. Was Tessa blackmailing you?"

"Tessa? What did she have to do with it?"

"Probably nothing." Colt tapped his fingers on the bar, determined to get answers. "Anybody squeezing you for cash lately?"

"Why the hell would I give anybody money because I banged a hot-looking broad who, by the way, was a willing participant?"

"Did you kill my sister?" Lainey reached over and grabbed his sleeve.

Porter jerked it away. "Now wait a minute, missy. I had sex with a married woman. That's not a crime in my book. No one said anything about murder."

Colt slid between the stools, his back to Lainey. The last thing he needed was for the oilman to take a drunken swing at her. By his count, the guy was on his second double, and who knew how many he'd had before Colt arrived. "Answer her question, Porter. Where were you the night Tessa Moretti was killed?"

"Jesus! You, too?" He wiped his brow. "I had no cause to kill that woman. I was about to get what I wanted with or without her."

"And just how were you going to do that, may I ask?" Lainey's voice dripped with anger.

Colt felt her lean forward, felt the faint brush of her breasts against his back as she grabbed his shoulder and moved her body to the left, probably to glare at Porter. He bit his lip and inched forward slightly to keep from reacting to the message his brain was sending south of his belt buckle.

For the first time, the man's face flashed a hint of fear. "Look, Sheriff, you're talking to the wrong guy. I had nothing to do with that woman's death."

Lainey leaned closer, and Colt stifled a gasp as her body pressed hard into his back. "How were you going to steal her company without her knowing it?" she asked.

Unable to take any more of Lainey's torture without embarrassing himself, Colt backed out from the space between them. He missed having a gorgeous woman, or any woman for that matter, stirring up those kinds of feelings in him. Since his divorce from Tessa, he'd thrown himself into his work and taking care of Gracie. An occasional dinner date had sometimes ended in bed but not often enough. The way his body reacted to this woman both surprised and terrified him. He took another step away from her, but he could still smell the flowery perfume she was wearing.

"The lady asked you a question, Porter. I'd like to know the answer myself. How could you buy Spirits of Texas without Tessa's consent?"

The Houston man sniffed, raising his hand for another drink before meeting Colt's eyes. "Roxy and I were working on it. She was wearing her husband down, and I was checking out other angles."

"Like what?"

The cowboy lowered his voice. "Nothing illegal. I was talking kickbacks to some of her clients if they changed suppliers. I figured if the cash flow petered out, she might be receptive to a deal that would keep her rich for the rest of her life."

"You scumbag!" Lainey shouted. "No wonder my sister hates you so much."

Colt swiveled to face her. "I thought you said you hadn't spoken to Tessa in years."

Lainey's eyes widened as she drew a sharp breath. "Carrie told me."

Colt turned his attention back to Porter. "Okay, let me get this straight. You were working a deal with Roxy Moretti to buy the winery, and no one was blackmailing you. Is that correct?"

"Yes," Porter admitted. "I had no idea someone was watching us. I don't think Roxy knew, either."

"And you're sure you were in Houston Tuesday night? Before you answer, let me warn you. That's easy enough to check out."

"I was in Houston curled up in bed when Moretti's ex bit the bullet. My lovely wife will vouch for that."

"Don't be so sure of that, asshole. When she finds out about your little tryst with a porn star, no telling what she'll say. Then we'll see what kind of bullet you'll be biting." Lainey's nostrils flared with fury.

Colt grabbed Lainey's arm and gently eased her off the stool. "We're done here. I'll walk you to your room." As he shoved her toward the door, he glanced back over his shoulder at Porter. "Let my office know when you come back into town. I may need you to stop by the station for a few more questions."

Silently, he guided Lainey out the door toward the elevator. Only after he punched the up button did he turn and face her. "What floor?"

"Sixteen." She stared straight ahead, unwilling to meet his eyes.

Alone in the elevator, he finally let go of her arm. "So, are you going to tell me what the hell you were doing here tonight?"

She glanced up, her eyes challenging. "I already did. I wanted a night cap, remember?"

"Cut the crap, Lainey. You're forgetting who you're talking to. I can spot a lie a mile away. Need I remind you about the Carolyn Winters fiasco?"

She lowered her gaze, the bravado dissipating. "I only wanted to talk to him to see if he knew anything. I had no idea he and Roxy were in cahoots behind Tessa's back." Just then the elevator stopped, and she faced him. "Do you think he killed her, Colt?"

Giving a civilian details about an ongoing investigation broke every rule in a cop's manual, but the pain in her eyes got to him. He softened. "My gut says no, but I'll pull up his cell phone records to see who's been talking to him lately."

That seemed to satisfy Lainey, and she turned and exited the elevator. He followed her down the hall in silence. When she stopped at her room, she looked up at him, her eyes questioning.

For a split second, he thought she was going to invite him in. Mentally, he scolded himself for hoping she did. "I'll leave after you're safely inside." He couldn't resist adding, "You seem to have a penchant for getting into trouble."

She inserted the keycard and opened the door. As they walked in, his eyes caught a glimpse of something on the floor inside the door.

Hesitantly, Lainey bent down to retrieve it. When she tried to speak, her voice wavered, "Colt?"

Her eyes met his as she held the folded paper in her hands. "Open it," he said, a bad feeling coursing through his body.

The color drained from her face as she read. Without a word, she handed it to him. He met her eyes and saw the fear before he glanced down at the paper. A wave of icy panic gripped his body as he stared at the four words cut from a magazine and pasted on the single sheet of hotel stationery. Four words that tore at his gut, slicing him open with the cold reality that there was still a killer loose in Vineyard. He reread the note.

GO HOME OR DIE.

He stepped toward Lainey and shoved her behind him. "Stay here," he commanded, drawing his gun, acutely aware of her trembling body pressed tightly into his back. Without a sound, he pulled away and searched the room to make sure whoever had left the note was not lurking, waiting to attack. Confident they were alone, he holstered his weapon.

"No one's here now. Probably never was." He glanced around the room a final time.

"Why would someone want me out of town, Colt?" Lainey's voice was barely a whisper between gasps of air, as she stood rooted to the same spot he'd left her.

In one swift move, he was beside her, his arms encircling her, pressing her close to stop her shaking. Like a mother comforting a child, he stroked her silky hair, still piled high on her head. "My guess is you've gotten a little too close for comfort with your questions," he whispered, hating that his reaction to her body molded into his was the same as in the bar.

She stayed that way until he felt her breathing slow. Finally, she inhaled then pulled away. "I made a promise to help bring Tessa's killer to justice. It's going to take a lot more than a single sheet of paper to scare me off."

His fingers lingered on her forearm for a few more seconds before he let them drop. He tried to decide if she was really unafraid or just trying to convince him of it. "I'll find out who did this, Lainey. I promise."

He had no idea how he would do that, but he vowed to find a way. With the exception of a murder-suicide last winter involving an elderly couple and a death pact, Vineyard's usual crimes consisted of shoplifting and petty theft and every once in a blue moon, someone pounding on their wife. For the first time since he'd joined the police force eight years ago, Colt felt out of his league.

"I'll have the hotel manager pull up the security tapes. Maybe we'll get lucky and recognize someone."

"It couldn't have been Porter," Lainey said, finally showing a trace of the attitude he'd seen earlier when she'd confronted the Houston man. "He was in the bar the entire time."

"Don't rule him out yet. He could have paid the bellman to deliver the note." Colt picked up a discarded blouse from the floor, probably thrown there when she dressed to meet Porter. "You can't stay here tonight," he said, handing her the rumpled shirt.

Panic flashed in her eyes momentarily before she recovered. "I'll be fine. The door has a dead bolt."

"No," he said much too quickly. "Whoever sent you this warning probably intended only to scare you, but I'll be damned if I'm going to gamble with your life to find out." He glanced at his watch. It was after midnight. Thank God, Gracie was at his mom's.

He pulled out his cell phone. "Start packing and I'll call one of your sisters to let them know you're on the way."

"No."

He turned to face her. "No?"

"Maddy moved to a two bedroom condo after Robbie was killed in Afghanistan. There's barely enough room for her and Jessie as it is." She pulled her suitcase from the closet and plunked it on the bed. "Kate lives with two other residents. No way I can go there. I'll call the Hilton down the road."

"That wouldn't solve anything. You'd still be by yourself. What about Deena?"

Lainey opened her mouth to respond then quickly closed it.

"What? Deena has a four-bedroom house. Surely, one of those is not in use."

Lainey narrowed her dark eyes. "A long time ago, I told Deena I saw Mike with another woman at Billy Bob's. When she confronted him, he made up some bullshit excuse, and she believed him." Lainey paused. "I don't blame her. They'd only been married a little over a year. I should never have told her. Anyway, Mike hasn't spoken to me since." She shook her head. "It has to be the Hilton."

Colt drew a breath. "You can stay in the guest quarters at the ranch. It's close to the main house, and the dogs guard the perimeter like they own it. You'll be safe there."

Lainey's eyes widened. "I can't do that, Colt. Really, I'll be fine at the Hilton."

"It'll only be for a few days." He rose from the chair. "It will give Gracie a chance to get to know her long-lost aunt."

Nice touch, he thought, mentally patting himself on the back. He couldn't resist adding, "Besides, it's obvious I need to keep my eye on you in case you decide to do any more of your Nancy Drew impressions."

"Ha!" she exclaimed, throwing a stack of blouses into the suitcase. Suddenly she froze when there was a loud knock at the door, a gasp escaping her lips.

Colt's eyes met hers, and he put his finger to his lips to silence her. For the second time, he reached for his gun. "Who's there?" he asked, inching toward the door.

When there was no answer, he waved his arm signaling Lainey to go into the bathroom. Cautiously, he opened the door, but no one was there. "Hello," he yelled down the hall.

Nothing.

"Police! Come out slowly, hands in the air." He was about to head down the hall to investigate when a man appeared from around the corner by the elevator.

"Can't find my room." The words were slurred. "Could have sworn it was on this floor."

Just then, the elevator stopped and the man disappeared. Colt stood in the hall, debating whether to go after the guy and question him further. Unwilling to leave Lainey alone, he walked back into the room and shut the door "You can come out now, Lainey. It was just a drunk from the bar who can't find his room."

Even as he said it, he couldn't stop the feeling that it might be more than that. He punched in a number on his phone and waited. Lainey emerged from the bathroom, her face still ashen. He related the details to a sleepy Flanagan and instructed him to call Rogers and get down to the Conquistador ASAP.

"I'm through arguing, Colt. Let's get out of here."

———

The moment the elevator door closed, the man blew out a sigh of relief. *That was a close one.* He wasn't getting paid to go head to head with the law. No sir! The two grand in his pocket only covered scaring the TV bitch back to wherever the hell she came from.

Too bad that's all he was supposed to do. He'd watched her all night in the dress that barely covered her ass. He would have loved a couple of hours with those legs wrapped around his neck.

He had no idea why they wanted her gone, but who was he to ask questions? He was only getting paid to put the note under her door, wait for her to return, then knock once to scare the shit out of her. The money didn't cover a hayseed sheriff with a big-ass gun. He'd reached for his own automatic when the guy surprised him, then smartly reverted to the old, I-can't-find-my-room bullshit.

When the elevator stopped in the lobby, he exited toward the bar, shrugging uncomfortably in the suit. He hated suits, never wore them, but tonight he needed to blend in with the other businessmen in the bar. He'd eyeball Porter one last time so he could include it in his report, then he'd head to Dallas and pick up a quick blow job on Harry Hines Boulevard before driving back to Waco. He patted his wallet, fatter with the extra grand they'd given him for keeping tabs on the oilman who was now so drunk he was having trouble staying upright on the barstool.

They wouldn't be happy when they heard that. The quick and easy job he'd signed on for now involved the local pigs and a drunken cowboy. In his vast experience, that always spelled complications. He reached into his pocket for the phone and flipped open the receiver, his eyes trained on Porter, who was now proclaiming his

TEN

"Damn it! I knew he was a loose cannon." He slipped out of bed, careful not to wake up the woman spooning him. Once the door closed behind him, he spoke into the receiver, his voice low. "Where is he now?"

"In the bar downing double scotches like he'd just spent three weeks in the Sahara. What do you want me to do?"

"Get him out of there before he starts shooting off at the mouth about our deal. I don't care how you do it. Just get it done."

"Not a problem, boss, but I only stopped back to check on him before I left for business in Dallas. I've already earned my pay tonight. Anything extra will cost you."

He frowned, the lines creasing his brow. This wasn't the first time this joker had come back with his hand out, and it was starting to be a problem. But the extra money didn't even come close to the millions that would go down the toilet if Porter fucked up the deal. "Don't I always make it worth your while? Keep him in sight and call me the minute he's back in his room."

"Can do, but I expect the compensation to be worth what I'm giving up."

"You know I'm good for it," he said, more annoyed than he wanted to let on. "Just do it."

He slammed the receiver and opened the bedroom door. "God-damn it," he swore under his breath as he crawled under the covers. There would be no more sleeping until after the next call.

———

Jerry Moretti stared at his wife as she sashayed out of the bath-room wearing a long dark fur coat. When she was directly in front of him, she did a slow turn to give him a better look.

"Isn't it gorgeous, lambkins? Russian sable." She ran her hands down the rich brown fur provocatively. "See the silver threads? That's how you can tell how expensive it is." She made a graceful pirouette in front of him. "I got it for a steal."

Jerry took a deep breath, trying to calm down before he spoke. "Do you really need one more mink coat to go with the other four hanging in your closet, darling?"

Roxy pouted, her lower lip protruding in the cute way that usually made him putty in her hands.

Not this time!

"Vladimir was only in town one day. The trunk show at Market Hall was by invitation only. It's an honor to be on his short list." She opened the front of the long coat to allow him a peak at what she was wearing, or more correctly, what she wasn't wearing.

His mouth watered at the sight of his naked wife, still turning him on after two years of marriage. Quickly, he looked away. "Goddamn it, Roxy. Where were you the other night when I explained money would be tight for a while?"

Roxy stepped toward the bed until she was standing right over him. In a quick motion, she heaved herself on the bed and straddled him, moving her hips suggestively as she touched the expensive mink to his cheeks. "A man like you deserves to have a woman next to him wearing the most expensive fur in the world, doesn't he?"

She purred as she replaced the fur rubbing his cheeks with one of her breasts. "A coat like this tells the world you must be one helluva stud to have a woman like me. You do want people to think that, don't you, angel face?"

Damn her! She knew he couldn't resist those tits. He opened his mouth and suckled the huge brown nipple.

"See, baby, I'm worth every penny you spent on this coat."

"You are, Roxy. No argument there," Jerry said between licking and sucking. He wiggled her other breast out of the coat and squeezed. "It's just that until we get Tessa's brat paid off and I get the vineyard back in my family where it belongs, we need to go a little easy on our spending." He closed his mouth on the second nipple, tracking his hand past her cleavage and down the length of her body. "You're wrong, though, dumpling. This is the most expensive fur in the world," he murmured as he grabbed her crotch.

"Ooh," she squealed. "You can't have one without the other, sweetheart. You knew the day you met me I wouldn't come cheap."

Tell me about it, he thought, right before her hand snaked down and stroked him. "Oh, Christ, keep the fucking coat," he said between fast choppy breaths. He flipped her on her back and positioned himself above her. There was something to be said for sleeping buck-ass naked.

Shoving her spread legs over her head, he entered her. Slowly, at first, before he pumped, rocking with her in perfect harmony.

He stopped grinding and looked at Roxy after a shrill ringing nearly scared him out of his skin. "Shit!"

"Don't answer it," she whispered hoarsely. "You've got me wetter than an ice sculpture in the middle of a Texas heat wave. Keep going, Jerry, please." Roxy tightened her ankles around his neck and pushed her lower abdomen into his.

"I have to take this call," he said, raising up and reaching for his cell phone. "I've been waiting all night." He walked into the hallway before he gripped the receiver. "Yeah."

"You remember that problem we talked about today?" The words were slurred.

It was all he'd been able to think about.

"I had a nice visit with your new partner tonight before the sheriff interrupted. I think he wanted some of that action himself. Before they left, she mentioned needing money to get out of Texas. She'll be an easy sell."

He took a deep breath as he flipped the receiver shut. The man was three sheets to the wind, but if what he said was true, if he could get full ownership of the vineyard before the big deal, Roxy could get ten of those damn coats if she wanted.

"Where was I?" he said, walking back into the bedroom. The unmistakable anger in his wife's emerald eyes wiped the smile off his face. He would have to grovel.

"Goddamn it, Jerry, you know how hard it is for me to get off without a vibrator! I was almost there when you had to go answer that stupid phone. What could be more fucking important than me coming all over you?"

He raised her legs up again and entered her for the second time. "Right off the top of my head, I can think of two million things. All green." He reached for the vibrator that stayed permanently plugged in and turned it to the highest mode. "Get ready, sugar. Daddy and his Big Mac are gonna make your day."

————

As soon as Colt drove through the gate, the dogs appeared out of nowhere, barking in near harmony as they escorted the car down the gravel driveway like Secret Service protecting the President.

"How many dogs do you have?" Lainey asked, remembering Colt had always loved animals, had even planned to go to veterinary school before his father died.

Colt laughed. "Only two, but they're fiercely protective. Once they decide they like you, they won't even let me get close."

"Maybe that's a good thing," she blurted before she could stop herself.

That was stupid! All night there'd been this electricity between them, especially when he'd held her in his arms at the hotel, but whatever she'd felt, it was gone now. He was simply the town sheriff doing his job to keep her safe. She was an idiot for bringing it up when he obviously blew if off. Keeping her distance was definitely a good idea until she left for Florida in a few days. The man had generously offered his home to her. The last thing she wanted was to make him uncomfortable.

"That probably is a good thing," he answered, turning to flash that drop-the-panties grin Tessa had warned her about. "The sooner we get you out of that dress, the better." He stopped the car in front of a small brick cottage situated a few feet from the main house, then turned to her, a touch of mischief in his eyes. "That really didn't come out the way it should have. I meant—"

"I know what you meant," Lainey interrupted. She opened the door and slid out. Forget getting out of the dress. The faster she got away from him period, the better. The faint smell of his musky aftershave was messing with her mind. "Nice place. Who lives here?" She bent down to pet the two dogs lapping at her heels and was immediately subjected to the wettest kisses she'd ever received.

"Fred! Ginger! Leave her alone," Colt commanded as the dogs jockeyed for her attention and now had her flat on the ground. "I'm so sorry. They aren't usually this overwhelming."

When the dogs finally moved away to sit obediently next to Colt, Lainey sat up, swiping at the slobber that covered her face and pulling at the dress that had ridden up her thighs. "Some watch dogs you have, Winslow."

His shoulders relaxed when he realized she was kidding. "They don't get to see women out here very often. Apparently, they like that dress as much as the suits at the bar did." He grabbed her arm and helped her up before walking back to the car and opening the trunk. "Come on. I'll give you a tour of the place."

He hauled her small suitcase out with one hand and closed the trunk with the other. "And to answer your earlier question, no one lives here. It used to house the ranch foreman, but after I bought the place from Josh Keating, I turned it into guest quarters. My mom stayed here after her knee surgeries."

"You run the ranch by yourself?"

"Not hardly," he said with a grin. "I rent out the back pasture to a neighbor who raises longhorns. We passed his place when we turned off the main road. The arrangement works for both of us.

He gets to have more cattle, and I make a little extra without all the hard work." He pointed to the barn on the other side of the house, his face lighting up with pride. "I use the revenue for the upkeep of my horses. Gracie is becoming quite the quarter horse expert."

"Her mother loved horses, too." As soon as the words left her mouth, Lainey wished she could take them back. "I'd love to see Gracie ride," she added, hoping to get his mind off the earlier remark. From what everyone said, Tessa and Colt's friendship had been a casualty of the divorce.

He met her gaze momentarily before walking up the two steps. At the door, he turned. "Come on in. You must be exhausted."

———

He answered the phone before the second ring, springing out of bed and racing to the door. A backward glance confirmed she was still asleep. Must be all the wine she'd drunk earlier. "Did you get him to the room?"

"Yeah, but there was a problem."

Dammit! It was too late in the game for problems. "What kind?"

He heard the other man laugh nervously. "I told you he was shit-faced, didn't I?'

"You mentioned it."

"Well, when I finally got him to his room, he started fighting me. He wanted to toss back a few more with another drunk he met downstairs. I poured him straight bourbon from the mini bar, but he wasn't interested."

He rubbed his forehead, trying to ward off the migraine now building on his left side. "You got him in bed, right?"

"Not exactly. With all that booze in him, he thought he was Muhammad Ali."

His head started to throb. "I'll deal with him in the morning."

"Ah, boss, like I said. There was a problem."

"Spit it out. What kind of problem?" He never did like this guy. Never really trusted him.

"He's dead."

The color drained from his face. "What the fuck did you do?" he screamed, then opened the door to see if he had awakened her. Her gentle snoring was a testimony to the wonders of alcohol.

"He came after me like a fucking bull. Even took a swing at me and busted my lip. When I shoved him, he fell into the nightstand and cracked his head. There was blood everywhere."

This morning everything was right on track. A dead body definitely changed things. "Are you sure he's dead?"

"His head was split wide open. Brains and shit were hanging out. I nearly puked."

"Where are you now?"

"In the hotel parking lot trying like hell not to smear his blood all over this rental car." The man paused. "By the way, my fee just went up another twenty-five grand, and I need it now so I can skip town and lay low until this blows over."

The rage only made his head pound harder. "I don't have that kind of money lying around."

The man laughed. "Sounds like you have a problem then. I'd hate to have to tell the cops about you if they catch up with me."

"Is that a threat?"

"Take it any way you want. I just need my damn money."

After a moment he said. "Meet me in the alley behind the hotel in twenty minutes. I'll bring the cash."

"Wise move. I'll be waiting."

He disconnected and walked back into the bedroom. His clothes were strewn across the chair exactly where he'd thrown them last night while she was still sober enough to be worth anything. He didn't bother to wake her to tell her where he was going.

Porter was never really a player in the deal. He'd just let him think he was, promising to allow the drilling if he got Tessa and Jerry to agree to sell. His plan was to make Moretti think the Houston man was the only one interested in the vineyard because he knew neither Tessa nor Jerry would consider what his investors would do with the land. He should have known Porter couldn't keep his mouth shut, should have realized making him part of this was a mistake, especially since he was one of only a few who could identify him. Now he was dead and there were other problems to contend with.

He pulled out the hidden compartment in his nightstand and grabbed the Beretta on his way out the door.

ELEVEN

I've slept with a lot of dogs in my life, but never one that actually barked.

Lainey shot straight up in bed at the sound of her sister's voice. "Where have you been? You hung me out to dry at the bar with Bozo."

You obviously handled yourself pretty well.

Lainey glanced at her wrist. Just as expected, a purplish bruise had formed on the inside where Porter's fingers had pressed. "Yeah, I was freaking Rambo," she deadpanned.

Ginger lifted her head from her curled-up position at the end of the bed and sniffed. Fred opened his eyes, looked up, then immediately went back to his loud snoring, snuggling closer to Ginger on the thick comforter.

Just like a man, Tessa said. *Fun to look at but not too bright. Kinda like a lava lamp.*

"Did you know someone shoved a threatening note under my door at the hotel last night?" Lainey asked, ignoring the quip.

Tessa's smile faded. *Is that why you're here?*

Lainey propped the pillow behind her and leaned back. "Someone wants me out of town in a hurry."

Welcome to my world. Every woman in Vineyard would have loved to ship my ass off to Timbuktu or some damn godforsaken place.

"No, seriously, Tessa, Colt thinks I'm getting too close for someone's comfort."

I wish I knew who that someone was. Tessa crinkled her nose. *I can't believe you slept with these mutts. They smell like old lady Roberts every time she wore her fur coat.* She flashed the famous Tessa smile that Lainey knew always preceded a wise crack. *Remember how we called it her wet coyote mink?*

Lainey smiled. She did remember that coat. "It rained pretty hard last night, and I felt sorry for them." She reached down and rubbed Ginger's head. "They're sweet dogs."

Colt always did have a soft spot for animals. It killed him when he had to leave A & M to come home and take care of his mother after his dad was killed.

Lainey turned away. That was the year her world had fallen apart. She'd come home on spring break and discovered Tessa had stolen her journal. They'd never really gotten along, but when Tessa found out about her crush on Colt, her teasing turned relentless. Then Tessa got pregnant and the next thing Lainey knew, she and Colt were getting married. The day Tessa told her, eyes flashing victory, was the day Lainey left Vineyard and never looked back.

Suddenly, both dogs jumped up and ran to the door, their barks deafening. Instinctively, Lainey moved closer to Tessa, unable to stop the horrified gasp that escaped her lips.

"Wake up, sleepyhead. Breakfast is served in five minutes."

Hearing Colt's voice, way too cheery this early in the morning, Lainey let out the breath she'd been holding.

Not once in all the time I was married to that man did he ever fix me breakfast.

———

Lainey stared down the driveway, waiting, wondering how Gracie would react when she found out she had to spend the morning with an aunt she didn't even know existed until her mother died. It was not the ideal way to get acquainted. Lainey remembered when she'd found out her own father had died. She'd known he'd been sick and had spent a lot of time in hospitals, but she'd fallen apart the day he didn't come home. She'd been angry for several weeks—at her mother, at God, at anybody who would listen.

"Go back and get him," she'd shouted, blaming her mom for coming home without him. Granted, she'd been a little older than Gracie, but the loss nearly killed her. She hoped Gracie would have an easier time with her grief.

She moved closer to the window, feeling the chill of the March morning, her breath fogging the glass. The rain had clumped the leaves around the base of the big oak tree that shaded Colt's porch almost like a blanket protecting it from the nip in the air. She pulled the oversized gray sweater tighter around her body. Colt's sweater. Somewhere in the middle of the bacon, eggs, and biscuits and gravy, she'd mentioned she was cold. Within minutes, he had the big sweater draped over her shoulders, unaware his touch on her neck had sent chill bumps up her arms. He'd assumed her sudden shiver was from the low temperature, and he'd upped the thermostat.

She stepped back from the window and took a good look at Colt's house. Like him, it was warm and masculine, but definitely lacking a woman's touch, although he did say his mother had selected the curtains. Dark green with burgundy trim, they kept the house cool and dark. Probably just the way he liked it.

Lainey's gaze took in the kitchen in one sweep. A little on the small size for her taste, it had proven adequate for the lumberjack breakfast he had whipped up. Scolding herself with every bite she'd stuffed in her mouth, she'd cleaned her plate and even scarfed down a cinnamon bun afterward. No doubt, she'd have to spend at least a month or two of hard work in the gym to get rid of the extra pounds she had to be packing on.

Hell, the chicken-fried steak the other day probably added a whopping five pounds, and that didn't include the mashed potatoes and gravy. Oh Lord, she'd forgotten about Ruby's bread pudding. For sure, she needed to get some exercise. Thank God, she would be back in Savannah late Friday, and she could work off her overindulgences.

She pulled the chair away from the kitchen table and sat down with a fresh cup of coffee. Why did everyone else's coffee taste better than hers? Maybe it was because she was always running late, grabbing the instant stuff on the way out the door. She took another sip, then spied a picture on the mantel of Gracie sitting on an absolutely gorgeous black horse. Moving closer, she was surprised to see Tessa standing next to her, also staring at the picture.

I bought her that mare two years ago when she showed an interest in rodeo competition.

Lainey reached up and examined the picture. "She's the spitting image of you, Tessa. You must be proud."

Tessa sighed. *She's the only thing I ever got right in this world.*

"Why'd you give her up, then? Why'd you let Colt have full custody if you loved her so much?" Lainey raised her hand. "Don't answer that. It's none of my business. I know you must have had your reasons."

Long story. Someday, I may tell you, but for now, let's just say I loved her enough to know Colt was the better parent.

Lainey bit her lip to keep from saying she found that reason hard to swallow. Whatever Tessa wanted, she got. It didn't matter who got trampled in the quest.

Where's Colt?

"He had to run down to the station to sort out some new evidence from last night. Porter said he was home in bed with his wife when you were poisoned. He has to check that out, plus find out who left the note at the hotel."

So, you're going to hang out here all day?

"I'm taking care of Gracie until Colt gets back."

She heard Tessa's sharp intake of breath, saw the sudden sadness sweep across her eyes. *Where is Gracie?*

For the first time since she could remember, Lainey felt a genuine stab of empathy for her sister. "Colt's mother is dropping her off. She was supposed to keep her today, but her knee's acting up. The doctor's going to squeeze her in for a cortisone injection."

A car rounded the corner, making its way toward the house, and Ginger sprang to life. She raced toward the end of the driveway with Fred at her heels.

"That must be them now." Lainey opened the door and walked to the top step, hoping this wouldn't turn out to be a disaster.

The Chevy sedan pulled to a stop. Gracie, looking so small in the big car, trained her eyes on Lainey. Surely, her grandmother had warned her that her dad had to work for a few hours.

"Hello, Mrs. Winslow," Lainey said as soon as Colt's mother stepped out of the car. "It's nice to see you again."

"Call me Delores, Elaina. I'm sorry I'm interrupting your day, but I really need to see Dr. McCullough."

"Don't give it another thought. I'm looking forward to getting to know my niece. Hopefully, you'll feel like a new woman after the shots."

She huffed. "Hope so. I must have twisted my knee somehow last night when Gracie and I went out to dinner. I was awake half the night trying to find a comfortable position. If nothing else, I'll sleep all day."

Lainey walked down the steps just as Delores opened Gracie's door. "Hi. Remember me?"

The child nodded, then stared at Lainey's chest. "Hey, that's my dad's sweater. Does he know you're wearing it?"

Lainey tugged on the collar as a faint whiff of fabric softener reached her nose. "Yeah. I was cold this morning, and he let me borrow it."

Gracie stepped out of the car and bent down to receive Ginger and Fred's wet kisses while Delores opened the trunk and pulled out her small suitcase.

"Let me," Lainey said, taking the suitcase from her. "You go on to the doctor. The sooner you get help for that knee, the better."

She held her hand out to the little girl. "Come on. Let's go see what kind of trouble we can get into before your dad gets home."

The child's eyes lit up. "We can play on Daddy's computer. I'll show you the letter I got from the Mickey Mouse Club. It has my name on it, and all the Mouseketeers signed it."

That wasn't so hard. Mentally patting herself on the back, she grabbed Gracie's hand and guided her up the steps. "I can't wait to see it." At the top, they both turned to wave as Colt's mother made a U-turn and headed back down the drive with a two-dog escort.

"Let's go put your clothes away first, then we'll take a look at your dad's computer."

Gracie stopped and looked up. "What was your name again?"

Lainey's breath caught in her throat. She was beautiful. Tessa's shining accomplishment. At the thought of her sister, Lainey whirled around to see if she was still there. She wasn't. She turned her attention back to Gracie. "I'm Lainey. You don't have to call me Aunt Lainey if you don't want to."

"We'll see," she said, sounding much wiser than her eight years. She was smart enough not to commit too early. She'd make a great businesswoman.

"Sounds like a plan. Now lead me to your room and we'll get these clothes put away."

Gracie raced ahead of her up the stairs. By the time Lainey made it to her room, she had already flopped down on the bed. Slightly out of breath from trying to keep up, Lainey flopped down beside her. "Wow. What a great room."

"Mommy helped me decorate."

It figured. Tessa always had a knack for this sort of thing. The room was bright with pinks, greens, and purples everywhere. Draped with hot pink toile, the canopied bed looked like every stuffed animal in the state of Texas was propped against the pillow shams.

"You did a fantastic job." Lainey opened the suitcase and Gracie pulled out her dirty clothes and dumped them in the hamper. She added two more stuffed animals to the zoo across her pillows.

"Come on, Aunt Lainey, let's go play on Daddy's computer." Gracie giggled. "I called you Aunt Lainey." Grabbing Lainey's hand, she raced back down the stairs to the study and pulled up an extra chair next to the computer.

The day flew by as Lainey and Gracie got to know each other and played on the computer. Colt had done a great job raising her. When he called to tell them he was on his way home, Lainey felt a twinge of disappointment. One look at the child's face told her Gracie did, too.

It had been a fun morning. The only time Lainey left her chair was to phone her agent to tell him to move her interview to the following week. She hoped they'd understand when he told them her sister had died. It was already Wednesday and after spending time with Gracie, there was no way she'd let Jerry Moretti screw her niece out of her rightful inheritance. She'd make it a point to get involved with the negotiations along with Tessa's lawyer.

"Please, please, please, Aunt Lainey, can we look at my Mickey Mouse letter one more time before Daddy gets home?" The longing in her eyes was too compelling to ignore.

"Okay, but we have to hurry. He was already leaving the station when I talked to him." She pulled up Outlook Express again and clicked on the Gracie folder. Her squeal when she saw the letter was worth the risk of Colt catching them on his computer.

"Look at all the people who signed it. This one is my favorite Mouseketeer." Gracie leaned across Lainey to touch the signature on the bottom, then lost her balance and fell forward, landing hard on the keyboard.

"Oh, no." Her eyes quickly filled with tears as they stared at the blank screen. "I've ruined it."

"No, no sweetheart. You just accidentally deleted it. We can get it back, I promise." Lainey said a quick prayer to Saint Anthony, the patron saint of lost things as she opened up Colt's Delete file. All her efforts to get closer to this child would be wasted if she couldn't get that letter back. Short of calling Mickey on the phone, she would find a way.

With a smile, she located it and moved it back to Gracie's folder. "There. It's back where it belongs." About to click on the folder to show her, another deleted e-mail caught her eye. It was from Tessa ,dated approximately two weeks before her death and had the word "Gracie" in the subject line.

Curiosity overcame her better sense. "Gracie, can you get me a glass of water from the kitchen? I have a tickle in my throat."

Gracie stood up and hugged her neck. "Sure, Aunt Lainey. I'll be right back."

The moment Lainey was positive Gracie was out of the room, she opened the e-mail, wishing she hadn't. Tessa wanted Cole to agree to joint custody of Gracie. Obviously, he hadn't been willing to do that. The last line, in all capital letters and underlined, caught her attention.

DON'T MAKE ME GET A COURT-ORDERED DNA TEST FOR YOU AND GRACIE. I GUARANTEE YOU WON'T LIKE THE RESULTS.

Ohmygod! Was Tessa warning Colt that Gracie was not his? Even Tessa wasn't that cruel, or was she? Why hadn't Colt said anything?

Lainey slammed the laptop shut when she heard Colt's voice at the front door. She took a few calming breaths before she greeted the man who very well may have been responsible for her sister's death. Watching the way he picked up his daughter and swung her around, Lainey realized he had one damn good reason to want Tessa out of the way.

TWELVE

"Hello, Mike. Deena's expecting me." Lainey greeted her brother-in-law, her lips tipped in a half smile.

He stepped aside to let her pass, his dark eyes boring into her.

Guess he's still pissed after all these years.

"I'll call later, honey." He grabbed a jacket off the hook next to the door, still glaring at Lainey. "Need me to pick up anything on the way home?"

Deena appeared and hugged Lainey. "If I think of something, I'll call. Have fun at the racetrack." She tugged at Lainey's jacket until it was off. After hanging it on the hook where Mike's coat had been, she nudged her toward the kitchen. "I made King Ranch Chicken, your favorite."

Lainey's eyes lit up. "It smells wonderful. I haven't had that since…" She stopped before she blurted that their mother had fixed it the night Tessa announced at the dinner table she was getting married.

Deena kissed her on the forehead. "I know. Come on, you can help Maddy with the salad while I fix our drinks. Kate's stuck in Dallas traffic."

Lainey walked around the table to hug her older sister then picked up the potato peeler and the biggest cucumber she'd ever seen.

"Don't get any ideas," Maddy joked when Lainey stared incredulously at the vegetable.

"Jeez! Did they use steroids to grow this thing?" She turned to face her sister. "And for the record, Maddy, you're the one who hasn't been laid since the Stone Age."

"Yes, she has," Deena said as she handed them each a Margarita Swirl.

"No way!" Lainey exclaimed, using her finger to mix the Sangria with the frozen Margarita before taking a sip. "Yum. You always did make these better than any bartender, Deena."

"Damn straight," Deena replied before turning to Maddy, her lips quivering as she tried to hold back a smile. "Tell her about it, big sis. I haven't had a good laugh in a while."

"Anyone I know?" Lainey pushed aside the barstool and moved closer to her oldest sister.

Maddy flushed as she took a swig of her drink and shot Deena a look that should have at least wounded her. "Nothing to tell. I had a date. We went to bed. End of story." She reached for another wedge of lettuce and plunged the sharp knife down the center.

"Tell her why it was the end of the story," Deena prompted.

"You have a big mouth, Deena. No wonder I keep some things secret from you."

Deena faked a pout before the grin returned. "If you don't tell her, I will."

"Okay. Okay," Maddy said, pointing the knife at Deena. "Then I'm going to tell her about you and that old fart at the nursing home."

"Quit stalling, Maddy. I need details."

"It was Dusty Robinson."

"The hottie from Lakeview?" Lainey's eyes lit up with recognition. "The one who drove the 'Vette and had all the Vineyard girls fighting for a chance to try out him and that car on Inspiration Rock?"

"Yep," Deena answered.

Lainey turned to Maddy. "You sly fox! My sister Maddy actually hooked up with the biggest catch in town. Yes!" She raised her arm above her head. "So how was he?"

"A dud," Maddy replied, trying to sound annoyed but unable to hide her own glee when Deena burst out laughing.

Pencil dick is a better word.

Lainey did a 180, nearly slicing her finger with the peeler. "How would you know, Tessa?"

Tessa smiled. *Do you honestly think I wouldn't know about the best-looking guy in the county? Seriously, Lainey, are you forgetting his dad owned the biggest ranch in Texas?*

"Tessa slept with Dusty Robinson?" Both Maddy and Deena inched closer to Lainey.

Hell, yes. All my friends were wild over him, so I had to do him. Shit, he was like a Texas snowstorm. You never know when they're coming or how many inches you'll get.

Lainey shook her head. "Where do you come up with those?"

If I remember correctly, drop-dead gorgeous Dusty shot his wad way early, and I didn't need even half a ruler for an accurate measurement. Can anyone say premature ejaculation?

Lainey burst out laughing.

"What'd she say?" Maddy asked.

"Dusty was a little quick on the draw, Maddy?"

"Damn her! She did have sex with him," Maddy shouted before she broke out in a grin. "Let's just say his trigger finger never actually reached the trigger, but the gun went off anyway."

Trigger finger, my ass. That boy only had a sawed-off shotgun, and he wouldn't know what to do with that trigger finger even if it came with pictures and an instruction sheet.

Lainey was barely able to repeat Tessa's words, and before long, the sisters were doubled over with laughter.

"What's so funny?" Kate asked, throwing her coat and purse in one of the chairs as she walked into the kitchen from the hallway.

"Do you remember Dusty Robinson?" Maddy was still having trouble talking.

Kate grinned. "Say no more. His reputation is well known around here." She shoved a crouton in her mouth then turned to Lainey. "Maddy dated him a few times, you know?"

"That's what we're laughing about," Deena said, handing her youngest sister a drink. "Come on. Let's eat while the food is still hot. Lainey can tell us about her trip to the bar last night."

At the mention of the last twenty-four hours, Lainey turned to Tessa, her smile fading. "You and I need to talk in private later." For some unexplained reason, she wasn't ready to tell her other sisters what she'd discovered on Colt's computer.

Like we don't always talk in private?

"You have a knack of disappearing when it's convenient for you."

One of the benefits of being dead, little sister. Tessa tried to sound flippant, but her furrowed brow and narrowed eyes gave her away.

Good, let her worry about it, Lainey thought as she followed Deena into the dining room.

They sat down at the table and began chatting like they hadn't seen each other for years. Nobody mentioned anything about their secret investigation until the dishes were cleared and Deena had served her famous coconut cream pie.

"God, I'm going to be as fat as a cow when I get back on the air in Savannah," Lainey said, licking the whipped cream off her upper lip. "Speaking of my job, I had my agent reschedule the interview in Florida until next week." She shoved another bite into her mouth.

"Good idea," Kate said. "There's no way we're anywhere close to finding out who killed Tessa."

"Obviously someone thinks we are," Lainey began.

An hour later over a second cup of Irish coffee, she had related the events of the night before, without mentioning seeing Tessa's e-mail on Colt's computer. She'd deal with Tessa later. She'd also held back telling them about the way her body had responded when Colt held her in his arms at the hotel. She loved her sisters, but they'd think she was an idiot for even thinking about that.

"Ohmygod!" Kate exclaimed when Lainey got to the part about the note under her door. "We have to stop this right now before you get hurt." Her eyes filled with tears that threatened to spill. "Please, let Colt deal with this."

Lainey turned to Tessa, who had moved close to Deena at the head of the table, unusually quiet since the sisters sat down.

Tessa nodded. *It has gotten too dangerous, Lainey. You should listen to Kate. Let the cops handle it.*

"Like hell I will. It's gonna take more than a jerk like Porter and whoever else is trying to run me off." Lainey paused, ready to plead if she had to. She was determined to see this through. "We're getting close. I can feel it."

"Porter's way up there on our Potential Killer List. Do you think he paid someone to slip the note under your door?" Maddy squirted another shot of whipped cream into her coffee. "Maybe he had Roxy do it after one of their sexcapades."

"Don't ask me why, but for some reason, I don't think he's our guy. He talks a tough game, but he crumbled when Colt questioned him." She turned toward her dead sister. "You agree, Tessa?"

Hmm! He definitely gave it up faster than a five dollar hooker. I think you're probably right. The man's like a Mounds candy bar— no nuts.

"What did Colt say about the note?" Deena asked.

"I think it shook him up a little. People around Vineyard want to believe whoever killed Tessa had a grudge against her, Colt included. The note moved it out of that category and into more sinister motives."

"Like what?" Kate grabbed the Irish whiskey and poured a dollop into her coffee. "Porter was the only one who wanted the vineyard, and from what he said at the bar, he was about to get it, with or without Tessa."

"I don't know." Lainey rubbed her forehead. "Maybe it really was someone Tessa pissed off."

"What about the security camera at the hotel? Surely a hotel like the Conquistador has one on every floor?"

"They do," Lainey replied. "Unfortunately, someone spray painted it black. You can't see anything."

"Jeez! Didn't the desk clerk notice that?"

"Apparently he was on the phone to his girlfriend for two hours. He didn't realize it until the cops showed him the camera. Needless to say, he is no longer a Conquistador employee."

"That brings us back to square one, but it doesn't make it any safer for you, Lainey." Kate sipped her coffee. "Actually, it probably makes it more dangerous."

Lainey swiveled her chair to face Tessa. "We have to be missing something, Tessa. Who wanted you out of the way badly enough to kill you? Think about it. How could someone poison you without you knowing how they did it?"

"Ask her to tell you everything she ate starting with dinner that night. Colt said cyanide works fast, so it couldn't have been lunch," Maddy said.

Just the Chinese food, but I wasn't very hungry. I barely tasted it.

"A little Chinese," Lainey told her sisters before turning back to Tessa. "What were you drinking?"

Tessa's forehead crunched. *I remember I wasn't feeling so great. I was dizzy and I could hardly catch my breath.*

"That's what cyanide does to you," Deena said after Lainey repeated Tessa's comment. The other sisters stared at her. "What? I Googled it!"

The Viognier! Tessa exclaimed. *I had a glass of Viognier.*

"Viognier?"

It's a new white wine we were researching to see if we wanted to add it to our catalog.

"Where'd you get it?" Lainey straightened up in the chair, visibly excited.

Tessa shook her head. *It wasn't the wine.*

"Where'd you get it, Tessa?" Lainey repeated the question, her voice escalating an octave.

Tessa looked up and took a slow deep breath before blowing out the air. *A few years ago, I tasted the wine at a small vineyard in northern California. I was so impressed, I knew it would be a big seller here in Texas. Convincing Jerry to import the grapes wasn't so easy, though. He had this macho thing about only using our own Texas-grown crop. We nearly came to blows over it.* She paused. *Our vintner was extra careful to keep the oxygen out of the barrels because it would have ruined it. He was as excited about it as I was.* Tessa smiled. *It turned out fantastic, almost as good as the one I sampled in California. I knew we were on to something.*

"Tessa," Lainey interrupted, her voice harsher than she intended. "Who brought the wine?"

It was straight out of the barrel. Tessa's eyes clouded over with sadness. *Jerry dropped it off.*

THIRTEEN

COLT REREAD THE REPORT Flanagan had laid on his desk a few minutes earlier. It was the final toxicology report from the ME's office. As he suspected, Tessa had enough cyanide in her blood to kill a small village.

"What?" he asked when he glanced up to see Maddy standing over his desk.

She handed him another report "This just came in. It's the laboratory analysis of Tessa's stomach contents." Despite trying to sound detached as if she were discussing another victim instead of her dead sister, the slight catch in Maddy's voice said otherwise.

He met her stare before he began to read. He knew that look. She had something on her mind, and she was not about to leave until she said it. Quickly, he scanned the new report, not in the mood to hear the latest office gossip.

Tessa had a small amount of undigested chicken and rice in her stomach. No surprise there since Lainey mentioned Tessa had

Chinese food delivered that night. Chicken fried rice had always been her favorite.

A conversation two days ago with Joey Winters who'd delivered the food had verified Tessa's food choice, and after a chat with both Joey and his mother, Carolyn, Colt had reached the same conclusion as Lainey when she and her sisters decided to track down Tessa's killer on their own. His gut told him the Winters family had nothing to do with the poisoning, but he wasn't ready to cross either of them off his list just yet.

Lainey and her sisters were a whole different headache. After what happened at the hotel the other night, hopefully the Garcia girls would move out of police work and into something less dangerous. It would sure make his job easier.

He smiled, thinking how nice it was having Lainey in the guest house. He loved watching Gracie get so excited in the morning waiting on Lainey to come to the house for coffee. If he didn't know better, he'd swear the two of them shared some kind of secret, the way they giggled when he was around. Truth be told, he looked forward to the mornings more than he liked to admit.

He glanced down at the paper in his hand, embarrassed Maddy had seen the smile that tipped his lips. Thankfully, she had no way of knowing what had made him grin. He cleared his throat and concentrated on the report. Tessa had consumed a small quantity of some kind of white wine. Again, no surprises. His ex-wife was in the winemaking business and preferred white over red.

He looked up to find Maddy still leaning over his desk. "You gonna tell me what's on your mind, or you just gonna stand there all day?"

Maddy pursed her lips and shrugged before she turned and stepped toward the door. "They were researching a new wine to see if they could market it," she said, pivoting to face him again. "That's what Tessa drank that night."

Colt laid the file on the desk and squinted. "Now, how would you know that, Maddy?"

She chewed on her lower lip, as if she were measuring her words carefully before she spoke. "I talked with Tessa about seven that night. She was waiting on dinner to arrive, and she mentioned the new barrels of wine. She was really excited because she was going to try it for the first time."

Colt eyed her suspiciously. "When'd you say you talked to her?" He rummaged through the file for a report. When he found it, he frowned, lines creasing his forehead. "Your number doesn't show up on her phone records."

Maddy looked away, shifting uncomfortably from her left foot to her right. If he were a gambling man, he'd bet the farm this woman was lying through her teeth, and he was determined to find out why.

"Maybe it was earlier when I talked to her," Maddy said. "I stopped by on my way home from work to see if she wanted to go to dinner with Jessie and me after Jessie's soccer game."

Colt observed her shifting her weight back to her left leg.

"And you think maybe the cyanide was in the wine?" He made a mental note to Google winemaking as soon as he was alone. Although Vineyard was famous for its wineries and even had an annual grape stomping festival, he knew nothing about the mechanics of his own hometown's number-one industry. Was it possible an entire barrel had been contaminated somehow?

"I don't know, Colt. I never really got into all that technical stuff with my sister. All I know is the grapes were imported from California, and Tessa was about to get her first taste."

Colt's eyes narrowed. "Seems strange she didn't invite you in."

Again Maddy shifted. "She did. Like I said, Jessie had a soccer game that night, and I was already running late."

"So did you at least taste the wine with her?"

He saw a look of panic flash momentarily in her eyes. "She didn't have it yet when I was there."

Colt straightened up. "Where'd she get it?"

"I can't be sure. I didn't stick around to find out." Maddy leaned farther across the desk and lowered her voice. "I really think the poison was in that wine."

"Until the lab confirms it, we can't be sure." He picked up Tessa's phone record again and studied it. Other than the original call to the Chinese restaurant, there had been no phone calls in or out.

"You should talk to Jerry about this."

That got his attention, and he leaned forward, his hand on his chin. "Why Jerry?"

Maddy glanced down at the floor and licked her lips, a maneuver he recognized as her stalling technique when he asked something she didn't want to answer. "Tessa couldn't go out to dinner that night with Jess and me because she was waiting on him. He was supposed to bring over a bottle of the new wine after he tapped the barrel." She turned and walked out the door before he could question her further.

Reaching for the file, he flipped through the police reports until he found his notes on the initial interview with Jerry Moretti. He didn't remember Jerry mentioning he'd stopped by Tessa's the night of the murder, and he wanted to make sure before he confronted him. After rereading the report, he leaned back in his chair, eyebrows furrowed. This was strange. Not only had Moretti not mentioned it, he'd made it a point to say he went straight home from the office that day because he'd hurt his back lifting barrels. He'd mentioned it three different times.

Colt definitely needed another face-to-face with Mr. Moretti. He was reaching for the phone just as Landers opened the office door and stuck his head in.

"Better put a hold on that call, boss. The head honcho at the Conquistador is on the other line waiting to talk to you. You need to hear what he has to say." He pointed to the blinking light on the phone. "You're not gonna like this."

Colt blew out a whiff of air. The day had not started out great after they discovered the security tapes from the Conquistador were useless. They weren't any closer to finding out who put the note under Lainey's door than they were the night it happened. Hell, for that matter, it had been nearly a week since Tessa was killed, and they still had no one who even remotely looked good for the murder. From the sound of it, his day was about to get worse.

He picked up the receiver and punched the blinking button. "This is Sheriff Winslow."

"Sheriff, this is Joel Lakota at the Airport Conquistador. We spoke yesterday when I gave you the tapes from the sixteenth floor…"

"Yes, we're still examining them, Mr. Lakota. I'll get them back to you as soon as I can."

"That's not why I'm calling, Sheriff. One of my housekeepers made a gruesome discovery a few minutes ago."

Colt braced himself. "Go on."

"She attempted to clean one of the rooms even though it had a Do Not Disturb sign on the door. When she went in, she saw a body on the floor, blood everywhere. She freaked out. We're still trying to calm her down."

"Keep the door shut, and make sure no one touches anything until we get there with the crime scene guys. Don't let the housekeeper leave, either, Lakota." He made eye contact with Danny Landers who was still half in, half out of the room, a knew-you-wouldn't-like-it look on his face. "Any idea who the dead person is?"

"The room's registered to a Quinton Porter from Houston."

So much for the day getting better.

———

Lainey parked the rental car in the visitor spot at Spirits of Texas, even though Tessa's empty space at the back of the building was closer. Making her way to the front door, her mind was already formulating what she'd say.

Last night, after Tessa revealed Jerry had brought over the bottle of wine that possibly contained the poison, the sisters had chosen Lainey as the one to confront him, given her experience with interviews. Later today, Maddy was going to tell Colt about the wine, allowing Lainey time to question Jerry first.

Carrie Phillips glanced up from Tessa's desk, unable to hide the surprise in her eyes when Lainey walked through the door. With the phone cradled between her tilted head and her left shoulder, she motioned for Lainey to sit as she resumed flipping through a pile of reports.

"I know you were supposed to get the new wine last week, but it wasn't ready. It's in the bottling phase now," Carrie said, rolling her eyes when she looked up. "Probably another couple of weeks," she continued, tapping her fingers on the desk. "I'm sure the substantial discount you'll receive on the first shipment will more than make up for your continued patience."

After a few more minutes of conversation, she hung up and faced Lainey. "Why do people always want everything yesterday?"

Lainey laughed. "The story of my life." She glanced around the outer office as Carrie stood and walked to the beverage bar.

"Coffee?"

Something was different about the room, but Lainey couldn't say what. "No thanks. I'm meeting Deena and Maddy later for lunch." She pointed to Jerry's office. "Is he in yet?"

Talk about the story of my sex life with that man!

It shouldn't have surprised Lainey to see Tessa sitting beside her since her sister appeared at will, but she jumped anyway.

"Are you okay?" Carrie asked staring at Lainey with a confused look on her face.

You gotta work on that startle reflex, sis. You should be used to me by now.

"I'm fine," she answered Carrie, ignoring Tessa. She pointed again at Jerry's office. "I need to talk to him."

Carrie pushed back a stray curl that had fallen over her right eye. "He's pretty busy this morning."

"This can't wait," Lainey responded, more emphatically than she wanted. She met Carrie's stare until the older woman turned away and picked up the phone. Tessa's best friend seemed nervous, not her usual bubbly self.

144

She looks like she hasn't slept in a week. Tessa commented. *Wonder if she and David are on the fritz?*

"I know you told me not to disturb you this morning, Jerry, but Lainey Garcia is here and insists on seeing you," Carrie said into the receiver.

Like he's doing something worthwhile. The man spends his days surfing porn on the Internet.

Carrie held her hand over the phone and looked up. "Jerry won't be free until after lunch. Wants you to come back, say two-ish?"

Lainey crossed her arms and leaned forward. Dan would say this was her get-comfortable-and-hang-onto-your-ass position. She'd interviewed a ton of arrogant men in Savannah. One more rich boy would be a piece of cake.

She smiled, allowing a swoosh of air to escape. "Could you remind your boss I own half this place? Then tell him I'll just wait in Tessa's office until he can see me." She picked up a *Wine Country* magazine and pretended to read the cover before glancing back up. "Oh, and could you ask him to bring me the books for the past year? It will give me something to do while I'm waiting."

Hot damn, Lainey. You're better than I thought. I almost feel sorry for my ex.

———

The minute Colt walked into Room 817 at the Conquistador, he knew who the victim was. Even with half his skull exposed, there was no denying the loud cowboy shirt or the skin-tight jeans. "Obvious head trauma," Colt deadpanned. "Got anything else?" He bent down to make eye contact with Mark Lowell, the crime scene expert Vineyard shared with four neighboring cities.

Mark picked up a fragment of skull from around the dead man's head with tweezers and deposited it into a clear plastic forensics bag. "Not so far. Looks like this guy put up a good fight, though. I'll scrape his nails and run a DNA on the blood all over his hands. I'm betting it's not his."

Colt watched Mark roll the body over. It was definitely Quinton Porter. "Time of death?"

"Not sure," Mark responded. "My best guess would be sometime between midnight and six this morning."

A knot formed in Colt's gut. He and Lainey had left the hotel around one. It's possible they may have crossed paths with the killer. He racked his brain trying to remember if anyone looked suspicious. Except for the drunk who couldn't find his room, there was no one. An uneasiness washed over him and had him wishing once again he had questioned the guy.

"I can narrow that timeline down a bit, Mark," he said to the CSI. "I saw Porter around one. Granted, he probably would have blown a point 02, but he was very much alive and still drinking."

He'd glanced into the bar one last time on his way out to make sure Porter hadn't snuck up to Lainey's room and put the note under her door. He'd heard him even before he'd looked in, laughing with two or three other drunks at the bar.

"I'll make a note of that." Mark stood up and motioned to the man near the door. "Tell Jacko he and Rollins can take the body to the morgue," he said before turning back to Colt. "We've printed everything in the room that we could. Probable scenario is there was a violent struggle, and this guy was pushed into the night stand at just the right angle with a lot of force." He pointed to the edge of the oak stand, still covered with blood and hair and obvious gray matter.

Colt turned as Flanagan and Rogers walked into the room.

"The night clerk said Porter left the bar alone around one-thirty this morning. The manager is pulling the security tapes now," Rogers said.

"Shit!" Colt raced to the door and flung it open. Halfway down the hall, his suspicions were verified. The camera at both ends of the long hallway had been spray-painted black just like the ones on Lainey's floor.

"Have our guys print the cameras," he said as he walked back into the room, knowing it was probably useless. "Is that Porter's?" He pointed to a cell phone in another forensics bag.

"Probably. It was on the desk."

Colt picked up the plastic bag and turned it over, hoping to see something on the screen that might identify the phone as Porter's. Only the date and time were displayed.

"Hand me some gloves," he commanded. When he had the gloves on, he pulled out the phone and flipped open the receiver. He clicked Calls Sent. Along with several numbers with a Houston area code, there were a few with Dallas interchanges. The last call was made at one in the morning.

Colt hit redial and waited, tapping his finger on the desk.

"Hello," a soft female voice drawled.

"This is Sheriff Winslow. To whom am I speaking?"

"Well, my goodness, Sheriff, you don't have to be so formal. What can I do for you?"

"Who is this?" he repeated.

She giggled. "Everyone says my voice is sexy, Colt. I'm surprised you don't recognize it." When he didn't respond, she continued, "It's Roxy."

Colt froze. Why in the hell was Porter calling Moretti's house at that time of night? Then he remembered the pictures of Roxy and Porter they'd found on Tessa's computer. A booty call? "Did you talk to a man named Quinton Porter last night?"

"Who?"

"I don't have time for games, Roxy. I know you and Porter had a thing. I don't care about that right now. I only need to know if you talked to him last night."

After an awkward silence, she responded, the giggle in her voice totally gone. "I heard the phone ring last night, but Jerry answered. You're not going to tell him, are you?"

"Not unless I have to," Colt said. "Was it Porter on the phone?"

"I don't know. Jerry got out of bed and went into the living room to talk. I had a little too much to drink last night, and I went right back to sleep." She paused before asking, "What's this all about, Colt?"

"Probably nothing," he lied. The last thing he wanted was for Roxy to alert Jerry before he had a chance to question him. A person's initial reaction to something like this was always priceless in an interrogation. "I'll try to catch him at the office. Everything okay your way?"

"Peachy," she said. "I'll tell Jer you called when he gets home tonight."

"You do that." Colt disconnected and turned to his two detectives. "Where's Landers and Romano?"

"Danny's waiting to hear back from you. Said you wanted him to pull Jerry Moretti's phone records for some reason."

Colt sighed. "Damn!" He'd forgotten Maddy had told him Jerry was the one who delivered a bottle of wine to Tessa the night she was killed. He'd been about to call and ask him about it when he got the news of a dead man at the Conquistador.

He turned back to Mark Lowell. "You guys done here?"

"It's all yours." The CSI closed the container with his equipment and stood up. "I'll call when I know something."

When they were alone in the room, Colt barked out orders. "You two start interviewing the staff as well as the guests. I'll have Maddy fax over a picture of Porter. See if anyone heard or saw anything this morning that might help."

"On it," Flanagan said, and then he and Rogers exited.

Colt flipped his phone open and dialed the station. "Send Landers over to the courthouse. I need a warrant signed for Spirits of Texas and Jerry Moretti's house. Then have him and Romano meet me at Jerry's office ASAP," he said as soon as Maddy answered the phone. "We have probable cause."

FOURTEEN

THE AMUSEMENT IN CARRIE'S eyes faded as Lainey's thinly veiled threat to inspect the books registered. Her eyes narrowed as she took her hand off the receiver. "She said…" Carrie stopped as if she had been interrupted. Then she turned to Lainey. "Jerry is rescheduling his morning appointment. He'll see you in a few minutes, Lainey."

Oh, she's pissed! Tessa said, standing up when Lainey did. *I know that look.*

Lainey stopped at the door to Jerry's office and turned back to Carrie. "Let's do Happy Hour one day this week. I'd love to catch up." Despite Carrie's smile, Lainey recognized the unmistakable flash of anger in her face.

Her eyes moved beyond Carrie to the wall behind the beverage bar. No pictures! That was what was different about Tessa's office. Someone had taken down all the photos of Tessa and Gracie, and that angered Lainey. Her sister was barely in the grave—actually, she wasn't, but still, it was a bit early to ditch her things.

"I'd like to have the pictures you took off the wall." Lainey didn't wait for Carrie's response. She turned and reached for the knob just as the door opened.

Her surprise at seeing Tessa's lawyer leaving Jerry's office was as obvious as his unmistakable look of a cat caught with the family bird in his mouth.

"Nice to see you again, Miss Garcia. I was just going over some things with Jerry about Tessa's will."

Why did he feel an explanation was needed? "Nice to see you too, Mr. Prescott." She extended her hand. When he reached for it, she glimpsed the look that passed between him and Carrie.

"I'll need to come by later this week to finalize what we talked about the other day," Jerry shouted out to him.

Prescott cleared his throat. "Call the office anytime," he mumbled, placing his hat on his head and walking out without telling Carrie or Lainey goodbye.

Strange, Lainey thought as she walked into Jerry's office. Why was Tessa's lawyer having a conversation with Jerry without her there?

A quick scan verified Jerry had the bigger office since Tessa had split hers to build the apartment in back. Tessa had definitely been the better decorator.

Whoever picked out this office décor must have been high, Lainey thought as her eyes moved from the orange-red couch in the corner to the solid orange chair in front of Jerry's massive ornate desk.

Jerry glanced up and smiled, motioning for her to sit in the chair that up close looked like someone had barfed after eating a dreamsicle. "So what was so God-Almighty important that it couldn't wait until after lunch? Charlie and I were going over some legal stuff that needed to be taken care of immediately." Despite the smile, his cheeks were flushed with anger.

Lainey perched on the edge of the ugly chair and Tessa moved behind it. "First off, I know you're not happy with Tessa's decision to leave me half this winery."

"Damn right, I'm not."

I don't know what makes this guy so stupid, but whatever it is, it works.

"Regardless of your opinion, I intend to take my responsibilities seriously."

The smile faded. "And you think your experience in front of the camera qualifies you to waltz in here and pretend to know what the hell you're doing?"

About as much as watching naked women on your computer qualifies you, ass wipe.

"I'm a fast learner." Lainey moved forward in the seat. "I didn't come here to discuss that, Jerry. I came to find out if you had anything to do with my sister's death."

The smile disappeared completely. "What kind of jackass question is that? I admit there were times I wanted that woman out of my life, but killing isn't my style."

Oh, please. Like you have a style.

Lainey decided to jump right to it. "What was in the bottle of white wine you dropped off at Tessa's the night she was killed?"

His face flamed. "I was nowhere near your sister's house that night. Working with her eight to ten hours a day was more than anybody should have to tolerate. I sure as hell wouldn't let her ruin my evenings, too."

Lainey forced her lips to part in a curved stiff smile. "We both know that's not true, Jerry. You brought her a bottle of the new batch of Viognier, but conveniently, you didn't stay to taste it with her."

He jumped up, his knee connecting with the edge of the humongous oak desk. "How the fuck would you know that?" He grimaced as he rubbed his knee.

Lainey cringed under his rage and slid back into the chair. Had she miscalculated what he might do? She began to rethink her decision to question him by herself.

Tell him Paul Ridley told you.

"Paul told me." Lainey had no idea who Paul was.

Slowly, Jerry lowered himself to his chair. When his eyes met Lainey's again, she could tell he'd calmed down somewhat. "Our vintner is mistaken. We did taste the new wine together, but that was the night before."

This SOB is lying like a rug.

Lainey shrugged, deciding to play nice cop. "People sometimes get confused about those kinds of things. It's possible Paul mixed up the two days."

The beginning of a smile again formed on Jerry face. "I'm pretty good at remembering things like that."

Bullshit! You can't count your balls and come up with the same number twice.

Lainey laughed out loud before she could stop herself. Picturing Jerry using his fingers to count was too much, and she giggled again. "Sorry," she apologized. "I was just thinking I was pretty good at that myself." She bit her lip to try to look serious again. "So, you're saying you didn't stop by Tessa's the night she died?"

153

"Hell no!" He leaned forward. "My Roxy thought I still had a thing for your sister. I'm not stupid. I would never take a chance on getting caught at Tessa's…"

Both he and Lainey turned toward the door as a male voice bellowed outside. Before either could speak, the door flew open and banged against the wall hard enough to rattle the picture hanging over the couch. Colt breezed past Lainey and stopped in front of Jerry's desk.

He glanced first at Lainey, then Jerry, his blue eyes slit in anger. "Someone wanna tell me what this little meeting is all about?"

"She was just—"

"I stopped by to discuss my new role as partner." Lainey finished Jerry's sentence while returning Colt's stare.

Jerry let out the breath he'd been holding. He looked relieved, probably thinking she wasn't going to tell Colt about the wine. Her lips tipped in a smile before she quickly turned away. It might be fun watching Jerry squirm as Colt grilled him, but she was already running late for the lunch date with her sisters.

She stood up. "Unless there's something else, Jerry, we'll continue this conversation later." She flashed him a grin then turned to Colt. "I'll see you at the house."

Colt reached for her arm and gently held her immobile. "Hold it, Lainey." He squinted. "You're sure this was strictly business?"

He was standing so close that when she looked up, she noticed a tiny knick on his chin. He must have cut himself shaving this morning. She zeroed in on his lips, afraid he'd see right through her lie if she looked into his eyes.

Big mistake! She found herself lost in those luscious lips, envisioning what it would be like to have them all over her face, her body.

"Lainey!"

She jerked upright, a rude ending to the wonderful fantasy. "Of course, it was business. What else could it be?"

He stared hard, as if searching for the truth beyond her eyes. Lainey gulped, knowing she was busted, waiting for him to blast her for interfering in his investigation.

Again!

When he didn't, she pulled out of his grasp and walked to the door. Before she exited, she glanced back as Colt slammed a piece of paper in front of Jerry.

"I need you and Carrie to sit quietly in the front office. This is a warrant to search the place."

Jerry's mouth fell open wide enough that a quarterback could have used it to practice his throws. When his eyes met Lainey's in an accusatory stare, she flipped her finger off her forehead in a salute and exited. She couldn't wait to tell her sisters.

———

By the time Colt and his men finished with Spirits of Texas, he was craving a long tall one. He glanced at his watch, wishing it was closer to the time he could actually indulge himself. Today had been one for the record books. He hadn't seen this much action in Vineyard in the eight years he'd been on the force.

"Now that you've torn the place apart and found nothing, I suppose you'll go on over to the house and tear that up, too," Jerry snarled, his eyes sending daggers.

"Don't need to. My men are there now."

"Goddamn it, Colt! I told you I had nothing to do with Tessa's death. Why can't you believe me?"

Colt whirled around to face him. "Oh, I don't know, Jer. Maybe because just about everything you've told me so far has been a lie. Makes it kinda hard to believe anything you say."

Jerry opened his mouth, then must have thought better of it and slammed it shut, crossing his arms tightly across his chest instead. "I'm telling the truth, Colt. You can ask Roxy."

"I already did." Colt knew he shouldn't enjoy watching the outrage spread across Jerry's face as much as he did.

"What's going on here?" David Rivera asked as he pushed through the front door. "Looks like every police car in Vineyard is parked out front."

"Not all of them," Jerry commented, sending more daggers Colt's way.

"I called David to talk some sense into you, Colt," Carrie said. "Why in the world would you ransack this office? What could you possibly be looking for?"

Colt acknowledged David with a nod before turning to Carrie and Moretti. "Did you know a purchase of cyanide was made from Tessa's laptop two weeks ago?"

"I knew it," Jerry shouted, jumping up from the couch. "The bitch went and killed herself just to spite me."

Colt took a step toward Jerry who slumped back down on the couch. "That's one angle. More likely someone used her computer and the company credit card."

"Tessa would never kill herself," Carrie said, standing up and moving toward David. "You must be mistaken, Colt."

"Oh, yes she would if she thought it would hurt me somehow," Jerry said.

"Not everything is about you, Moretti," Colt reprimanded.

"Are you through here, Colt?" David asked. "I'd like to take Carrie to lunch unless you have other plans for her."

Colt met his stare. If there was ever any doubt whether or not David still held a grudge after all these years, his body language coupled with the double entendre made it crystal clear. Once best friends, they rarely spoke now.

Colt's expression grew somber as he remembered the old David. Six feet four, he'd been the star wide receiver, as well as district All-American point guard for the Vineyard Panthers. He had it all—good looks, decent grades, and the prettiest girl in Vineyard by his side. Then he blew out his knee in the state semifinals senior year, and suddenly, he was no longer a "big man on campus."

Graduating with honors several months after Tessa and Colt's wedding, David then moved back to Vineyard and worked his way up the city management chain. Colt had tried to rekindle the friendship, especially after he and Tessa divorced, but David wanted nothing to do with him.

Who could blame him?

"Carrie can leave," Colt said, choosing the high ground and not commenting on David's last remark. He turned to Jerry and flipped his thumb toward the office. "I need to talk to you in there, Moretti."

"Come on." David reached for Carrie's arm. "Let's allow the sheriff to earn his salary." His face curved in a grin, but his dark eyes remained angry.

Good thing the people of Vineyard voted me in as sheriff, Colt thought.

157

If David was able to use his power as city manager to have a say so over the police department, Colt knew he would be out on his ass for sure. A disturbing thought crossed Colt's mind as he realized he wasn't trained to do anything else. He'd left school in the middle of his senior year after his father died, leaving behind his dream of becoming a veterinarian.

Before it was all said and done, he'd realized what The Rolling Stones sang about years ago—*You Can't Always Get What You Want*—was true. He'd gone back to UT Arlington for his criminal justice degree and never looked back.

At the time, leaving his mother alone to struggle through the funeral and all the legal stuff that followed had not been an option. His mother had been lost, had no clue how to even pay bills.

He'd planned to go back to school the following semester after he'd taught her enough to survive until he graduated. That was before she fell and broke her hip. An only child, the responsibility for her had fallen squarely on his shoulders, not that he'd minded. He loved his mother and would have done anything for her.

But even his mother couldn't help him through his grief over the loss of his father, couldn't stop the loneliness that ate at his heart. While his friends were partying at school, he was stuck in Vineyard taking care of his mother. If it hadn't been for Tessa also leaving school, Colt knew he would have gone stir crazy.

Waking up beside her after an all-night pity party had scared the hell out of them both and in the end, ruined their friendship. He'd found himself more alone than ever, responsible for an unborn child as well as an invalid mother and filled with resentment for having to give up his dream.

But he'd thrown himself into his own investigation to find the person who had run down his father on the back road by their house and left him there to die. After six months, he'd discovered an out-of-the-way body shop and managed to get friendly with the owner who bragged about getting paid double for doing after-hours body work on a Mercedes in some guy's garage. Colt found out the man was an attorney with two prior DWIs that had been pleaded down to misdemeanors.

When the police closed in on the guy with a receipt Colt had lifted from the body shop, even his denial hadn't mattered. All the evidence Colt had relentlessly gathered was enough to convince a jury. How fitting he was now the police chief and the lawyer was rotting away in Huntsville serving out the life sentence he deserved.

"Can we get this over with, Colt? I'm gonna have to spend a lot of money on Roxy to make up for you guys trashing the place."

Colt snapped back to reality when Jerry rose from the couch and headed for the office.

After sending Flanagan and Rogers back to the station, Colt followed Jerry and plopped down on the ugliest couch he'd ever seen. Somehow, sitting where Lainey had been a short while ago made him smile.

Christ, she'd looked hot in that two-piece sweater set. The turquoise blue made her dark eyes jump out as she looked into his face and lied right through her teeth when he'd asked why she was meeting with Jerry. If Maddy knew it was Jerry who delivered the wine to Tessa, chances were pretty good Lainey did, too. The odds were even better that despite his warnings, she was still poking around in something that could get her shot.

"What's on your mind, Colt? I've answered your questions twice already."

Colt reached for a notebook from his shirt pocket and pulled the pen out from the metal rings. "Who called your house last night around midnight?"

Nothing like jumping right to the point.

As he expected, a look of sheer panic crossed Jerry's face. "Wrong number," he snapped, his lips pursed.

"That's not what Roxy said. Why'd you drag your sorry ass into the living room to talk to a wrong number, Jer?" Colt flipped through the notebook. "Talking for over two minutes to a stranger seems odd."

Jerry's color faded and he blew out a breath. "Okay, don't mention this to Roxy, but I'm seeing someone on the side."

Colt laughed out loud. "Since when did you quit chasing skirts and start hitting on Houston cowboys, Moretti?"

Jerry reached for the phone, his face somber. "Do I need a lawyer?"

"You might," Colt responded. "Right now, we're just having a conversation."

"I suppose you already know who called?"

"I do."

"Shit!"

Colt smiled again, thinking he'd love to get this man in a high-stakes poker game. "Why'd Quinton Porter need to talk to you so late?"

Jerry stared out the window for a few seconds before he turned back to meet Colt's intense stare. "You know my wife, right, Colt?"

When Colt nodded, he continued. "A woman like that doesn't come cheap, ya know?"

Again, Colt nodded.

"Porter promised me a lot of money if I could help him get the okay to set up his equipment in the far corner of the vineyard." Moretti sniffed, shaking his head. "Hell, we don't ever use that land anyway. Too rocky for vines."

"So, you and Porter were in cahoots with Roxy?" Colt asked, fishing to see if Jerry knew about his wife's extracurricular activities.

"Roxy? What the hell does she have to do with anything?"

Question asked and answered.

"Tessa hated Porter. She wouldn't talk to him when he came by the office. She even complained to Rivera about him. Said he was harassing us."

"David Rivera?" Colt shot up in his seat. "Why did she go to him? What could he do?"

"He and Tessa met occasionally for a drink." A smile formed on Jerry's face as he apparently realized he knew something Colt didn't. "You know everybody figured David would end up with Tessa instead of you." When Colt didn't respond, Moretti continued. "Apparently, she thought he could help her get rid of Porter, him being the city manager and all."

"Did Carrie know?"

"Know what?"

"That her fiancé was meeting his old girlfriend on the side?"

Jerry leaned back in the chair, his hands clasped on the back of his head. "It only happened once or twice. Carrie was usually out of town." Then he grabbed the edge of the desk to keep from tipping over.

This guy was the same doofus he'd been back in high school. All that money couldn't buy him class. What had Tessa ever seen in him?

Colt grinned. Anyone who had spent five minutes with his ex-wife knew Tessa had loved the finer things in life. She could afford them with Jerry's money. That's what she'd seen in him.

"So, back to you and Porter. Did you talk to him today?" Colt knew the answer but watched for Moretti's expression.

"He's back in Houston by now. We're gonna sit down with Lainey and discuss his offer in a few weeks. Maybe by then, she'll be ready to get out of Dodge and head back to her life, wherever the hell that is." Jerry shook his head. "For the life of me, I can't figure out why Tessa left her half of a business she loved to a sister she hadn't talked to in years."

Colt's eyes perked up at the mention of Lainey. "You're counting on Lainey leaving town soon?"

"Sooner or later, she'll realize selling her half to me is the smart thing to do."

"Did you want that badly enough to threaten her, Moretti?" Colt felt a sudden anger, remembering how scared Lainey had been the night she'd found the note. Remembering how vulnerable she'd felt, her trembling body pressed against his.

"Threaten her? Hell, Colt, she's a barracuda, a carbon copy of her sister. I learned the hard way with Tessa. Don't screw with women like that." He chuckled. "I'm just gonna wait it out. It won't take long for Vineyard to bore a big city girl to tears."

Colt processed his comment. For some reason, he believed Jerry had nothing to do with the note. Call it gut.

"Speaking of your ex-wife, Moretti, did you put the cyanide in the bottle of wine you took to her house the night of the murder?"

FIFTEEN

"That bitch!" Moretti's hands shook as he pointed toward Colt. "She's lying, Colt. I'll tell you exactly what I told her. I wasn't anywhere near Tessa's that night."

Colt's face flamed. *Damn her!*

Lainey was poking around in the investigation behind his back again. It was past time he had another chat with his ex-sister-in-law. With Gracie sleeping over at Maddy's house with Jessie, tonight would be the perfect time to confront Lainey. Knowing how much his daughter had responded to her newfound aunt's attentions, more than likely, he would end up the bad guy in Gracie's eyes if the conversation heated up.

And he was pretty sure it would.

He pushed Lainey from his mind, determined to crack Moretti. "Nowhere near Tessa's, huh, Jer?" He stared across the massive desk, ready to nail him. "That's funny. Your vintner explicitly remembers you coming in right before he left that day and asking him to tap one of the barrels so you could check it out. Said you were so excited after tasting it, you insisted he fill a bottle to take to Tessa's."

Jerry looked defeated. Finally, he leaned forward. "Okay, Colt, this is the truth for real now. I did take Tessa a bottle of the wine, but there's no way the poison was in it. Paul and I both sampled the Viognier from the bottle before I hand-carried it to her."

"Why'd you lie about it?"

"Hell, if Roxy found out I went over to Tessa's, she'd kick my ass. I wouldn't get laid for a year."

Colt contemplated this. His radar for reading people was pretty good, and unless Jerry was a master liar, he believed his story.

"Where were you between midnight and seven this morning?"

"With a wife who looks like Roxy, where the hell do you think I was?"

"And Roxy will verify this?"

"Of course she will. Where you going with this, Colt?"

"Porter's dead." Colt stared into Moretti's eyes, hoping to catch his reaction.

"What?" Jerry's face turned whiter than his laser-treated teeth. "How?"

"Someone shoved him into a nightstand. Did a number on his skull."

A smidgeon of color returned to Jerry's cheeks, and he leaned forward, eyes squinted. "And you think I might have had something to do with it?" He tsked, holding up his thumb and second finger. "Jesus, Colt, I was this close to doing business with the man and making a ton of money."

"Can you think of anyone else who might not be so crazy about the guy?"

Jerry thought for a moment. "I barely knew…" He paused. "Wait a minute. I do remember him saying he had another deal in the works. Said that's why he was making so many trips to Vineyard lately."

"What kind of deal?"

"I have no idea. I assumed it had something to do with drilling for oil."

Colt's ringing cell phone jarred him from his intense study of Moretti's face. He flipped up the receiver. "Winslow."

"I think you'd better make a detour on your way back to the station, Colt," he heard an excited Flanagan say. "We've got another body at the Conquistador."

———

The minute Colt exited Freeport Avenue and turned into the Conquistador lot, an uneasy feeling gripped him. Was this somehow connected to Porter?

He parked the cruiser. Walking to the entrance, he was mobbed by what looked like every guest in the hotel, all talking at once, all demanding answers. With the details of Porter's death splashed across the news media, this latest murder had everyone in a state of panic.

The hotel manager spotted Colt as he came through the revolving doors, and scrambled over, bringing at least five TV crews with him.

"Sheriff Winslow, is there any connection between the man you found in his hotel room this morning and the most recent victim?" the hot chick from Channel Eight asked.

Another reporter shoved a mic in his face. "Sheriff, could this be the work of a serial killer?"

"Should the people of Vineyard take steps to protect themselves?" The Channel Four guy nearly whacked a colleague on the head trying to get his mic closer.

Lakota shrugged. "They're going crazy. Apparently, someone from my staff alerted the TV stations right after I called you," the manager said, clearly exasperated.

Colt waved off the reporters. "I'll make a statement after I have a chance to see the body and check out the crime scene. I'd appreciate if y'all will step back and allow me and my men to do our jobs. You'll know something when I know something." He turned back to Lakota. "Where's the body?"

The man looked ready to break into tears as terrified hotel guests swarmed, still demanding answers. "In the alley behind the dumpster. Your men just arrived and are out there now." He pointed to an Employees Only door down the hall. "That's the quickest way."

The crowd slowly separated to allow Colt through when his narrowed eyes threatened consequences if they didn't. He pushed through the doors that opened directly into the back alley. Lifting the yellow crime scene tape his men had used to cordon off the area, he stooped under it.

Danny Landers knelt beside the body and glanced up when Colt approached. "Looks like a single gunshot wound to the back of the head." He pointed to the area.

Colt squatted for a better look. The victim was about five-ten and dressed in a dark blue suit. He certainly could have been any one of a number of business travelers who stayed near the airport every night on business. But what was left of the vic's buzz cut caused a flash of recollection in Colt's mind. He remembered seeing a man with a buzz cut sitting at the bar when he'd confronted Porter. With the man's back to him, Colt hadn't seen his face.

"Any I.D.?" Colt asked, noticing a scar slightly below a path of blood that had dried after streaking across his cheek. He glanced down the alley at the blood trail, now puddled in a pothole about ten yards from the body.

"We've got to stop meeting this way, Winslow. My wife's getting suspicious," Mark Lowell said as he arrived with two of his men. He bent down and made eye contact with Colt. "What the hell's going on in Vineyard?"

After nodding to Mark, Colt rose and backed off to allow the CSIs access to the victim.

What the hell *was* going on in Vineyard? He turned to Landers and Romano. "Anybody see or hear anything?"

"No," Landers said. "Maybe the perp used a silencer."

Colt mulled that over, glancing up. The Conquistador was directly in the path of ascending airplanes. "More likely, the noise up there would have covered up a gunshot."

Just as he said it, he caught a glint of something in the sunlight, and he hustled over for a closer look. "Over here," he shouted to the CSI assistant bagging the evidence. "Another one here." He pointed to the two used shell casings near the fence surrounding the dumpsters.

"Looks like a nine millimeter," the CSI commented as he picked it up with tweezers and deposited it into a clean forensics bag.

Colt rubbed his cheek. "That's interesting."

"Why's that?" Mark's young assistant asked.

"A nine mil is not the preferred weapon of gangs or run-of-the-mill shooters. It's used primarily by homeowners for protection." Colt inched closer to the body. "Can you guesstimate the time of death, Mark?"

The CSI chief glanced up. "I'd say around the same time span as the guy from this morning. Somewhere between midnight and seven. I'll know more after the ME finishes."

"Can you turn him over?" Colt asked.

The assistant bent down and helped the chief roll the body on its back.

Caught off guard, Colt was unable to stop the gasp that escaped.

"You recognize him, Colt?" Mark asked, as everyone turned to stare.

Colt tilted his head for a better look at the dead man's face. It was him!

Dammit! Why didn't I go after him?

He knew keeping Lainey safe had been the right move, but he'd missed a golden opportunity to question the guy. "He knocked on Lainey's door last night right after she found the note. Said he was drunk and couldn't find his room."

"He may not have found his room, but he definitely found trouble." Mark reached into the man's back pocket and pulled out his wallet. He flipped it open. "Kenny Thornton. Says here he's from Waco."

Colt was no longer paying attention to Lowell. He leaned closer and zeroed in on the multiple scratches on the man's left cheek. He'd bet hard-earned cash he was staring at a perfect DNA match to the scrapings Mark had bagged that morning from under Porter's fingernails.

"I'm sorry. Do what you have to, but I need another week off, Dan." Lainey parked her car in front of Colt's guest house and climbed out, adjusting the hands-free headset. She smiled as Colt's two "watchdogs" covered her with wet kisses that smelled like beef jerky.

"I don't see how staying in Texas an extra week is going to help," Dan argued. "We're getting pounded with e-mails. Your adoring fan base wants to know when you'll be back."

"I'm sure Angie is holding down the fort," Lainey replied, unable to stop the huge grin from spreading across her face. Angie Summers would probably take over her job one day, but Lainey was secretly overjoyed her true-blue fans would not take it lightly.

"She's doing okay," Dan said. "But that's not the point. I've got my hands full trying to convince the producers to be patient." He paused before adding, "Especially since there's a good chance you're going to leave us anyway."

There it was—finally out in the open. They'd been dancing around it the entire fifteen minutes since he'd called.

"Is that really what this is about, Dan?" She opened the trunk and lifted the bag of groceries she'd picked up at Kroger's on her way home, noticing how beautiful the Texas sky was with the flaming orange sun beginning its descent directly beyond Colt's rooftop. "Dan?"

"I'm here," he said after a few seconds. "Damn it, I miss you, Lainey."

She softened. Dan Maguire was one of the nicest guys she'd ever met. Why couldn't she give him what he wanted? What held her back? "I know. I miss you, too." It was only a half lie. The truth was she had totally forgotten to call him the last few days. A flash of guilt stabbed at her heart when she realized she had to tell him how she felt. He was too good a man as well as a friend to string him along.

"Dan, I—"

You brought the Viognier! Ohmygod, I can't wait until you taste it.

Lainey whipped around, nearly dropping the phone nestled on her shoulder as she hobbled up the steps and into the kitchen.

And brie! Oh God, I wish I could eat, Tessa said. As excited as a teenager on her first date, she peeked into the grocery sack when Lainey placed it on the table.

"I have to go, Dan. I promise I'll call tomorrow with an update." She'd been on the verge of telling him about the note. Knowing how stubborn she was, he would have understood why she couldn't leave Vineyard now. Still, he'd have insisted she come home now before she got hurt.

"I love you," he said, his voice sad with regret.

"I know. Me too." She did love Dan, just not the way he wanted her to. She disconnected and blew out an audible breath.

Was that the guy you've been sleeping with?

Lainey shot Tessa a look. "How do you know about Dan?"

She shrugged. *Just guessing.* She turned away. *You might not want to burn your bridges with a guy like that, Lainey. There aren't too many good ones left.*

"Isn't that the sad truth?" Lainey said, speaking more to Tessa's first comment. Maybe she shouldn't ruin what she and Dan had until she was absolutely sure she couldn't learn to love him the way he wanted her to.

Hey, where'd you get the Viognier?

"I stopped by the winery and talked to your vintner after I left Jerry's office."

Did he tell you Jerry picked up a bottle of wine for me that night?

"Yes, but he said both he and Jerry sampled the wine from your bottle. It couldn't have been laced with poison."

Shit! Back to square one again.

"Not necessarily. What if Jerry added the cyanide after he left Paul?"

Tessa rubbed her chin. *Hmm. I never thought about that. Does Colt know?*

"Oh yeah," Lainey said, shaking her head. "He walked in on my meeting with Jerry while we were discussing it. I have a feeling I'm gonna get another lecture when he gets home."

Tessa smiled. *I always thought Colt was the most adorable when he was pissed about something. His blue eyes get all steamy and his eyebrow goes up like this.* She hitched her left brow up in a comical grimace, exactly the way Colt did.

Lainey laughed out loud. "You have it down pat. I'm probably going to see that tonight, and thanks to you, it will be hard to keep a straight face."

She pulled the cork from the bottle and poured the Viognier, then raised the plastic cup in a mock toast to Tessa before she took her first sip. "Oh, my! This is fantastic, Tessa."

Told you. Despite trying to look only casually interested, Tessa's eyes said otherwise. This wine was her baby.

172

"What did Paul do different to get it this smooth?"

Tessa frowned. *If you're going to run the winery, Lainey, it's time for a little education.* She moved closer. *Every type of wine comes from a different grape. Chardonnay, merlot, pinot, they all have their own grape.*

Lainey took another sip. "You definitely hit onto something special when you grew this one."

You can't grow Viognier grapes in Texas, my not-so-smart sister. It's too freakin' hot. We imported them from a small vineyard in northern California. That was one of the knock-down, drag-outs between Jerry and me. He wanted things to stay as they were.

"I'm glad you convinced him." Lainey poured another glass. "I don't think I've ever had a white wine this smooth."

Tessa beamed. *Even Jerry was amazed. We're gonna sell this at fifty bucks a bottle, wholesale. Only the finest restaurants in the area will serve it.* She paused and lowered her eyes. *I hate being dead. I hate that you and Jerry will sell it, not me.*

Lainey poured her third helping, noticing Tessa's raised eyebrows. "What? These cups are small."

I know you, little sis. You'll be drunk before Colt gets home. She giggled. *I once read an article in a magazine about the dangers of heavy drinking. Scared the shit out of me, and I never read that magazine again.*

Lainey shook her head. As irritating as Tessa was, she made her laugh, but hearing her mention Colt's name reminded her they had unfinished business. She swallowed the sip of wine and placed the cup on the table. "Sit," she commanded.

Tessa's eyes questioned before she plopped down in a chair opposite Lainey and giggled. *We never really did this, you and me. Are we about to have some kind of sister talk?*

"Is Colt Gracie's father?"

Tessa gasped. *Now why would you ask a stupid question like that?*

"Cut the crap. I saw the e-mail you sent him."

Tessa folded her arms across her chest and glared. *I never figured you to be a snoop, Lainey. Since I know Colt would never show that to anyone, I have to assume you looked into his personal things.*

Lainey opened her mouth to defend herself then decided against it. "Does it really matter how I found out? What's important is whether it's true or not."

Tessa took a deep breath then exhaled slowly. *It is.*

Lainey stood up, knocking the chair backwards. "How could you do that to him, Tessa? Even for you, it's unconscionable. And why would you tell him after all these years? He was the only parent Gracie had, real or not."

Tessa quickly dropped her lashes but not before Lainey saw the hurt. "I'm sorry," she said softly. "That was a low blow. I know you loved Gracie and wanted custody of her. I get that, but to threaten Colt with the only thing in life he lives for..." She paused, unable to go on, sitting back down instead. Reaching for the wine, she tilted her head back and drained the glass.

I have no excuse, Tessa said softly. *I know I was a shit. Hell, I was a shit to everyone. I was used to getting my own way no matter what I had to do.* She paused. *Remember when I told you my life was going to change big time?* When Lainey nodded, Tessa continued. *I thought I would get joint custody and start acting like a mother for once. I had big plans for Gracie and me.*

"Who is Gracie's father?"

Tessa studied Lainey's face for several minutes before her mouth half-curled as if she couldn't quite complete the smile. *I'm the Whore of Vineyard, remember?*

"So, you're saying you don't know?" Lainey tried unsuccessfully to hide her disgust then chastised herself for being so judgmental.

Tessa shook her head.

"But she could be Colt's, right?"

Again, Tessa shook her head. *Colt's not the father. End of story.*

Then she disappeared, leaving Lainey alone in the room. "Tessa, come back here," she demanded, knowing it wouldn't happen.

Her head was swimming with unanswered questions. If Colt wasn't Gracie's father, then who was? Did Colt know the man?

It was too much to think about after a day like today. She tried to clear her mind and think about the job offer in Florida. Gracie's image kept popping into her head.

She leaned back in the chair and propped her feet on the table. Then she reached for her fourth glass of Viognier and chugged it.

SIXTEEN

COLT SLID INTO THE chair behind his desk and exhaled. Talk about the day from hell.

"This just came in, Colt."

He glanced up when Maddy laid a report on his desk. Despite her effort to come across as all business, Colt noticed her reddened eyes. He'd deal with that in a minute, he thought, reaching for the report.

Earlier, when Maddy had first suggested the possibility the cyanide could have been in the wine Tessa had drunk that night, he'd called the CSI lab about the pieces of glass recovered from the ruins at Tessa's house. Although they hadn't found any large chunks of the bottle, there were thousands of tiny shards. He'd almost felt their eyes rolling when he instructed them to test even the smallest pieces a second time, despite not holding out much hope they would find anything.

This report proved him wrong.

He made eye contact with Maddy, sure this was the cause of her pain. "You may have been right. They were able to find a trace of some substance other than the wine from a few of the shards."

"When will we know for sure?"

"Probably in a few days." He got up and walked around his desk to stand next to his ex-sister-in-law. "You've had a pretty rough day, Mad. Why don't you go home and put your feet up. You've already stayed an hour past your shift."

"I wanted to talk to you about this before I left." She cleared her throat. "Does this mean Jerry killed my sister?" Her voice choked on the words.

Colt saw her tremble. "Not necessarily. We don't even know if what they isolated from the glass was the poison. It could just be something that was added when they fermented the new wine."

Colt's eyes caught Danny Landers outside his office, pressing a piece of paper against the window and pointing excitedly.

"Now go home and relax. That's an order." He turned her body around and walked with her toward the door. "I promise I'll let you know the minute I have confirmation from the lab."

The second the door opened, Danny squeezed through. "Here's what I got so far on the dumpster vic."

When Maddy stopped, Colt gently nudged her. "Go home, Mad. You're gonna have your hands full with Gracie and Jessie tonight. Gracie's so excited, she's piled all her stuffed animals into the sleeping bag." He was grateful no one had told her about his suspicions that the latest victim might have something to do with the note under Lainey's door or Porter's death. He could never have talked her into leaving if she'd known. "I'll see you in the morning."

The minute the door closed, Danny handed his notes to Colt. "I ran his name through the database and found out he's a small time hood from Waco." He pointed to the printed list. "He's got a sheet a mile long—everything from aggravated assault to man one. He just got out of Huntsville last December. Apparently, he's got quite a temper. Roughed up a few of his fellow inmates while he was there."

"Pull any phone records you find registered under his name," Colt instructed. Although they hadn't found a cell phone on Kenny Thornton's body, maybe they'd get lucky and find a clue in his home phone records, that's if he had a home.

When they'd confirmed a car in the parking lot at the Conquistador had been rented to the dead man that day, they'd been able to lift blood and hair samples along with some pretty decent prints. The blood and hair were still at the lab. Colt felt certain the DNA from the blood would come back as Porter's since they'd found a can of black spray paint in the back seat of the car.

"What?" Colt asked, glancing up.

Danny hadn't moved, a smug grin on his face as he showed Colt the other piece of paper he held. "I already pulled his phone records. Look." He pointed to a Dallas number called four times from Thornton's home phone. "Now check this out. Luckily, the guy's cell phone was registered." A grin covered Danny's face as he showed Cole the mobile phone records. The same number was highlighted seven or eight times, the last one around one that morning.

"Good work, Danny." Colt patted the young officer's back. "I'm gonna make a good cop out of you yet."

Landers beamed. "What's next, Chief?"

"See if you can find out who Thornton was talking to in the Dallas area."

"Already did. The number came from a throw-away."

"Damn!" Colt let out a frustrated breath. No one said it would be easy, but he'd hoped they would catch a break.

He walked behind his desk and sat down, glancing once again at the phone records. "Try to find out where the prepaid phone came from, Danny. Maybe we'll get lucky and some 7-Eleven cashier will remember who he sold it to."

Landers raised an eyebrow in a good-luck-with-that look before he turned and exited the office, leaving Colt alone for the first time that day.

If his hunch was right, Thornton had killed Quinton Porter. But why? Obviously, the Waco man was a hired gun, but who wanted Porter dead? From the information he'd gathered from Jerry, Porter had ridden into town like an economic savior flashing big bucks at Jerry and possibly someone else. That is, if what Jerry said about the oilman having another deal in the works was true.

Maybe Porter's death was a robbery gone bad. Colt picked up the file labeled with the Houston man's name and scanned the report. Porter's wallet had been in his back pocket when they discovered him, and it still held nearly a thousand bucks. It was highly unlikely the attack had been a robbery with that much cash untouched.

So, was there a connection between Thornton and the person who shoved the threatening note under Lainey's hotel room door last night? Or was that just another coincidence? Maybe he was actually the one who left the note. Or maybe the Waco guy had really been just a drunk looking for his room. Wrong place, wrong time?

Colt shot down that theory quickly. The fact that Thornton was not a registered guest at the hotel plus the can of paint in his car ruled out coincidence. But what did all that have to do with Elaina Garcia?

At the thought of Lainey, Colt remembered he still had to confront her about sneaking around asking questions regarding Tessa's murder. He glanced at his watch before straightening his arms over his head to stretch. It was after nine. No wonder he was tired. He'd still been awake at three that morning, unable to sleep, thinking about everything that had happened since Tessa died.

He stacked Landers' notes and placed them in a blank folder. It would be a day or two before the test results started coming in. Scribbling Thornton's name on the folder, he placed it next to Porter's file.

Suddenly feeling his lack of shut eye, Colt got up and grabbed his jacket. Flipping the light off, he walked through the station, nodding to the night crew, busy at their desks. It was deceptively quiet now compared to the earlier excitement in here. Joe Saldonna, sleeping off a drunk and disorderly in the back cell, was the only action.

"See ya, boss," Jeff Knight, the newest officer on the force, said as Colt passed. "We'll call if something comes up we can't handle."

Colt smiled. "Try to hold down the fort, guys." He exited the station and walked to his car, his instincts telling him he would hear from them before the night ended.

The words of his CSI echoed in his head as he slid into the front seat.

What the hell *is* going on in Vineyard?

Colt toweled his hair dry and wrapped the terry cloth around his waist. The shower had given him a second wind, breathing new life into his weary body after an incredibly long day. Now all he needed was a cold Bud for his soul.

He started across the bedroom toward the dresser but got sidetracked at the window. The moon, two-thirds full, shone down on the pond in the pasture, its beams glistening like diamonds dancing on the surface.

Even though late March temperatures sometimes dipped into the low forties at night, Colt opened the window. The rush of cool Texas air coupled with the smell of turned earth in the adjacent field warmed his soul and reaffirmed his decision to plant his roots in this small corner of God's country he called Gracie's Acres.

He glanced toward the guest house to his right and noticed a light on in the kitchen. Lainey was still up even though it was after eleven. Pulling off the towel, he quickly threw on a pair of old jeans and his Cowboys jersey.

Might as well get this over with. He slicked back his wet hair with his hand, not wanting to waste time blow drying it.

Somehow, he had to convince Lainey to leave the investigating to him. Maybe if she found out about Porter and the hired gun, she'd finally realize someone out there wasn't playing games.

He grabbed a beer on his way out the door and headed toward the guest house, unable to put his finger on why he felt like a pimply-faced teenager. Sure, his ex-sister-in-law was easy on the eyes, but he knew a lot of pretty woman. Hell, he'd even dated a few now and then, although then was probably a lot closer to the truth.

He stopped to pet Ginger, who had positioned herself at the bottom of the steps, which to a stranger might look like the first line of defense against an intruder. A smile formed on his lips thinking of Lainey teasing about his guard dogs. Half a second later, Fred rushed from the back of the house at a full clip and nearly knocked him on his butt, bombarding him with another round of wet kisses.

Teddy must be feeding them treats again, Colt thought as a whiff of dog breath blew his way. A retired farmer, Ted McDougal made extra cash mowing Colt's lawn and keeping the few bushes around the perimeter from dying. Despite Colt's warning he didn't want the dogs to get fat, Ted couldn't resist. Even carried treats in his truck without owning a dog himself.

Colt straightened and walked up the steps of the guest house. He knocked once lightly on the door, but after getting no response, tapped harder. Hearing a commotion inside that sounded much like a chair slamming against the wall, he stiffened, cursing that his gun was up in his bedroom locked in the nightstand.

The door flew open and a sleepy-looking Lainey, still wearing the turquoise blue sweater she'd had on earlier, stared out at him. "Hey, Colt." She rubbed her eyes and stretched. "What'd you need?"

Colt tilted his head to see past her into the room. Convinced she wasn't in danger, he allowed his shoulders to relax and concentrated on her face. Her shoulder-length hair had fallen across her eye, and she swiped at it almost comically. Up this close, he noticed her olive skin was smooth and nearly flawless, setting off her dark brown eyes.

He stepped between her and the door and walked into the room, picking up the chair that had fallen backwards, apparently when Lainey jumped up to answer the door.

"Sorry, it's a mess," she apologized. "I had a long day and must have dozed off."

"You don't say," he drawled, semi-amused as he eyed the empty bottle of wine. "There's not a chance Tessa's wine had anything to do with it, right?"

She blushed, and he stifled a grin, mentally scolding himself for teasing her and enjoying it so much. She looked so irresistible when she was embarrassed.

"Okay, maybe I did have one glass too many, but believe me, Colt, you would have, too. It's the best wine I've ever tasted." She blushed again. "Sorry. There's none left for you."

He lifted his bottle of beer and took a long cold swig. "I'm not much of a wine guy." He eyed her curiously. "Where'd you get it?"

"Where'd I get what?" She yawned again. "Sorry," she said before she erupted into a fit of giggles. "I'd forgotten how little it takes to get me tipsy and how soon after the tipsy part the dozing off takes over."

"You didn't answer my question."

"Oh, the wine." She looked away. "Maddy told me about the Viognier, and I stopped by and talked Paul into letting me try it. It's as good as Tessa said it was."

His eyebrows hitched.

"I mean as good as Maddy said Tessa told her it was."

"So, did you ask the vintner if Jerry took a bottle of it to Tessa that night?"

Lainey burst out laughing.

"What's so damn funny?"

"Nothing, really."

When he stared daggers at her, she stopped laughing, but her eyes were unable to hide her obvious glee. "Okay, it's your eyebrows. Are you aware only your left eyebrow hikes up when you're mad?"

The beginning of a smile brought his eyebrow down. "Tessa used to tease me about that." He glanced at the kitchen table. "Have you put anything in your stomach besides the wine?"

When she shook her head, he slid the grocery sack across the table and pulled out the Brie and a loaf of French bread. Then he walked over to the kitchen counter and retrieved the sharpest knife he could find.

Thank God, his mother had stocked the place before she had her surgery and moved in. He walked back to the table, pulled out a chair. "I haven't eaten, either. Do you mind sharing?"

"I'm not hungry," she said. "But you go ahead."

"Sit, Lainey," he commanded. "Unless you want to spend the rest of the night hugging the porcelain throne, you need to eat something."

She did as he said and plopped down across the table from him. Feeling her eyes watching his every move, he unwrapped the Brie and cut away the hard white covering. Pulling a chunk of the bread from the loaf, he smeared the rich white cheese on it and handed it to her.

She hesitated only a moment before reaching for it and taking a bite. He watched her chew, enjoying the way her tongue flicked across her lips. By the time he had a piece ready for himself, she'd already devoured hers.

"Here." He handed his bread to her. "I'd forgotten how much you can put away."

Again she blushed, and again he scolded himself for enjoying it so much. He coated another piece of bread with the cheese and popped it into his mouth. Before long, the entire wedge was gone and only a small piece of bread remained. Colt couldn't remember ever eating only bread and cheese and being this full. The French obviously knew what they were talking about.

A glance Lainey's way showed a tiny bit of color had returned to her cheeks as she leaned back in the chair. It felt good sharing a meal with her and sitting quietly afterward, but he had come for a reason. As much as he hated destroying the moment, he had to get things out in the open.

"Did you know Quinton Porter was killed last night?"

He studied her face. Other than a hint of sadness, she didn't look surprised.

"Maddy told me," she said, shaking her head. "The guy was a jerk, but he didn't deserve to die." She hesitated before she looked up, her eyes questioning. "Unless he was the one who killed my sister."

"I don't think he was," Colt reassured her. "But that remains to be seen." He pressed on. "Did you also know we found another body at the Conquistador this afternoon?"

Her eyes widened. "Another body? Whose?" She struggled to hide her confusion.

"A small-time thug from Waco who more than likely was the one who killed Porter."

After her sharp intake of air, he debated whether to tell her about his suspicion that Thornton was the one who put the note under her door. He decided against it. "We'll know more when the test results come back."

Reaching across the table he grabbed her hand. "The point is, we are no longer looking for some disgruntled woman who thinks Tessa screwed around with her husband. It's become more serious." He was suddenly aware he had been massaging the top of her hand, and he jerked his fingers away. "It's dangerous, Lainey. I can't have you and your sisters jeopardizing my investigation, not to mention putting yourself on the killer's radar."

She met his stare, and for a minute, Colt thought she would deny everything.

Instead, she stood up. "Okay."

He couldn't believe it. He'd come here expecting a fight, or at the very least a little resistance, and all she had to say was okay? "I mean it, Lainey."

"I heard you. I'll stay out of your way." She pointed toward the door. "I'm sure you've got a busy day tomorrow, and so do I, so let's call it a night."

His face flamed.

Damn this woman. She had no intentions of backing off.

He stood, jerking the table in the process and headed for the door. As he passed her, she stepped back and stumbled. He caught her just before she crashed into the wall. "Whoa!" His anger dissolved when he realized this was his fault. "Maybe you'd better sit down for a minute."

But she didn't move. He was acutely aware of the way she felt in his arms, her breasts burning a hole in his chest, her lips dangerously close to his.

"Colt?" She looked directly into his eyes as if she could see into his soul and read his mind. "Kiss me."

He took several quick breaths, all the while still watching her. Had she read his mind she would have known he wanted to do more than kiss her. He wanted to possess her, to hear her cry his name when he brought her to a thundering orgasm.

But he couldn't.

She must have sensed his hesitation because she raised up on her tiptoes and brushed her lips across his, gliding her tongue over his lower lip in a way that sent tingling sensations everywhere south of his eyebrows.

"Lainey," he protested.

She answered by pressing her body farther into him.

God help him, he tried, but it was a losing battle. He reached behind her head and dug his hand into her hair, loving the silky feel as he pulled her mouth to his. This time there was no gentle touch as his tongue met hers and probed, licked. It had been so long and this woman smelled so damn good.

Then he remembered not only was she feeling a buzz from the wine, she was also his ex-wife's sister. He pulled his lips from hers. "We can't do this." He released her and headed for the door, not willing to take a chance and look back at her.

Afraid he would be lost if he did.

Hesitating only momentarily while his self-control went the last round with the ache in his groin and won, he pushed open the door and walked out. In all his thirty-two years, he'd never taken advantage of a woman who had consumed too much alcohol despite many opportunities to do just that. He was not about to start now.

He bent down to give both Ginger and Fred one last pat on the head before he forced himself to move toward his house, away from hers. Behind closed doors, he reached up and touched his lips still burning from her kiss. He would have to be extra careful around Lainey until the investigation was over and she moved out.

He had come damn close to picking her up and carrying her to the bedroom, and that was absolutely not acceptable.

For godsakes! She was family.

SEVENTEEN

LAINEY REACHED INTO HER purse for the ibuprofen bottle and twisted off the cap. The little man hammering away at her forehead was a painful reminder never to drink a whole freakin' bottle of wine alone.

She popped three pills, then gulped them down with the icy cold water she'd picked up at the 7-Eleven on the way over, along with the gigantic black coffee.

Leaning back in the driver's seat, she held the water bottle to her forehead as she stared at the front door of Spirits of Texas. She wanted one last go at Jerry, convinced he knew more about the wine than he'd let on yesterday. While she was at it, she intended to find out why Tessa's lawyer had stopped in for a secret meeting with Moretti. He was supposed to be working for her, not Tessa's partner.

After Maddy called last night with the news that a foreign substance had been isolated from the pieces of glass found among the ruins of Tessa's house, Lainey realized Jerry might well be the one who had killed her sister. Not even Colt's lectures warning her to butt out could keep her from digging for the truth. It's what she did for a living, what she was good at—getting people to slip up and say things when they didn't mean to.

At the thought of Colt, she felt a warm flush climb up her face, further encouraging the little man in her head to play his bongo drums. She lifted the cold bottle again to her forehead, leaving it there as she breathed deeply, begging the medicine to do its thing.

Unfortunately, the hangover was not her only regret from last night. What in the hell had she been thinking when she'd kissed Colt? That he would kiss her back, and they would live happily ever after?

Funny how alcohol did that to you. The words of the country song popped into her brain, the one about tequila making your clothes fall off. Substitute wine for the tequila.

Thank God, Colt had already left for the station before she woke up. She didn't know how she could have faced him. It was embarrassing enough *she'd* actually kissed *him* but outright humiliating that he'd basically said, "Thanks, but no thanks."

She took another deep breath, grateful the headache was beginning to slack off. She'd sit here for a few minutes longer before confronting Jerry once again. Moretti and a blinding headache were more than she could stomach.

Her thoughts meandered back to Colt and the look on his face after the kiss. To him, Lainey reasoned, she was just Tessa's little sister. She'd seen it in his eyes.

But who kisses a younger sister the way he'd kissed her last night?

She ran her fingers across her lips, remembering the fire he'd ignited when he'd pulled her mouth to his, the burn of his five o'clock shadow brushing against her cheeks. Her breath caught as she thought about the way his body had meshed into hers, the unexpected bulge in his jeans letting her know he wanted her.

Wanted her? Not hardly. Otherwise he wouldn't have turned and walked away without a word after she so blatantly threw herself at him. All that heat, all the electricity was apparently just a guy thing. Somewhere, she'd heard women need love and emotions. Men simply need a naked woman.

Remembering how provocatively she'd offered be that naked woman, like some damn cat in heat, she wondered how she would ever be able to look him in the eyes again. What did it say about her that he'd turned her down flat? She didn't know what hurt worse, her hangover or her crushed ego.

She glanced down at the empty coffee cup. *Add a full bladder to that mix.*

She'd waited as long as she could before confronting Jerry. The man was a jerk, had always been a jerk, and probably would die a jerk. She wasn't looking forward to another sit down with him, but nature was calling—with a bullhorn.

When she couldn't wait any longer, she opened the door and slid out of the seat, hoping to make it inside without embarrassing herself. She made a mental note never again to drink that much liquid while scrunched in a small car.

Her first thought when she opened the door to the winery and walked into the empty room was that she'd wasted her time and gasoline driving there. Then Roxy emerged from Tessa's office, the look of surprise on her face as obvious as the fact she wasn't wearing a bra. Lainey tried not to stare, but her boobs were gigantic, like two water balloons ready to burst.

Tell her the garden club called and said they're missing a 'ho.'

Lainey was getting used to Tessa sneaking up on her and barely flinched. She gave her sister a cursory glance, narrowing her eyes in a look that said "be quiet and let me handle this." No such luck!

Great body! Too bad its only purpose is to keep her useless head from flopping off.

"Good to see you, Roxy."

Liar!

Lainey pointed to the bathroom. "Excuse me a minute." She nearly ran to the other side of the room.

When she came back out, Tessa was standing beside Roxy holding two fingers behind her head, her adolescent attempt to make Lainey laugh.

Lainey ignored her and focused on Roxy. "Jerry around? I need to go over a few things with him." Lainey did a quick scan of the most recent Mrs. Moretti.

Dressed in a tight red mini that didn't begin to cover her long tanned thighs and a sequined black sweater that showed off where she'd invested her money, Roxy smiled, then held out her hand.

"Elaina, isn't it?"

She knows damn good and well who you are.

Lainey agreed. It was a ploy she'd used many times herself to make someone think she wasn't impressed enough to remember their name.

She grabbed Roxy's extended hand. "Call me Lainey." Then she nudged her head toward the other office. "Jerry?"

"He's not here," Roxy said, unable to hide the tinge of fear that crept into her eyes. "Two cops picked him up and took him down to the station about an hour ago." She flopped in the chair behind

Carrie's desk. "I'm sure I can help you, though. I've been promoted to Vice President of Marketing."

Wonder how many blow jobs that took? Tessa eased down in one of the chairs facing Roxy and pointed to the other. *Sit, Lainey. I have a feeling this is gonna get good.*

Lainey kicked around the notion of bursting Roxy's bubble by reminding her she owned fifty percent of the company and therefore, had fifty percent of the voting rights. Roxy wasn't a VP unless Lainey said she was, and the last she remembered, nobody had asked.

She decided it might be to her advantage to pretend Roxy was an equal in the company, practicing that more-bees-with-honey thing her mother had always preached.

"Congratulations. I'm sure you've earned it."

She glanced sideways as Tessa mouthed, *Blow job.* Then she used both hands to make an exaggerated imitation of peeling a banana before she put her hand on the back of her head and shoved it down on the imaginary fruit.

Despite herself, Lainey laughed out loud at Tessa's imitation, noticing the sparkle in her sister's eyes when she did.

"Sorry," she apologized to Roxy. She was definitely sorry, but not because of laughing. Her little outburst nearly brought back the guy with the hammer. She rubbed her forehead, wishing for the ice-cold bottle as she tried to get the image of Tessa and her banana out of her head. "Where's Carrie?"

"She had some errands to run this morning. Said she'd be in after lunch."

"Why'd Colt need to talk to Jerry again? He was just here yesterday." No sense beating around the proverbial bush.

"You'd have to ask Colt that."

"Do you think your husband had anything to do with my sister's murder?"

Roxy jumped up. "Are you out of your fucking mind? Jerry wouldn't hurt a flea."

Yeah right. If Jerry's a nice guy, then I'm not freakin' dead. He'd kill his own mother if he thought he could sell tickets to the funeral. Tessa huffed. *Hell, I wouldn't be surprised if he made money at my funeral.*

Lainey ignored her sister's ranting and propped her elbows on the desk. "What about you, Roxy? Did you hate Tessa enough to poison her wine?"

For a minute Lainey thought the woman was going to come around the desk and smack her up the side of the head, but then Roxy smiled. "It wasn't me." She eased back down into Carrie's chair. "Don't get me wrong. I hated your sister as much as everyone else. Suspected she still had eyes for my Jerry. Working with him every day, she must have realized what she'd let slip through her fingers. The man is a ball of fire in everything he does, if you get my drift."

Christ! She's kidding, right? He's so dull, some nights I had to put a mirror under his nose to see if he was still breathing.

"Funny how things work out, right, Rox? Two weeks ago, my sister died. Now you've not only taken over her office, but you also have her old job title."

"Now wait a minute, sister, before you go flapping at the mouth and saying things your ass can't back up."

Whoa! You've hit a nerve.

194

Lainey glared, unwilling to give Roxy the satisfaction of staring her down. If she wanted a cat fight, she was ready. "What makes you think I can't back up my claims?"

Roxy's color went from strawberries to beets in a micro minute. "What could you possibly have on me that would make you think you can waltz in here all high and mighty and spout off asinine accusations? This is my company now," she said, then added, "Mine and Jerry's."

Lainey smiled. She had Roxy exactly where she wanted her. Mad enough to say things without thinking. "Are you forgetting I own as much of this company as you and Jerry combined?"

Roxy let out an audible breath. "I never figured you to be a bitch like your sister."

Those are fightin' words, Lainey. Rip her a new one.

"There're a lot of similarities between my sister and me you can't even pretend to know. For instance, we were both aware you were doing Quinton Porter at the Shady City Motel."

Roxy gasped. "Colt told you?"

"I was there the night Porter admitted it to Colt. Who was black-mailing you with the pictures?"

Roxy's mouth dropped, but no sound came out. Finally, she closed it and leaned back in her chair, a resigned look on her face. "I don't know."

"I don't see you and Porter having much in common, Roxy. What'd you want from him?"

"The same thing he wanted from me." She made a sweeping motion around the room with her arms. "This place is worth millions, but Tessa and Jerry were so against letting Quinton's company come in. He tried to convince them it wouldn't hurt the vines, but they wouldn't listen. We were only trying to figure out a way to make them come to their senses. One thing led to another..." Her voice trailed off.

"So, you have no idea who blackmailed you?"

Roxy stood abruptly and walked into Tessa's office. When she returned, she held a manila envelope with her name printed on the front. "This came this morning. They want me to take five grand to a post office box in Lakeview before noon."

She handed the envelope to Lainey. Inside were the same pictures Maddy had shown her at the police station, the ones they'd found on Tessa's computer along with a typewritten instruction sheet.

"I thought it was Tessa. She's the only one I know who was hateful enough to do something like this. Plus, I think she overheard me one day talking to Quinton."

Lainey glanced toward her sister who was shaking her head.

Wasn't me, I swear. I would have gone after Porter with the Polaroids, not Roxy.

"Unless you believe in ghosts, I doubt that." Lainey lowered her head to hide the smile.

I'll be damned. You do have a sense of humor behind all those brains.

Lainey relaxed in the chair as she thought about what she should do next. When she looked up, Roxy was beside her. "You're not going to tell Jerry, are you? There's really no reason he has to know, with Quinton dead and all."

Lainey saw the sadness flash in her eyes as she spoke about Porter. This woman had genuinely cared for him. It shouldn't have surprised her, but it did. That old saying there was someone for everyone must be true.

"Can you get your hands on five thousand dollars in the next hour or so?"

When Roxy nodded, Lainey continued, "Okay, here's what I want you to do."

———

Lainey shifted in the front seat of the rental car, her eyes trained on the Lakeview Post Office entrance, her mind racing in anticipation.

"Let me have a look," Deena pleaded from the back seat.

Lainey had called her sisters the minute the idea popped into her head. Maddy and Deena had insisted she pick them up from work, but Kate couldn't get away. Lainey had to promise to call her the exact minute they found out anything.

"What if whoever it is knows we're here?"

"How could they?" Lainey answered. "We're parked far enough away no one would suspect what we're doing."

"We're actually on a stakeout." Maddy giggled. "Colt is gonna kick our butts."

Hearing Colt's name brought a fresh blush to Lainey's cheeks. Thank God, her sisters didn't know about her little seduction disaster the night before.

"But what if they don't show?" Deena asked. "What if they think the money isn't going anywhere and decide to pick it up after work?"

"Or after dark," Maddy chimed in. "We can't wait here all day. I'm starving."

"Here." Lainey pulled a small package of doughnuts from her purse. She'd picked them up that morning at the 7-Eleven, then quickly decided her stomach felt too queasy to chance it.

"Give me one of those," Deena demanded, grabbing the bag out of Maddy's hand.

"Hey!" Maddy protested.

For a minute, Lainey took her eyes away from the binoculars they'd picked up at Walmart on the way over and watched her older sisters bicker over the doughnuts. This is what she'd missed the most when she'd left Vineyard.

If they had time for lunch later, she'd spring and take them to the new Olive Garden off the interstate. It was Maddy's favorite restaurant, and she owed them for hanging out with her today. Besides, there was nothing like eight hundred breadsticks to take the edge off her hangover, which was finally starting to feel like just a nuisance headache.

Lainey tried to focus on the front door of the post office again, but she was distracted by all the Mercedes and Beemers passing by. She'd always known Lakeview had a higher median income per family, but she didn't realize just how wealthy this community was.

Situated about ten miles north of the airport, Lakeview had a population of nearly forty thousand. Several of the Dallas Cowboys and a few Mavericks lived in this small city, known for its many high school football championships. Lainey said a prayer whoever was coming for the money wouldn't notice her rental car which stood out like a tall blonde in a roomful of short brunettes.

She glanced at her watch. It had been ninety minutes since Roxy had dropped off the money. They'd used a bright green envelope, hoping it would be easier to spot from this distance.

She put the binoculars up to her eyes again. "Ohmygod!" she exclaimed as she saw a familiar face going into the post office.

"What?" Both Deena and Maddy said in unison, scooting close enough to Lainey to blow her hair into her face.

"Hold on," Lainey pleaded, pushing her hair back and motioning with her hand for them to back off. "I want to be sure."

As they watched in silence, Lainey was aware of her own breathing, slow and audible. The minutes ticked off as they stared at the front door of the post office.

"There," Maddy shouted as a lone figure exited the building and walked to a blue Jaguar.

"Is that who I think it is?" Deena asked, leaning over the front seat so far, Lainey could smell doughnuts on her breath.

"Yep." Lainey handed off the binoculars to Maddy, slumped back in her seat and stared in disbelief.

Even without the glasses, there was no doubt they were watching Carrie Phillips slide into the driver's seat of Tessa's old car, the bright green envelope protruding from her purse.

EIGHTEEN

I'll be damned! If I hadn't seen it with my own eyes, I wouldn't have believed it.

Lainey twisted her head around in time to see Tessa plop down next to Deena in the back seat. "It's about time you showed up."

"She's here?" Maddy nearly pretzeled her neck to look, then eyed Lainey suspiciously. "She's not up here with us, is she?"

Lainey smiled. "She's cuddled next to Deena."

And if I say so myself, Deena, you've plumped up a bit. She made a face. *Move your fat ass over and give a girl some room.*

"She wants you to scoot over, Deena," Lainey repeated before she faced forward and looked into the binoculars again.

Carrie had backed the Jaguar out and pulled into the flow of traffic. The three sisters slid down in their seats when she passed.

Follow her, Tessa shouted before her lips twisted in a cynical smile. *I shouldn't have left her my Jag. We'll never catch her in this piece of shit.*

"Wanna bet?" Lainey started the ignition, shifted to drive and burned rubber pulling away from the curb, cutting off a Lexus SUV.

Damn, girl!

Lainey glanced into the rearview mirror to see Tessa shaking her head, a huge grin on her face as the outraged Lexus driver laid on the horn.

Oh, blow it out your ass!

Lainey made a U-turn, thankful there were no cops around and jammed her foot on the gas pedal. She figured Carrie was on her way back to Vineyard and headed the rental car in that direction.

As they rounded the corner of Main and Carroll, Maddy cried out, "There she is getting on 114."

Although they kept Carrie in sight, Tessa was right. The rental car was no match for the blue Jaguar, and they quickly fell back eight or ten car lengths.

Exiting off William Tate Boulevard, Lainey followed Carrie as she headed toward the winery. Right before the turnoff to Spirits of Texas, Carrie pulled into Starbucks' parking lot. The sisters watched silently when she exited the car and walked into the store.

Then Lainey eased the car next to the Jag and turned to Tessa. "You coming?"

You're kidding, right? Not even Brad Pitt in a Jacuzzi could keep me from seeing the look on Carrie's face when she sees us. Mischief flickered in her eyes. *Okay, maybe if he was naked.*

The sisters climbed out of the car and walked into the coffee shop just as Carrie paid for her drink and shoved her wallet into her purse.

"Hey, Carrie, what a surprise seeing you here," Lainey said while the others surrounded her.

Carrie's eyes widened as she glanced from one sister to the other. "It's no surprise. Everyone knows I'm addicted to the Chai tea here."

Ooh, I love Chai tea, Tessa said, moving closer to stand next to Lainey. *It's like drinking a big slice of Mom's pumpkin pie.*

Maddy stepped forward. "Lainey wasn't talking about being surprised that you're at Starbucks, Carrie."

Deena pushed her older sister to the left to squeeze in between her and Carrie. "The mystery is why you waited to get back to Vineyard to get one. Lakeview now has a great new Starbucks." Her eyes strayed to the display of blueberry scones before she turned back. "Actually, it's just a block from the post office."

If this wasn't serious stuff, Lainey would have laughed at the way Carrie's eyes opened to full circles. Her eyebrows furrowed as if searching her brain for a response.

"Good to know," Carrie countered before adding, "As nice as it is to see all of you, I really have to run. I have a bear of an afternoon at the office."

"I'll bet," Lainey said. "It must be hard trying to figure out how you're going to spend Roxy's five grand."

Carrie gasped then recovered enough to attempt a smile she didn't quite pull off. "I have no idea what you're talking about."

Deena pulled the bright green envelope from Carrie's purse before the smaller woman snatched it back.

She always sucked at lying, Tessa said. *Watch how she drums her fingers on the counter.*

"It might be a good idea if we all sit down and have a little talk," Maddy said.

Carrie smiled, but her eyes remained cold. "No can do. That killer afternoon, remember?"

This time Maddy stepped close enough to Carrie that she almost lost her balance and fell into her. "Right now, we're the only ones who know about this, but I can't promise I won't let it slip out when I get back to the station." Maddy raised her eyebrows. "You understand, right?"

Carrie's smile disappeared, and she took a deep breath. Without a word, she turned and walked to the far corner of the store. The sisters followed and pulled up chairs while Carrie slid into the fourth. Tessa stood beside Lainey, her eyes burning into Carrie's face as if trying to figure out what kind of game her friend was playing.

"How long have you been blackmailing Roxy?" Lainey blurted, leaning forward.

Carrie blew out a long breath, sending her bangs upward in the breeze. "Did you know she and Porter were working a deal worth millions?"

When no one answered, she continued, "I couldn't let that happen to Tessa. Figured I'd get Roxy to give up some of her money before I went to Tessa and Jerry with the proof." She tapped the table with her coral-tipped nails.

Yeah, right. How stupid does she think we are?

"What kind of proof?"

Carrie took a drink of her tea, slowly licking the foam from her lips. "Roxy got her hands on a list of all the wine distributors who were tight with Tessa. She gave Porter a few names at a time." She paused. "Guess she wanted to keep him on a string, keep him as her boy-toy as long as she could."

Ew!

"Anyway, Porter would get the names and contact them to offer a kickback if they'd quit buying from us."

"How'd you find out?"

"I got a call from one of our biggest clients wondering what was going on." She took another sip. "I think Tessa was giving him more than wine, if you get my drift."

Lainey looked up at Tessa, her eyes questioning. After Tessa scrunched her face and shook her head as if she'd just tasted something sour, she mouthed *No way!*

Lainey turned back to Carrie. "So, you expect us to believe you figured this out after one phone call?"

"Hell, no." Carrie shouted. "Three other clients called and said the same thing. It didn't take long to put two and two together, especially when I noticed how Roxy turned into a horny bitch every time Porter came to the office."

"So, you found out about the affair and then blackmailed her?"

"I set a trap. It was so obvious. Roxy must have been sex-starved. I guess she's used to the bigger boys from her porn days." Carrie winked. "Tessa always said Jerry's size thirteen boots were grossly misleading." Her eyes moved from Lainey to the other two sisters. "Any one of you would have done the same thing."

Maddy and Deena might have, but you're too much of a goody-two-shoes, Lainey.

Lainey shot Tessa a look before skewering Carrie with the same one. "Did Jerry know?"

Carrie finished her tea, then leaned back in the chair. "Of course he knew. When you marry a woman who has raunchy sex with strangers in front of a camera, you can't expect her to suddenly become Mother Teresa." She sniffed. "Jerry wasn't Mr. Wonderful-Husband himself. He was banging anything in panties."

Same old Jerry. Tessa sighed. *He has two emotions, hungry and horny. When I saw that look in his eye, I'd hurry up and make him a sandwich.*

Lainey put her finger to her lip to silence Tessa. They were getting to the heart of this matter, and she didn't want to start laughing at one of Tessa's remarks. She pursed her lips then faced Carrie again. "How about you, Carrie? Did you and Jerry have a thing?"

Carrie threw her head back and laughed. "Besides being one of the biggest losers I know, Jerry was off limits to me. I would never go for one of Tessa's castoffs."

All three sisters made eye contact before Maddy turned her gaze to Carrie. "Are you forgetting David Rivera?"

At the mention of her fiancé, Carrie's eyes hardened. "Tessa and David were high school sweethearts." She forced a laugh. "If I excluded everyone Tessa slept with in high school, I would've had to leave town to find a date."

You bitch!

"Morning, ladies."

All five of them, including Tessa whirled around to face Colt Winslow, wearing his police uniform and a smile so fake, he could have passed for a car salesman.

"Hey, Colt." Maddy glanced at her watch. "I still have a few minutes left on my lunch break."

Colt ignored her and centered his attention on Lainey. "Obviously, you have a short memory. I guess I'll just have to haul your pretty little ass in for obstruction of justice."

"Hold on, Colt. There's no obstruction of justice going on here. We just happened to wander into Starbucks for a pick-me-up after our big lunch, and we ran into Carrie," Maddy said.

Colt turned his angry eyes on her and she slumped a little in the chair. "Really? I suppose you just *happened* to be sitting in a parked car outside the Lakeview Post Office, too."

Carrie's hand flew to her mouth, but not fast enough to stop the gasp.

Colt turned to her. "I'll take that green envelope now." He held out his hand, and reluctantly, Carrie handed it over. "You're lucky Roxy refuses to press charges, or you'd already be on your way to the station. Blackmailing is a felony."

My best friend calling me a whore should be against the law, too.

Carrie crossed her arms and glared at Lainey. "As I was telling them, I was only trying to keep Roxy from sabotaging Spirits of Texas. Apparently, Lainey and her sisters decided to get in on the action."

Hell's bells! I had no idea she could lie this well. Tessa shook her head in amazement. *I'm developing a new respect for her even though she said I was a ho-dog.*

Colt stepped closer to the table. "Can the lies, Carrie. Roxy called me the minute she was in her car heading for Lakeview. She told me everything."

"Why would Roxy call you?" Lainey asked. She'd gotten the impression Roxy didn't want anyone to know about her afternoon delights with Porter.

"Oh, I don't know. Maybe because I'm the police officer, and you all are merely a bunch of Angela Lansbury wannabes." He pointed to Carrie. "You and I will talk later when I come to the winery."

Then he spun on his heels to face Maddy. "You, I'll deal with back at the station."

I'd forgotten how damn sexy he is when he's madder than hell.

Halfway to the door, Colt turned back. "I'll see you at the house, Lainey. We'll settle this matter once and for all."

Oh, shit! Tessa said. *He doesn't get this pissed often, but when he does…* She rolled her eyes.

"Great," Maddy said. "I have to deal with another one of his talks where he tries to pretend I'm just another employee."

"You are just another employee, Maddy. It's been a long time since he and Tessa divorced," Deena reminded her, pushing her chair away from the table. "I'm starving. Anyone else want a scone?"

Lainey didn't hear her sisters. She was too busy watching Colt walk toward the door, fixated on the way his butt was outlined against the back of his uniform pants. A warm rush pulsed through her body as a smile crinkled her eyes despite the fact she knew she was in for the mother of all lectures back at Colt's.

He thinks my ass is pretty!

———

Colt didn't know whether he was more pissed because the Garcia girls had become a royal pain in the ass or because they'd found out Carrie was blackmailing Roxy before he even had a clue. When he'd questioned Roxy earlier she'd denied knowing anything about the pictures.

Obviously she'd had a change of heart. When she'd called to say she was on her way to make the drop exactly like Lainey had instructed her, Colt had slammed down the receiver and rushed from the station, wondering what the hell Tessa's sisters were up to now.

He should have known Lainey didn't intend to give up without a fight. Hell, she and Tessa hadn't even spoken in years. Why did she suddenly feel the burning need to solve her murder? Was it guilt? Or maybe she saw herself as an avenging angel.

The angel part would be right, Colt thought as he rubbed his lower lip, remembering how her tongue had slid across it last night.

Christ! What was he thinking kissing her back like that? She was Tessa's sister. His mind argued he and Tessa had never really lived as husband and wife—if you didn't count that one fling.

He shook his head to clear his mind, sliding into the front seat of the cruiser to head for the station. He had three murders to solve, and so far, he was doing a piss poor job on all of them. His gut told him they were connected somehow, but damn if he could figure out how.

Why would the guy who in all likelihood murdered Porter get offed the same day at the same hotel? Where did Tessa's death fit into the equation? Hers was premeditated.

And how did it all connect to Lainey and the "get out of town or else" note?

Right now he had no answers, but he was damn sure going to find them before one or more of the Garcia sisters ended up like Tessa.

He groaned at the lunch hour traffic that put him at the end of a long line stopped for a red light. He was tempted to turn on the siren but decided not to abuse the power.

Instead, he picked up his cell phone and called the station. When he heard Danny Landers's voice, his anger returned, remembering why Maddy wasn't there to answer it. He should have known something was up earlier when she'd rushed from the building like it was on fire.

"Hey, boss, where are you? Where'd you get off to in such a hurry?"

Colt ignored the second question. "I'm stuck at the light around the corner. I never got a chance to talk to you and Romano before I left. What'd you find when you checked the convenience stores?"

"A dead-end," Danny said. "No one remembers selling a prepaid phone to anyone who seemed unusual. Just your average 'live from paycheck to paycheck' kind of people."

"I was afraid of that." Colt tapped his fingers on the steering wheel. "This guy's too smart to get tripped up by something that simple." He inched forward a few car lengths, then cursed under his breath when the light turned red again.

"So, what's next?"

Colt rubbed his forehead. "Try checking the Lakeview and Kendal stores. You might even look at Roanoke." He sighed. "It's a long shot, but that's all we got."

"Will do, boss. After Phil and I grab some lunch, we'll head that way."

"Call if you uncover anything promising." Colt disconnected when the light finally turned green. He pushed his foot down and raced forward in time to get past before the yellow light turned red again.

Halfway to the station, he debated what he'd say to Maddy to make sure she got the message to give up the ridiculous hunt for Tessa's killer.

Damn!

He'd forgotten he needed to save his best arguments for Lainey. She seemed to be the one with all the big ideas and the free time on her hands to follow through on them.

The thought of another go round with her like the previous night stirred up mixed feelings. On one hand, he knew he had to convince her, even if it meant threatening to throw her in jail for a few days to keep her out of trouble. On the other, he wasn't ready to go up against another of those kisses.

A man only has so much willpower.

He pulled the car into his space and dialed his mother. She'd picked Gracie up from school to take her shopping for new spring clothes. Seems like the child had grown three or four inches overnight.

"Hey, Mom, how's it going?"

"Great, son, but I'm pretty sure you're not going to like it when you get your credit card bill next month." She clucked her teeth. "Since when did little girls' jeans cost more than a week's grocery bill?"

Colt laughed. "Welcome to the twenty-first century. Don't let her talk you into more than one expensive pair. A few cheap jeans won't kill her," he said, knowing his warning was falling on deaf ears. His mother spoiled his daughter worse than he did.

"Do you think Gracie can spend the night with you? I've got some business I have to take care of and won't be home until late." Okay, maybe that wasn't entirely true. He did have business, but it would take place at home and he didn't want Gracie around if it got out of hand.

"Great idea. She's got her eye on an adorable pair of pink pajamas. Since we won't have time to swing by the house to get hers, I'll have to charge that, too. They aren't cheap either." She laughed. "Oh well, gotta run. See you tomorrow."

He was still smiling when he entered the station. There was no reason why his mom couldn't run by the house to get Gracie's things.

Why was it he could face down a criminal any day of the week, but when it came to the women in his life, he became putty in their hands?

His daughter, his mother, Lainey.

———

"I've paid a lot of money, and so far, I have nothing to show for it," the man said, unable to disguise the anger.

"I know. I told you this wouldn't happen overnight. Don't get impatient and ruin everything." He hoped he could convince the man. He was so close to getting the job done and banking the rest of the three million they'd promised.

"When can I expect good news?"

He hesitated. Things had not gone as he'd hoped. With Porter dead and Thornton out of the picture, he only had two contacts left to work the deal.

And then there was Tessa's sister snooping around. He'd forgotten she was some kind of reporter. Thought she'd hightail it out of Vineyard after the note.

He'd been wrong. Now she was stirring up the shit along with the other three sisters. It was time to take off the gloves.

But his biggest problem was the Vineyard Police Department. He'd counted on Winslow's inexperience, but somehow, the man had risen to the challenge. He was getting too close for comfort. Fortunately, he had an insider reporting back on every new development in Tessa's murder investigation.

So far the body count was minimal—a whore who sapped the life out of every man she came in contact with, a drunken idiot who couldn't find his ass with both hands, and a wannabe gangster who started every conversation with his hand out for more money. If it came down to it he wasn't above arranging an accident for the sheriff. All he had to do was say the word, and the guy on the other end would get it done.

But he wasn't ready to kill a cop. At least not yet. More than likely, that would bring in the Feds, and he was positive his contacts wouldn't hold up under that much scrutiny. Although he'd taken a lot of precautions to keep his identity under wraps, it still could get messy.

"Well—when?"

He focused back on the question. "My sources tell me we should hear something in the next week or two."

The man paused. "You'd better be right, or you'll find out the hard way how I handle failure."

He held the receiver long after the other man hung up on him, taking slow breaths to calm his racing pulse. Now wasn't the time to panic. Not when he could smell the three million dollar payoff.

He knew exactly what he had to do to take care of Tessa's sister. The other problem would require more finesse.

A slow grin crossed his face as a plan hatched in his mind. He picked up the phone and dialed the police station.

NINETEEN

COLT EXAMINED JERRY MORETTI'S cell phone records and found six calls to Charles Prescott over the past two days. He didn't know what was going on between Jerry and Tessa's probate lawyer, but the phone calls had to be a conflict of interest. Prescott was supposed to be representing Lainey and Gracie.

He scribbled a note to himself as he glanced at the clock above his door. Nine-thirty already. He'd only meant to skim Porter's file but had ended up with everything he had on all three murders strewn across his desk.

Yawning, he stood and stretched. It had been a long day. Tomorrow was soon enough to confront both Jerry and Charlie about the phone conversations. More than likely, it would be something as innocent as a will or another pre-nup.

He walked into the main room at the station just as Phil Romano sauntered in.

"Hey, boss, anything new on the case?"

"Nothing much." Colt eyed his number two guy. Romano had been with the force about a year longer than Colt and had partnered with him those early years before Colt was elected sheriff.

Married with three kids, Romano was always searching for ways to make extra money. As much as Colt discouraged off duty work, he couldn't blame the man for taking the security job at the Texas Corral on the weekends.

Kids can get expensive, Colt thought, remembering his mother's comment about Gracie's jeans costing as much as her weekly grocery bill.

"Find out anything at the Conquistador?"

Rogers and Flanagan had spent the afternoon interviewing the guests and employees at the hotel, hoping one of them remembered something that might help.

"Nope. Most of the guests were already in bed and didn't hear a thing." Romano slumped into his desk chair. "Any luck on that prepaid yet?"

Colt shook his head. "We knew it was a long shot, but maybe we'll get lucky and someone will remember selling a phone like that. More than likely, whoever bought it used an alias, but you never know. I want you and Danny to expand your search to the surrounding cities." He picked up the duty roster. "You're not on tonight. Aren't you supposed to be working at the Corral?"

Romano pointed to the stack of files on his desk. "Yeah, but things don't get hopping until after midnight. They gave me a couple hours to catch up here."

Colt figured the owner would probably bend over backward for him. Despite the honky-tonk's reputation for drunken brawls and dance-floor shenanigans, Romano had whipped it into shape, and now, they rarely had to jail anyone. The year and a half Romano had been running security had changed the Corral into a respectable hangout, attracting crowds from across North Dallas.

"Besides, I'll get to sleep in tomorrow," Romano added. "Denise and the kids are spending the weekend with her sister in Fort Worth."

Colt laughed. "Ah! A little peace and quiet for a change."

"I heard that." Romano grinned back. "Have a great weekend, Colt."

"I'll be here in the morning," Colt responded, shaking his head. "You're not the only one with loose ends to tie up."

Romano's grin faded. "Aren't you the one who always harps about the importance of stepping away from the job occasionally?"

Colt shrugged. "Apparently, I'm better at preaching than practicing." He headed for the door, saying his goodbyes to the rest of the evening staff along the way. "Don't stay too long, Phil."

He exited the station, breathing in the brisk night air, enjoying thoughts of a long hot shower, which was exactly what his tired aching bones needed after the grueling day.

Then he remembered one last thing he had to do before falling into bed.

He had to convince his ex-sister-in-law to back off and that might mean playing hard ball with her.

———

Lainey threw another Milk-Bone toward Ginger before plopping onto the porch swing. Glancing toward Colt's sprawling acreage, she noticed the outline of several head of cattle grazing in the back pasture, barely visible in the fading light of dusk.

She wrapped Colt's sweater tighter around her as the cool air nipped at her body. She was glad she hadn't returned the sweater since the temperature had taken a dive after the sun went down.

Her attention was diverted when Fred's wet nose nuzzled her hand. Reaching for the box of treats she'd picked up on the way home, she threw one his way. "Okay, guys, that's all you get for now. I'm already in enough trouble with your daddy. If he thinks you're too plump to protect his ranch, he'll have my head," she explained to the doggie duo.

The sight of the canines sitting obediently beside her, tongues out and tails wagging, made her smile. Colt's adorable labs were about as threatening as a pack of toy poodles, even though each weighed over a hundred pounds.

Speaking of getting fat, what's up with Deena?

Lainey glanced over as Tessa slid onto the swing next to her. "Kate said Deena and Mike have been fighting a lot lately. Deena always was an emotional eater."

He's a jerk-off. She should have left him a long time ago. Especially after you told her he was making nice with what's her name.

"She loves him," Lainey defended. "A woman tolerates a whole lot more when her heart is involved."

Whatever! You should talk to her before she turns into a blimp. Feeding an empty heart is never a solution.

Lainey remembered interviewing the author of a book by the same name. She'd come away with a whole new outlook on eating when you're upset.

Dropping her foot to stop the swing, she turned to her sister. "Since when did you start reading books about emotions?"

Tessa lowered her eyes. *I'm just saying I hate to see her go through this alone like I did.*

Lainey attempted a smile. "No one who knows you would say your heart was ever empty—or your bed, for that matter."

Tessa's head snapped up. *Just because I slept around doesn't mean I didn't feel alone, Lainey.*

Lainey softened. Whatever Tessa had done wasn't her business, and she had no right to judge her. "I'm sorry. That didn't come out right. I just meant that to your friends and your family you always came across as confident and happy with your life."

Looks can be deceiving.

They sat in silence as Lainey contemplated Tessa's last statement.

God help her! She didn't want to go down this road, but something was pushing her. It was almost as if she had to know, had to get it out in the open in order to move on.

She lifted her leg and the swing began to rock again. "What really happened with you and Colt?"

Tessa raised her brows in surprise. *What does it matter? I'm dead now and out of the picture.* A veil of sadness washed over her face as her attempt to be glib failed miserably.

This was a side of her sister Lainey had never seen, and she couldn't let it go. "Were you always in love with Colt, or did you set your sights on him after you read my journal?"

Tessa laughed. *You think I married him to spite you?*

"Didn't you?"

Hell, no! Tessa turned away. *I married him because I had to. He—*

"I thought you said he wasn't Gracie's father?"

217

This conversation is old news, Lainey. Let's talk about something way more important, like how you're going to find out who killed me.

Same old Tessa. Even as a teenager, she'd always found a way to turn the attention away from herself when the situation got sticky.

"So, why'd you have to marry him?" Now that she'd started, there was no turning back.

You're not going to give up, are you? Tessa blew out a full breath. *Okay, here it is. Hope you get a big laugh out of it.*

Lainey waited. Something told her she wouldn't be doubling over.

I fucked up. End of story. Are you happy now?

"How? Your life was my dream."

Tessa's sarcastic laugh echoed in the quiet of the night. *Your life, little sister, was my nightmare.*

Lainey turned to stare at her. "Why do you hate me so much?"

The sound of the rusty chains sliding across the swing's hardware suddenly magnified as Lainey held her breath, waiting for an answer to the question she'd wanted to ask for over nine years.

I don't hate you, Lainey. Tessa's voice was low, full of raw emotions. *I spent three days in Savannah watching you, being proud of you and resenting you all at the same time.* She looked away. *I wanted to be you.*

There it was again. Both sisters dreaming about being more like the other. Both wasting precious moments fighting off the green-eyed monster.

Lainey decided not to pursue it. "You still haven't told me if you loved Colt."

Tessa smiled. *What's not to love about him? I knew he'd be the perfect father for Gracie.* She sighed. *I was right.*

"Who really fathered her?"

You're asking a helluva lot of questions that are none of your business, sis. Why not leave it at me being a whore and move on.

"I may have given up the opportunity of a lifetime by not heading to Florida for that job interview to maybe get shot or killed trying to find out who you pissed off enough to kill you. And for what, Tessa? So you can fade away into wherever the hell people like you go when they die?" She threw her hands in the air. "At the very least, you owe me an explanation."

Did you know Mom called me every time something good happened in your life? Tessa looked beyond the porch into the open field. *I don't even think she was aware of it, but she made sure I knew every time she received your grades from Mercer University, every time you won some stupid award for your stories.* She paused. *I got sick of hearing what a wonderful daughter you were and what a total screw-up I was.*

"Talk about old news, Tessa. Didn't we just have this conversation?" Lainey didn't wait for a response. "I can't help it if Mom did that to you. Hell, I wasn't even aware she was doing it. I only know every time she called me, I heard about how many rich boys you were hanging out with—how you were modeling for Macy's for extra money." Lainey ran her hands through her hair and sighed. "So our mother wasn't June Cleaver. Get over it."

Tessa glared at Lainey. *Did you know I flunked out of college the day you made the dean's list the first time?*

Lainey's heart softened, remembering how hurtful it had been to be compared to her beautiful sister and to always come up short. "I didn't know. I'm sorry."

I couldn't face Mom and tell her—at least not without a shit-load of booze in me. I found the alcohol easy enough in Waco on my way home from Temple, along with a married trucker who smelled like diesel fuel. She laughed. *Between him and the tequila shooters, I felt special until I woke up in the back of his cab with a bitch of a headache and a man I would normally never glance twice at blowing foul-smelling breath all over my naked body. Tell me, how much lower can you get than that?*

"We've all done things we regret," Lainey said, hating that she was now thinking about being sympathetic to a sister she'd spent so many years resenting.

You can't even imagine the regret, Lainey, Tessa continued. *By the time I hit Vineyard, I must have taken six showers trying to get his stink off my body.* She paused. *Six weeks later I discovered not only was I a whore but a pregnant one to boot.*

"Is he the father?"

Who the hell knows? Before it was over, I banged a few more lowlifes, all in the name of feeling special. She shrugged. *How ironic that a beautiful child like Gracie was the result of drunken sex.*

Both sisters glanced up as Colt's pickup rounded the corner and turned onto the gravel driveway. Lainey jumped up and headed for the door.

"I can't face him tonight," she said, but Tessa had already faded to wherever she lurked when things got heated.

Pushing the door open, Lainey scurried inside and leaned against it as soon as it closed. She was in no mood for another go round with that man. All she wanted was to crawl under the covers and rehash the conversation with Tessa, to try to make sense of it.

She had no idea her sister's life had been so messed up. She wondered why Tessa hadn't told any of her sisters about her dilemma. That's what sisters were for. If she hadn't had her younger sister all these years to confide in, to lean on, she would have been lost.

A sudden sadness rushed through her as she realized that Tessa had never felt close to any of them growing up. Lainey had Kate and the two older sisters were tight, but Tessa had always been the loner, keeping the others at a distance.

Why hadn't she at least confided in her best friend? Maybe she had. Maybe Carrie had been as judgmental as Lainey when Tessa told her.

She gasped and turned toward the door when Colt's knock interrupted her thoughts.

"Lainey?"

"I'm already in bed, Colt," she said quickly, then slapped her head. What kind of idiot excuse was that? He'd probably seen her scamper into the house as soon as he'd headed down the driveway.

"This won't take long."

She'd have to face him sooner or later. Might as well get it over with.

When she opened the door, his scowl might have scared off a lesser adversary, but she swallowed hard and met his gaze full on.

His eyes swept her body like a CT scanner. "You always sleep with your shoes on?"

Damn it!

She glanced from her feet to his face, feeling the rush of warmth move up her cheeks. She turned away and walked to the couch where she unceremoniously plopped down. "You might as well have a seat. I've been expecting this lecture. I have to warn you, though. I can only give you a few minutes. I've had a long day, and unless you plan on singing me a lullaby, the clock's ticking."

———

If she didn't look so damn sexy with that half-pout, half-mad look on her face, he might have laughed out loud before he engaged Lainey in battle. But he had no intentions of staging a command performance of last night's debacle. That meant he had to concentrate on what he'd come to say. Better for him if he got the hell out in a hurry.

"Maybe it's time you headed back to Savannah." He walked to the chair and sat down, waiting for her reaction.

"Excuse me?" Her voice conveyed her indignation. "I don't recall ever asking your opinion. If you want me out of this house, fine. I'll leave in the morning—tonight, if you prefer."

He met her eyes, even sexier with the new fire burning in them. "I have three unsolved murders and a killer running around who can't help but notice you're asking a lot of questions."

"I can take care of myself, but thanks for your concern." She stood up. "Now, unless there's something else…"

"Damn it, Lainey! You're not playing Clue with your sisters now. In my book, a nervous killer makes for an especially dangerous one."

"Is that what you think, Colt?" She laughed. "How is it I knew about the wine before you did? Or the fact that Roxy was dropping off five grand before you even questioned her?" She huffed. "My money's on Mr. Mustard in the office with a wineglass, by the way."

"That's not funny. You knew about Roxy because you're the one who planned that cockamamie scheme sending her to Lakeview in the first place," Colt shouted, unable to hide his frustration. He'd wondered how she knew those things. How she'd managed to stay one step ahead of his investigation. "And both you and Roxy could have ended up hurt—or worse—because of it."

He took a breath. "Stick to reporting, Lainey, and leave the police work to me."

She pointed to the door, not even trying to disguise her rage. "My long day, remember?"

He stood up and moved toward the door, then suddenly wheeled around on one foot for one last try at warning her, unaware she was right behind him. When she fell backward, he caught her wrist before she hit the floor, and he pulled her close, feeling her tense body relax in his arms. He stared into her face, trying to read her eyes.

"Do it," she whispered hoarsely. "We both know you want to."

TWENTY

CRUSHING HER AGAINST HIS body, Colt pressed his mouth to hers, a guttural moan escaping as his heart pounded in his chest. His tongue first traced the outline of her lips, then forced them open, sending shock waves through his entire body. He felt her shiver in response.

Every logical reason why he should walk away popped into his brain. Every argument why this shouldn't happen assaulted his senses, the unnerving voice in his head screaming Lainey could never be just another woman.

That scared the hell out of him. But when she moaned softly in his arms, his brain cried uncle. She smelled so damn good, like flowers on a windy day. Tasted so damn good, as he possessed her with his mouth.

Her breath came in short bursts as she teased back with her tongue, demanding, exploring. Somehow he found the strength to pull away from her burning mouth and tilt her head so his lips could reach her neck. In the soft fold at the base, he nuzzled, planting tender kisses.

A jolt of electricity spiraled through him as she rose on tiptoes and pressed her body closer, her firm breasts pushing into his chest.

Suddenly, he raised his head, held her in front of him, and stared into her jet black eyes now raging with the flame he felt shooting through his body. "Lainey?"

With cheeks already flushed from his five-o'clock shadow, she took a slow breath and released it as her tongue seductively licked her lips. "Don't stop now, Colt. I want you so badly, I ache."

He answered with his mouth, urgently tasting, nibbling first on her lips then moving to the tender lobe of her ear. With one hand in the small of her back, he pulled her closer, wanting her to feel his own desire while he slipped the sweater off her shoulders and let it fall.

There was no turning back now.

Fumbling, he unbuttoned her blouse, his hand lingering over her heart, now racing beneath his fingertips. He didn't bother removing it. Instead he slipped one hand behind her and unhooked the lacy black bra, the only barrier between his chest and her luscious breasts.

He cupped first one creamy mound, kneading her nipple until it was hard with desire before replacing his hand with his lips. Seductively, he caressed the swollen tissue with his tongue, causing a flashback of repressed desire in his own loins that nearly buckled his knees.

When he felt her hand brush the bulge in his jeans as she unbuckled his belt and moved to his zipper, he caught his breath.

In one fluid motion, he lifted her into his arms and headed for the bedroom, kicking the door open in his haste. Gently, he lowered her to the bed, his lips still holding her captive.

Then he hesitated, giving her one last chance to protest, praying she wouldn't.

Somehow, he knew what was about to happen would change his life forever, that this woman was different than the others he'd had casual sex with over the years.

But he was too far gone, his body no longer his to control. Only she had the power to stop him.

He watched as the hint of a smile crinkled her eyes.

God help him!

His mouth recaptured hers as he pulled back the covers and slid in beside her. This time, he removed her blouse and bra, throwing them across the room before surrounding her perfectly shaped breasts with his mouth. Slowly he licked, teasing her with his tongue, torturing himself with desire before he moved on.

She moaned softly as he released her swollen nipple and moved lower to her navel, fueling his intense need to possess her. Circling it with his tongue drove him mad as she writhed in obvious pleasure.

She wanted more.

He wanted more.

He was on fire, and she was the accelerant. There was only one way to douse the flame and that was to give into the raging desire that consumed him.

His hands fumbled at her waist, and she lifted her body high to allow him to unzip her jeans and slide them over her hips. When it was clear the skin-tight jeans wouldn't budge without assistance, he rolled over as she pushed them down over her thighs, wiggling her hips suggestively. He didn't think it was possible to be turned on even more.

He was wrong.

He took a moment to strip out of his own clothes. He wanted to feel her naked skin under his, to slide her silky white breasts against his chest. He glanced up, noticing she was watching his every move. Her eyes settled on the part of his anatomy crying out to be one with her, and she smiled.

Christ!

His mouth reclaimed hers, further igniting his passion already out of control. His fingers caressed her breast once again before moving lower, and he felt her body shudder under his fingertips. He tasted lavender as his tongue followed the feathery trail of his hands.

His lips reached the core of her womanhood, and she gasped, shattering any doubts he may have had. Relentless in his pursuit to pleasure her, he tasted, sucked. When he felt her hands in his hair, pushing him deeper into her, he nearly exploded, unable to take much more.

Slowly, he moved his body up the length of hers, sliding easily with the moisture of their lovemaking. Gently he lowered himself into her, becoming one body, one spirit with the woman beneath him.

Long forgotten were his fears as her body moved in perfect harmony with his. Nothing mattered but what was happening in this bed at this moment. Thrust after thrust, she met his passion, until they simultaneously erupted with the intensity of their climax.

His breathing, fast and frantic as if his body craved oxygen, finally became normal, and he slid off her. Staring at the ceiling, deep in thought, he knew he had just crossed the line, his own self-imposed line. Knew things could never be the same between them now.

Knew it and was terrified this incredible moment had been a disastrous mistake.

"Okay, then," she said, her voice still breathy as she broke the silence between them.

"Lainey, I'm—"

She reached across and put her finger to his lips. "Shh. Let's enjoy the moment. It is what it is. Nothing more."

"I never meant—"

"Colt, I'm serious. No apologies. We both know this didn't mean anything. Leave it at that." She giggled. "I gotta tell you, though, Mr. Winslow. You have a couple of major moves I wasn't aware of."

The mischief in her eyes forced him to smile. "And you, as well, Ms. Garcia." He sat up in bed, afraid to allow the afterglow to cloud his judgment. "I'll see you in the morning, Lainey."

She reached up and pushed him back down to the pillow. "Oh, no you don't. Stay and let me pay you back for your generosity." She winked.

He studied her face, trying to find a reason to go but drawing a blank. Why couldn't this just be two people enjoying each other's company, each other's bodies? Why did he have to make it out to be something it wasn't? She'd said it herself. It was what it was.

Sex!

Pure and simple.

Hot and wet.

He growled and reached for her again. "Enough talking. Payback time."

———

It was her wedding day, and her stepfather was walking her down the aisle toward the altar. Her dress was gorgeous, the long train flowing behind her, pink roses embroidered down the center.

After Johnny Lopez lifted her veil and kissed her, she glanced up at her husband who was waiting at the altar, his smile illuminating the entire church.

"Lainey."

She smiled back at him. "I do," she responded, thinking this was the happiest day of her life.

"You do what?"

Opening her eyes, she stared up at Colt, surprised he wasn't standing at the altar in a tux. She jerked her body into a sitting position, then grabbed the sheet to cover her bare breasts as the man in the dream she'd had so many times as a teenager offered her a hot cup of coffee instead of a wedding band.

She felt her cheeks flame. "I must have been dreaming."

The smile spread across his face. "I would love to have been a fly in that dream. You were smiling like you'd just won the lottery."

He sat down on the edge of the bed, and Lainey pulled the sheet closer to her chest.

That's rich, she thought, remembering what had happened the night before. After their third bout of lovemaking, both had fallen asleep, totally exhausted.

She glanced at the clock on the nightstand, amazed it was already after nine. She hadn't slept this late in years. She reached for the coffee from his outstretched hand and sipped. "How long have you been awake?" she asked, enjoying another sip. The man brewed a mean cup of joe.

Dressed in jeans and a blue plaid shirt that brought out his eyes, his hair still damp from a shower, Colt shot her a devilish grin. "About an hour. You were dead to the world, so I let you catch a little more shuteye."

He picked up the morning paper from the table and handed it to her. "Gotta run to the office for a few hours. My mom's bringing Gracie home around noon."

Her cell phone began to vibrate, skittering across the nightstand to hang precariously on the edge. Colt jumped, catching it just before it went over.

Lainey grabbed it from him and flipped the receiver open, irritated that one of her sisters was calling this early on a Saturday morning. Their rule had always been no calls before noon on the weekends.

"Hello."

"Hello, sunshine. Where've you been all morning? I've been trying to reach you for over an hour."

Her eyes met Colt's who hadn't moved from the side of the bed, his body language indicating he had no intentions of going anywhere anytime soon.

"I slept in this morning. I must have switched off the phone last night," she lied, her heart rate speeding up suddenly. "Why were you trying to reach me, Dan? Is something wrong?"

He chuckled. "On the contrary." He paused. "I need directions to get from DFW to Vineyard."

"You're at the airport?" Her voice elevated an octave. "What are you doing there?"

She glanced up when she heard the door shut behind Colt.

Colt had spent the last five hours going over the murder investigation files, growing more frustrated by the minute.

Damn it! I'm missing something that's probably gonna jump up and bite me in the ass when I least expect it.

He scratched his forehead as a disturbing thought occurred. What if the two murders at the Conquistador had nothing to do with Tessa? The only real connection he could make between her and Porter was the oil drilling contract, and Tessa had made herself perfectly clear on that subject. She had no intentions of selling Spirits of Texas to him.

Still, Porter had indicated he'd found a way to get around Tessa. If his plan was working, why would he need to kill her? And what about Carrie blackmailing Roxy? Did that fit into the whole picture or was it just a coincidence? Carrie had grown up in a poor neighborhood and had always schemed to get ahead in life. Maybe squeezing money out of Roxy was simply a way to get easy cash.

Roxy! He needed to take a second look at her, dig deeper. It was obvious to everyone except Moretti she'd only married him for his money, that she'd been sneaking around behind his back with Porter. Could she have had a serious disagreement with her lover and killed him?

What about Thornton? Was he just a thug Roxy had known from her porn days and hired to axe Porter? Then who killed Thornton?

He slammed the file to the desk and raked his fingers through his hair. The image of Lainey doing the exact same thing during their lovemaking marathon brought a smile to his weary face.

God! He didn't realize how much he'd missed sex.

The smile faded as the devil's advocate in his head reminded him last night hadn't been all about good sex. He'd been dancing around his attraction to her since the funeral. Even Lainey had picked up signals. "Do it," she'd said. "We both know you want to."

Obviously, he'd been so sex-starved she'd seen right through him. But it was more than that. Something about her got under his skin. Maybe that's why he'd been thinking about her since he'd left her talking on the phone this morning.

He pursed his lips wondering who this Dan guy was anyway? Colt didn't remember hearing that name before this morning.

He exhaled audibly in an attempt to blow away the twinge of jealousy he felt in his gut. No matter how much he hoped the guy turned out to be a gay friend or someone else's husband, Lainey's body language when she was on the phone had spoken volumes. He'd been a cop too long to miss the way she'd turned her back to him when she answered, the way she'd lowered her voice when she recognized the caller, and most telling, the look in her eyes when she'd finally turned around and met his gaze.

Whoever Dan was, he was definitely someone important in her life, someone she'd either shared or was still sharing an intimate relationship with. He scolded himself for wishing for the former. He had no business even thinking about going down that road, especially with his ex's sister. He and Gracie were getting along just fine without adding another relationship to the mix.

But his mind challenged his good sense that since he'd had a taste of her lips, her body, once would never be enough. Vivid snapshots of her squirming on the bed, moaning softly from his touch, brought another smile to his lips.

"You're not gonna be grinning like that when I tell you what I found out this afternoon, boss."

Colt jerked his head up, the smile fading as Danny Landers walked into the room and sat down hard in the chair.

"I was just thinking about something Gracie said this morning," Colt lied.

"Thought Gracie spent the night with your mom."

Sometimes he hated that his business was common knowledge in Vineyard. "I talked to her on the phone before I left the house." Colt shrugged. "So, what'd you find out?"

Danny leaned forward. "You know how I try to make it to all my nephew's soccer games?" When Colt nodded, Danny continued. "Well, this morning, they played in Lewistown." His eyes lit up with pride. "You should see him, boss. That little six-year-old can fly. He's faster than the bigger kids on the team."

"That can wait, Danny," Colt interrupted. "What did you find out that was important enough to barge in here?"

"On the way home, I stopped by a convenience store in Shakerville to get a slushy. Just for the hell of it, I asked the clerk if he'd sold any prepaid phones lately."

Colt's eyes narrowed. "Go on," he urged.

"As it turned out, he was the owner. Said he's thinking about taking them off the shelves because nobody's buying them anymore." Danny paused before explaining. "The phone companies have lowered their prices on the calling plans and most of them come with a free phone."

"Another dead end?"

Landers scooted to the edge of the chair. "Don't rush me. Everything needs a little foreplay."

Colt couldn't help chuckling. If his young officer only knew how close to home that remark hit after last night. "The day's only so long, kid. Get on with the story."

Danny glanced out the window at the three or four people milling around the station, then got up and shut the door. Instead of sitting back down, he leaned over Colt's desk. His voice dropped to a whisper. "He sold one about a month ago."

Colt's interest escalated. "Please tell me the guy used a credit card to buy it."

"Better than that." Danny beamed. "You have to register for a prepaid phone. Unfortunately, when I ran the guy's name through our computer a few minutes ago, it turns out he's been dead for six months. Heart attack."

"Dammit! I thought we were going to catch a break." Colt slid back in the chair. "Any relatives in the area that might have used the name?"

"The guy was staying at a hotel off Highway 114. Some kind of business conference. His family all lives back in Boston."

"Hmm," Colt mused. "Who walks into a 7-Eleven and buys a phone with an out of town dead guy's name and personal information?" He turned to Landers. "Did he use the Boston address or a phony one?"

"The Boston one."

Colt opened one of the files on his desk and read silently. When he looked up, Danny was staring, waiting for his follow-up instructions.

"Chances are slim this is even the phone we're looking for," Colt said, more to himself than the young deputy. "Find out who was at the conference, which hotel exactly. Then dig around to see if you can connect the dead guy to Porter or Thornton."

Danny flopped down in the chair, a self-satisfied grin on his face. "Don't need to."

"Damn it, Danny, this isn't a game," Colt reprimanded, unable to hide his annoyance. Danny Landers was a good cop when his youth didn't get in the way.

"The owner said he got nervous watching the man fill out the forms. The guy kept looking around to make sure no one was standing behind him. When he walked out, the owner glanced out the window more from curiosity than anything." Danny hitched his brows. "Here's where it gets interesting, boss. It was a cop."

Colt's body stiffened. "What made him think that?"

"The guy drove off in a Vineyard Police cruiser."

TWENTY-ONE

Out of breath, Lainey opened the door and stared at Dan Maguire as Ginger and Fred checked him out in their own unique way. She'd only had about thirty minutes to take a quick shower after he'd called from the airport, and her hair was still damp.

"You're beautiful without makeup," he said softly.

She rushed over and fell into his arms, enjoying the way he cradled her. "I've missed you, even though I forgot how good a liar you are."

When he bent down to kiss her, she turned her head slightly, and his lips brushed her cheek. The questions in his eyes tore at her heart. Dan was a beautiful man inside and out. She owed him the truth.

She pulled away and tugged at his arm. "Come over here and sit."

Reluctantly, he allowed her to drag him to the kitchen where she guided him to a chair.

"I'm sorry I don't have coffee, Dan, but there are a few packets of hot chocolate in the cupboard."

"I'm all coffee'd out, anyway," he replied. "Hot chocolate sounds nice. I didn't expect Texas to be this chilly."

She grinned. "By this afternoon, you'll wish you hadn't worn that long-sleeved shirt."

As she heated the water in the microwave, Lainey felt his intense gaze on the back of her neck. She dreaded what she had to do.

Setting the steaming cup in front of him, she slid into the chair opposite him and took a small sip of her own drink. This wouldn't be easy. She loved this man, just not in the way he wanted.

"Dan, I…"

He inhaled sharply. "I'm not sure I want to hear what you're about to say."

She fought to keep her brimming tears from falling. "You know I love you."

His eyes begged her not to add the "but I" part he obviously heard in her voice.

"I don't think I've ever met another man as totally unselfish as you. I will always be grateful I have you in my life."

"But?" he asked, his voice resigned.

She attempted to smile as a lone tear won the battle and slid down her cheek. "I'm not *in* love with you," she blurted, reaching across the table and taking his hand in hers. She massaged the tanned skin on top, kneading the soft palm underneath. "I'm sorry."

"How long have you felt this way?"

She sighed, releasing his hand. "I've been questioning myself for a while," she said. "I'm a coward and not nearly as unselfish as you. When I'm in your arms, I feel so safe, so secure. I want to stay there forever."

"Then why don't you?" His eyes sparkled with a ray of hope. "I love you, Lainey. I knew you were special the moment you walked into my office and convinced me you could send the ratings at KSAV through the roof. I just didn't realize how hard I would fall for you."

"I felt the same way about you, even with all the false bravado that day." She watched his steel gray eyes hold her captive, begging her to say what he wanted to hear.

She couldn't. She loved Dan too much to deceive him.

"But," she started.

"There's that negativity again," he said, turning away from her to dab his eyes.

She choked back her own cry, nearly losing her resolve to continue.

"Truthfully, I've known for a while," he finally said when he faced her again. "I felt it in your touch, saw it in your eyes. I just didn't want to believe it. I thought you would learn to love me as much as I love you." The hope disappeared from his eyes, replaced by a cloud of sadness.

"You can't make your heart feel something it doesn't," she said, her own heart aching with sorrow. "God knows, I've tried."

She stood and circled the table, embracing him from behind. For a while, neither spoke until Dan finally broke away.

"Are you still considering the Florida job?"

She shrugged. "They agreed to wait another week to interview me. I'm hopeful things can get wrapped up here in Vineyard by then." She had almost forgotten about the job interview. It had been rescheduled for this Friday.

Dan turned and met her gaze. A cold blade sliced through her heart with the sudden realization of what she was giving up. Reality hit her like a splash of icy water.

She pushed a stray lock of hair off his forehead. "Nothing's definite yet, Dan. I can change my mind all together and come begging at your doorstep before then. Who knows what will happen?"

Even as she said it, she knew it wouldn't happen. The driving force for their on-camera relationship had been the chemistry generated by their off-camera one. After today, that relationship was gone.

"Are you sure there's nothing I can say to change your mind?"

She shook her head. "As much as I'm gonna regret giving up on us, we both need to move on."

He glanced at his watch, then reached for his cell phone. She studied his face as he punched in a number, listening as he changed his plane reservations. When he disconnected, he almost looked relieved, as if he had known this moment was coming and was glad it was over.

Lainey smiled sadly. "You're leaving at eight tonight?" When he nodded, she sighed. "That gives me the whole day to show you around this little town I grew up in." Her smile faded. "Unless you'd rather not."

For the first time, he laughed out loud. "If you'll feed me before you drag me all over town, count me in. Peanuts just don't cut it," he said, springing up from the chair. "Come on, woman, tempt me with some of that great Texas food you're always gushing about."

"Ruby's!" she exclaimed. "You haven't lived until you've tasted her chicken-fried steak." Lainey grabbed her jacket and nudged him toward the door, stopping to plant a quick kiss on his cheek before closing it behind them.

As she slid into the passenger seat of his rental car, her mouth watered, thinking about Ruby's delicious home cooking. She prayed Colt wouldn't decide to have lunch there today. She wasn't ready to introduce the man she had been sleeping with for the past two years to the man she had slept with less than twelve hours ago.

She couldn't hide the grin that spread across her face. What did that say about her?

———

She jumped when her cell phone blared "Before He Cheats," nearly dumping a half full cup of Diet Dr Pepper into her lap. "Hello."

"Hey, babe, where are you?" a sleepy voice asked. "I rolled over and you were AWOL."

"I had to run a few errands before my hair appointment this afternoon. I didn't want to wake you, especially after you worked so hard last night." She was glad he couldn't see her face.

Worked so hard, my ass. All he had to do was plug in the damn vibrator and put it on the right spot. Even an idiot like Jerry could figure that out.

"Daddy knows what you like, don't I?"

Any moron can turn on the switch. "You sure do, baby. I can't wait to get more tonight."

"What time will you get back? Maybe I can sneak away from the office early, and we can do the nasty before dinner."

Even his voice irritated her. "I'd like that," she lied. *Fat chance of me making it home before dark.* "Gotta run if I'm gonna make that appointment. Love you."

"Hurry home, lambkins. Dirty Harry misses you already."

She hung up and huffed. Little Harry would be more like it, she thought, referring to the name he'd given his dick.

She raised the binoculars up to her eyes, just as Lainey and the guy who had arrived about an hour ago headed out the door. When Lainey reached over and kissed him, she smiled.

And they call me a whore!

She'd driven out to Colt's ranch to try to talk Lainey into selling her half of the winery. She thought maybe if she sweetened the pot with money on the side, it might work. From all indications, Lainey had no plans to stay in Vineyard despite what she told Jerry.

Her forced laugh was dry and cynical. She could spot a well-conceived plan a mile away, and Lainey definitely had a scam going to get Jerry to up the ante for what was rightfully his.

Rightfully hers.

Despite Jerry's promise to promote her after Tessa was out of the way, thanks to Lainey, that hadn't happened. He said she was the Vice President of Marketing, but she wasn't born yesterday. He was merely placating her.

Maybe he really had no intentions of making her part of management. If that was true, the man had a big surprise coming. Nobody screwed with Roxy Moretti and got away with it. She would get what was owed her no matter what she had to do.

Roxy shivered and pulled the jacket closer. When she'd left the house this morning, she didn't know she would be sitting behind a row of trees spying on Lainey. She'd only meant to wait until she saw Colt's car leave, then approach the woman for a talk. She'd been surprised to see Colt leave Lainey's house so early, still buttoning his shirt.

Lainey was so much like her sister it was a sin. *Even I don't go straight from one man's bed to another's.*

Who was this new guy anyway? Since she knew most of the men in Vineyard, she figured he must be an old lover from a neighboring city.

Ducking as the nondescript car backed out of Colt's driveway and headed down the gravel road, she waited a few minutes longer so the dogs wouldn't be alerted to her hiding place. She'd purposely stayed far enough away so they wouldn't pick up her scent.

Thank God for the binoculars Jerry kept in the car. He probably used them to peep into windows.

As she walked to her car, parked off the road farther down the highway, she thought about the way she'd tricked both Colt and Lainey into thinking she was stupid enough to allow Carrie Phillips to blackmail her. Hell, she'd known Carrie was behind that scheme almost the minute she found the pictures on her desk. Since no one else had entered the office, even a retard like Jerry could have figured it out.

It was a brilliant idea to throw them off, and it had worked. Quinton's death had screwed up the plan somewhat, but everything was back on track now. When she worked out the oil deal with Quinton's boss, Jerry would have to take notice and promote her to head of marketing for real. She'd worked too hard to accept anything less.

A smile spread across her face as an idea popped into her mind. She knew exactly how to get Tessa's half of the vineyard back into Jerry's hands and claim what was hers.

"What was so damn urgent you pulled me off the golf course, Colt?" Prescott's eyes flashed with anger. "It's not like I'm able to get away any day of the week to play."

"Sit down, Charlie. I need to ask a few questions." Colt pointed to the chair and waited until the lawyer was settled. "Let me see if I've got this right. You are the lawyer on record for Tessa's estate, right?"

"What's that got to do with anything?" Prescott shifted in his seat, a gesture Colt immediately recognized as a common occurrence when he made someone nervous.

"So, you wouldn't have any reason to be dealing with Jerry Moretti on anything while you're still acting as executor, right?" Colt saw a flicker of fear in the man's eyes.

"What are you inferring, Sheriff?"

A minute ago, he'd addressed him as Colt. A sudden shift away from a familiarity usually indicated he had broached a touchy subject. He shoved Moretti's phone records across the desk with the calls to the lawyer highlighted. "Maybe this will refresh your memory."

Prescott, suddenly looking older than his fifty-something years, grabbed the papers and fished in his pocket for his reading glasses. When he finally looked up, Colt noticed a drop of sweat beading on his forehead.

"Why is this important? It has nothing to do with Lainey or the will."

"Why don't you let me be the judge of that?"

Prescott took a deep breath and wiped at the perspiration now visible across his entire forehead. "You have anything cold to drink?"

Colt picked up the phone and asked Rogers to bring in a bottle of water. He sat in silence until Prescott had taken a long swallow.

"About a month ago, a man called my office looking to hire me to broker a deal on a future real estate project."

"What kind of real estate project?"

"I'm not in a position to divulge that information, Colt."

So, it's back to Colt now. "Who was this guy?"

Prescott finished the water in two gulps and placed the empty bottle on the desk. "I can't tell you that, either."

Colt studied the man he'd known all his life. The man whose only son had graduated with him from Vineyard High. He wished there was another way to find the facts, but he couldn't see it. "You are aware I'm investigating three separate murders, right?"

"I read about them," Prescott admitted.

"As a lawyer, I don't have to remind you how obstruction of justice works, do I, Charlie?"

The older man flushed. "Now look here, Sheriff. I know the law. What do I have to do with your murders?"

Colt leaned back in his chair with his hands clasped behind his head. "Maybe nothing. But that's my call, not yours." He smiled. "I have no qualms about throwing you into a jail cell faster than you can say 'Mulligan' unless you answer my questions. Or you could be headed back to the country club before anyone even misses you." He raised his hands in the air. "Your choice."

Awkwardly, Prescott cleared his throat. "His name's Marcus DuPont. Said he's the middle man for a conglomerate of foreign investors."

Colt tossed that around in his head. "What does this have to do with Jerry? Wasn't he working a deal with Porter to set up the oil drilling rig on his property?"

Prescott eyed Colt for a few seconds. "Before you go off on a tangent, let me explain. Never once did I let my involvement with Tessa's estate become a conflict of interest."

"Quit stalling."

The lawyer chewed on his lower lip. "They want to buy Jerry's land. All two thousand acres of it."

"Jerry and Lainey's land," Colt corrected. "What were they planning to do with it?"

Charles Prescott was visibly uncomfortable with the questions, making Colt speculate about what the man wasn't telling him. "The largest mall in the southwest, complete with office buildings, theme parks. The works."

"And Jerry was okay with this?"

"Oh yeah. Jerry was only playing hard to get to run up the asking price."

Colt seethed under a mounting rage. "More likely to screw Lainey and Gracie out of a helluva lot of cash." When Prescott didn't respond, Colt glared. "And you really don't see this as a conflict of interest?"

"I never saw it that way, no. Lainey would have had to sign on the dotted line right along with Jerry. There's no way to hide the purchase price."

"Come on, Charlie. I had you figured for a smart guy. Obviously, the feeling isn't mutual if you think you can spout this bullshit, and I'll accept it like gospel." Colt slammed his fist on the desk, then waved off his employees moving toward his office. "I should lock your sorry ass up on principle alone."

Colt took a few deep breaths to calm down. He had to take his personal interests out of the equation and treat this like any other investigation. The fact that this jerk was in on a deal that more than likely would hurt both Lainey and Gracie couldn't influence how he handled it.

"Did Tessa know?"

"Not really. She suspected someone local was trying to work a deal, but she had no idea who it might be." He paused before adding, "At least to my knowledge, she didn't know."

"What was your cut gonna be?"

For the first time, Prescott looked embarrassed. "Around three mil," he muttered under his breath.

"Three million?" Colt shouted. "Jesus, Charlie, how much money are we talking here?"

The lawyer met Colt's incredulous stare. "Somewhere around a couple billion."

There it was—the perfect motive for Tessa's murder. If Tessa opposed selling the vineyard, which he was pretty sure she had, there were a lot of people with a good reason to want her dead.

Two billion dollars worth of damn good reasons!

"Any idea who the local contact might be?"

Prescott shook his head. "I only know DuPont mentioned whoever worked the deal first would collect the booty. I have no idea who my competition was."

"Did you know Quinton Porter or a guy named Thornton?"

Again, Prescott shook his head. "I only know Jerry was pretending to be interested in the Houston guy's offer to make the other deal more lucrative."

Colt stood. "As much as I'd like to see you spend a few nights in my jail, there really isn't anything I can charge you with. Double dealing isn't a crime nor is being a conniving jerk, but hear me out, Charlie. I'm gonna make damn sure anyone who asks my opinion will not come knocking on your door for legal advice. After I think on this a bit, I may even give the state bar a call."

"I'm sorry you feel that way, Colt." Prescott lifted his overweight body out of the chair and walked out the door, leaving Colt staring in anger.

The words of the CSI jingled in his brain. *What the hell was going on in Vineyard?*

In the past few days, he'd dealt with murders, poisoned wine, blackmail attempts, and now this. He could only imagine what would happen to his town if a multi-billion dollar foreign entity bought the biggest piece of land in Vineyard and turned it into a goddamn recreational monstrosity.

He glanced down at his watch. He really needed to get home, although Gracie was spending another night at his mother's. She'd persuaded him to let her take her granddaughter to the movies today, then to church in the morning. She loved showing her off to her cronies.

Colt gathered up the files and stacked them neatly in the corner. Monday was soon enough to get back to them, especially since Danny wouldn't be able to get the phone records of all the employees until then without raising suspicions.

It still blew Colt's mind to think one of his men might have had something to do with this whole mess.

He turned out the light and headed out the door after making sure he didn't need to put out any fires before he left. On the drive home, he thought about Lainey again. He wondered how he'd feel if he discovered Dan whoever was spending the night in the same bed he'd slept in last night.

He'd called Maddy with some trivial work-related premise and casually asked who Dan was. The man was Lainey's boss in Savannah, but Maddy suspected there was more to the relationship—that he was also her boyfriend for the past two years. It definitely wasn't what Colt wanted to hear.

He scolded himself for allowing the green-eyed monster to surface. He and Lainey had nothing but a night of sex together, and she would be gone in a few days anyway. It was possible Dan had come here to talk her into going home now. Colt didn't like the way that prospect made him feel, either.

As soon as he turned into his driveway, he noticed the lights were off in the guest house. Was she in there under the sheets with her boyfriend?

He shook his head to clear his mind. He didn't want to imagine her doing the same things with this other guy that she'd done with him.

Three times!

Christ, he was acting like some teenager hopped up on testosterone.

He parked his car in the garage and walked into the kitchen. It was already dark, and he hadn't fed the dogs. Quickly he made a pit stop then filled their bowls with Kibbles 'n Bits. Just as he walked out on the front porch, he saw her car pull into the driveway. Scrambling into the shadows, he felt a bit adolescent spying on her, but unable to resist watching.

An odd thought struck him as her car pulled up next to the guest house and parked.

Where were his dogs?

He did a 360, but there was no sign of them. He resisted the temptation to whistle, not willing to risk her seeing him. The embarrassment alone would kill him.

He guessed the animals were out chasing the cows into the pasture. The labs thought they were Blue Heelers sometimes, herding the cows when they thought they were not where they should be.

He sucked in a breath as Lainey exited her vehicle and stood by the car door, her head turning in all directions. A sigh of relief escaped his lips when he realized she was alone. When she turned and faced his porch, he leaned closer into the shadows. She probably wondered why Ginger and Fred weren't there to greet her like always.

A flash of intuition rocked his entire body when Lainey approached the porch steps, and he pitched forward, dropping the dog bowls and screaming her name.

As if in slow motion, he watched, horrified, as the house exploded, sending Lainey across the driveway in a ball of fire.

TWENTY-TWO

COLT VAULTED OVER THE porch railing and rushed to where Lainey's limp body had landed about fifty yards from the guest house. Even at this distance, the intense flames scorched his face.

He searched for a pulse, breathing a sigh of relief when he felt one.

"Colt?"

He lifted her head slightly. "Don't move, Lainey." The terror in her eyes reflected his own fears.

In the distance he heard the wail of sirens approaching. He prayed whichever neighbor had called 911 after hearing the explosion had the good sense to ask for an ambulance.

He focused back on Lainey as she attempted to sit up. When she fell backwards and grabbed her left shoulder, he cautioned, "You probably only dislocated that shoulder, but until we know for sure, stay still."

Impatiently, he glanced toward the end of the driveway. Where in the hell were they? The blaze, fueled by the March wind, flared toward them.

When he couldn't stand it any longer, Colt positioned his arm under her good shoulder. "Stay flat," he instructed. "This is gonna hurt like hell, but you can't stay here. I have to get you away from the fire."

She screamed as he pulled her back another fifty yards or so. Although he still felt the heat at this distance, at least she was out of range of the flying embers.

He took a few minutes to scan her body. Except for a few bruises and black smudges covering her face and arms, there were no obvious injuries. "I'm no doctor, but I think your shoulder is the only problem, Lainey. You must have landed on it."

He shuddered thinking that had she been one or two steps closer to the door, she might have died. Or if he'd parked in front of his house instead of pulling into the garage, he might have smelled the gas in time to warn her.

The sirens grew louder, and both Colt and Lainey glanced up the driveway just as two fire trucks and an ambulance rounded the corner and raced toward them. Within minutes the trucks were parked and the firemen began pumping water on the guest house with hoses resembling huge serpents from where he knelt.

Colt stood as the two emergency technicians surrounded Lainey and began assessing her injuries.

"I'm okay, really," she protested. "If you'll help me stand up, I can get away from this heat."

"Hold on, ma'am. Let us do our job and make sure there aren't any fractures first."

After a few minutes, the two men flanked Lainey on either side and hoisted her to her feet. Disregarding her insistence she could make it on her own, they led her to Colt's porch and eased her down onto the swing. One of the EMTs ran back to the truck, returning with a sling he applied to her left arm.

Seeing that Lainey was out of danger, Colt scurried into the house for a blanket to throw over her knees. On the way out the door, he grabbed his jacket and draped it around her shoulders. He'd noticed her shivering and wasn't sure if it was because of the cool night air or the realization she'd come so close to dying.

The fact that she only wore a thin silk blouse suggested the former. A voice in his head taunted that she must have left the house before the sun went down and the temperature dropped.

Had she spent the day in Dan's hotel room?

Colt chastised himself for thinking about that now and concentrated on keeping her warm, but her shivering continued. He sat down and pulled her close, careful not to jar her injured shoulder. Together, they watched in silence as the firemen battled the raging fire.

Within minutes, the local news channels had satellite trucks lining the outer perimeter of Colt's property. Two of his men, Flanagan and Rogers, who probably dragged themselves out of warm beds to get here, were keeping onlookers at bay.

"I'm sure I didn't leave the stove on, Colt," Lainey said, her voice wavering.

He blew out a breath. He was pretty sure of that, too. "I know." When he saw the fear reappear in her eyes as the implication sunk in, he added, "Maybe there was a malfunction in the gas line under the house."

Even as he said it, he knew the chances of that were slim. As much as he hated the thought, a more likely scenario was someone had blown out the pilot light and turned on the gas stove, just as they suspected with Tessa's murder.

The disturbing thought stopped him cold. If true, it meant a killer was stalking Vineyard, one bold enough to walk onto his property and commit a felony.

"Where are the dogs?" Lainey asked, as the firemen finally began making progress extinguishing the flames.

He couldn't tell her what he suspected—that whoever had done this had dealt with Ginger and Fred beforehand. "Probably chasing a coyote somewhere," he lied.

She turned sharply, wincing as her shoulder jerked. "They would have come running when they saw my car, no matter what they were doing." Her voice dripped with sadness as if she'd read his mind.

He patted her good arm, unable to come up with any other way to reassure her. "I'm sure they're fine. We can't worry about them now."

Colt swallowed hard, trying to mask his mounting rage. He'd discovered as far back as his rookie years that being level-headed in an investigation was the best way to gather facts.

But whoever did this had made it personal.

When he'd convinced Lainey to move to the ranch so he could protect her, he'd felt confident he could do that. For the first time he worried it might not be so easy.

What if Gracie had come home and run to the guest house to say hello to Lainey like she always did? Colt shuddered at the thought, vowing to stop at nothing to nail the bastard who had done this.

He stared vacantly toward the pasture, trying to formulate a plan to find out who was responsible for this. His gut told him, despite everything Charles Prescott had said, it all boiled down to DuPont and someone local.

The possibility one of his four police officers might be involved squeezed his heart. Turning toward Flanagan and Rogers, who were doing a damn good job holding off the press, he forced that thought from his head. Both men had been with him since he'd been elected sheriff. Phil Romano was as close to a right-hand man as you could get, and Danny Landers was still a work in progress.

The obnoxious voice in his head kept taunting him, as if he needed a reminder that sometimes money made people do desperate things.

And three million dollars was a helluva incentive.

"Sheriff?"

His eyes followed the voice to a spot under the big oak tree shading the porch. A fireman who looked like he was right out of high school had retreated there for a break.

The young firefighter pointed to the barn on the other side of the house. "There's some kind of commotion going on over there. You might want to check it out."

Colt glanced quickly at Lainey, seeing a glimmer of hope in her eyes, before he bounded off the swing and raced toward the barn. Halfway there, he smiled as he heard his two labs barking in unison and beating the hell out of the barn door. As he drew closer, he noticed a dark spot on the metal lock. Careful not to touch that area, he unlatched it and pushed the door open. Both Ginger and Fred lunged at him, knocking him over and slobbering all over his face.

"Ginger! Fred!" Lainey screamed from the porch.

Hearing her voice, the dogs deserted Colt like he was a picked-over chicken carcass and bolted toward the porch. Colt walked into the barn to check on his horses. Reassured they were safe, he headed back to the porch to watch the firemen battle the last of the flames. His heart ached, staring at the crumbling ruins, the only thing left of his guest house.

Someone's going to pay for this!

———

She glanced at her watch. If she hurried, she could fix a snack before the ten o'clock news. Surely, the TV stations would have had plenty of time to rush out and take pictures.

She giggled like a teenager anticipating the scene—the massive flames enveloping the entire house, the firefighters battling in vain to keep the fire from spreading to the main house. The one she especially couldn't wait to see was the paramedic carrying out the dead body.

Who did Lainey Garcia think she was fucking with? She'd assumed she could waltz into town after all these years and pick up where her bitch of a sister had left off.

No way that was gonna happen! Tessa found out the hard way, and as of a few hours ago, so had Lainey.

She checked her watch again. She didn't want to miss the beginning, sure it would be the leading story on all the channels.

On the way out of the kitchen, she glanced down at the paper plate on the counter where she'd placed the four blue pills. They were nearly dry after she'd put a dropper full of cyanide on each one, and she slid them out of sight behind the coffee pot.

Good riddance to another asshole who shouldn't have fucked with me!

In the living room, she plopped down on the sofa and reached for the remote. The first station was showing the massive fire, with BREAKING NEWS crawling across the picture bottom.

She smiled. The devastation verified the explosion had been huge. But so far, there was no mention of a death.

She switched channels as she grabbed another handful of potato chips. Nearly identical coverage of the blaze flashed across the screen.

Still no mention of a body.

She turned up the volume just as the camera cut away to a reporter standing outside Colt's property. He said the cause of the fire was unknown, but it was believed to have been the result of a gas leak.

Ya think?

Shock yielded to fury as she listened to the man report there had only been minor injuries. She jumped up and slammed the remote on the coffee table, spilling her drink.

There was no friggin' body bag!

After a few minutes, she calmed down. Maybe that whore was alive tonight, but things could change in a hurry.

Tomorrow, she'd work on Plan B.

———

"Oh my God! How did this happen?" Maddy screamed as she and Deena pushed their way past the nurse into the examining room.

"I'm sorry, ma'am, you can't be back here. Ms. Garcia had a traumatic experience tonight, and the doctor hasn't finished with his assessment."

Screw the assessment. Are you okay, Lainey?

Lainey glanced quickly at Tessa who stood behind the other two, then back at the nurse. "I'm okay. They're my sisters, and I want them here with me."

The nurse held her ground. "Sorry. Hospital rules."

Remind Nurse Ratched whose money keeps this place running.

"It's okay, Sheila. I'll take full responsibility for it," Kate said, as she breezed into the room, nudging the others aside and grabbing Lainey's chart.

The nurse didn't budge.

Kate glared at her. "This is my sister. I said I'll be responsible if you get called on the carpet over this."

Finally, the nurse headed for the door. "I'll let Dr. Singletary know you're here, Dr. Garcia." She huffed, then walked out.

"Dr. Garcia," Lainey repeated. "That has a nice ring."

"Yeah, well, it might not sound so great rolling off the Chief of Obstetrics' lips as he reprimands me for pushing my weight around." Kate flipped through the medical records. "Looks like you lucked out. The shoulder's only bruised."

"Does that mean I get to ditch this stupid sling?"

"A bruised shoulder is as painful as a dislocation, Lainey. You have to wear it for a week or two." Kate turned to her older sisters. "If I get my ass chewed out for letting you two stay, there will be hell to pay."

"Three," Lainey said.

"Three what?" Maddy and Deena said in unison before Lainey's meaning sunk in.

Deena's eyes circled the room. "Tessa's here?"

"Right beside you."

Kate turned in that direction. "Do you know who did this to her?"

Tessa shook her head.

"She doesn't," Lainey told them.

"What the hell kind of ghost are you, just some kind of comedic relief?" Maddy pushed her hand through her hair. "I'm sorry, Tessa. It's just—I can't lose another sister."

She moved closer to the bed. "As of this minute, the Garcia girls are out of the murder-solving business. As soon as you're able, I want you on the next plane to Savannah, Lainey."

"Can't."

"Yes, you can," Deena echoed. "Even if we have to knock you out cold and stow you in the baggage compartment." She shook her finger. "It's gotten way too dangerous."

"It's not like we've made any great discoveries, anyway," Kate added, her voice harsh. "I don't know what I would do if I lost you, Lainey." Her voice caught.

"There's nothing in Savannah to go back to," Lainey explained, wincing as she reached across the bed for her water glass.

"Let me do that." Kate held the glass while Lainey sipped. The other three sisters surrounded the bed.

Deena leaned in. "Did you take that job in Florida?"

Lainey shook her head. "My producer was in town today, and we agreed it would be difficult for me to continue working for him."

"You broke up with Dan?" Kate asked.

"You had a thing with your producer?" Deena's eyebrows hitched.

"The breakup was mutual," Lainey said, ignoring her older sister's question. "Somehow our relationship slipped from passionate to comfortable. We both deserve more than that."

"Tell me about it," Deena said. "I can't remember the last time Mike and I had spontaneous sex in the kitchen like the old days."

"Ew!" Kate scrunched her face. "Remind me never to eat at your house again." She turned back to Lainey. "Are you okay with this?"

Lainey managed a smile. "Yeah. I spent the day showing him around Vineyard then dropped him off around seven-thirty at the airport. I knew as soon as I pulled away from the curb, I was losing a good friend."

"Someone may have been spying on you and knew you weren't home all day," Maddy said. "Did you see any strange cars when you left?"

The sisters jumped when the door opened and Colt walked in, his hair in his face, black smudges on his cheeks. After greeting Lainey's sisters, he moved to her side. "The doctor said I could take you home now. Your MRIs were all negative."

"Shouldn't she stay with me, Colt?" Deena asked.

"No," he snapped. "Whoever did this probably already knows she wasn't hurt. They might try again, and this time, I'd have you and Mike to worry about as well as Lainey." He leaned over and pushed a stray lock of her hair behind her ear. "She's going with me," he repeated.

Oh my God! You slept with him! Tessa laughed out loud. ***You little slut puppy!***

Lainey met her dead sister's eyes, expecting to see the-pot-calling-the-kettle-black look. Instead, Tessa had the biggest smile Lainey had ever seen on her face.

The nurse re-entered the room, her expression indicating she was still ticked Kate had overruled her. This time she refused to leave until she cleared the room so she could get Lainey ready for discharge.

Despite Lainey's protests, the two older sisters agreed to meet at Colt's in the morning to help her get bathed and dressed. Since Kate was in the middle of a long shift, she promised to meet them for lunch the next day. Some time during this exchange, Tessa had disappeared.

When the paperwork was finally completed, Lainey allowed Colt to grab hold of her good arm and lead her out the emergency room door. As he helped her into the front seat of his cruiser, his hand lingered on her arm for a few seconds before he walked around the car and slid in. During the fifteen minute ride to the ranch, neither spoke.

Lainey used the silence to ponder the last twenty-four hours. The day with Dan had been bittersweet, but knowing the pressure was off helped, and she'd nearly changed her mind at one point. When she'd kissed him goodbye at DFW, his eyes told her he would miss her, although they'd agreed to stay friends. Both knew the likelihood of that happening wasn't good. There had been too much history.

Coming back to face an attempt on her life had been an eye-opener. Maybe Maddy was right about her getting out of Dodge, but where would she go? She was in no shape to ace a job interview, not with all the distractions she had going on. An alternative might be to check into a hotel until she figured out what she wanted to do with her life.

"We're here," Colt said, jolting her back to reality.

He helped her out of the car and into the house where he led her to the spare bedroom down the hall from the master.

"Want something to drink before you go to bed?" he asked. "A Coke or maybe a cup of coffee?"

She shook her head. "I'm wiped out. This pain pill is only making me more tired. I just want to cuddle under the covers and not think about anything."

He looked into her eyes. "Me too." He pulled back the covers. "Wait here."

He returned with one of his sweatshirts. "That's the best I can do until we can replace your clothes tomorrow."

She took it from him. "This will feel good, Colt. I can't seem to stop my teeth from chattering." She reached behind and tried to pull the sling over her head.

"Let me help."

She shivered as he made contact with the tiny hairs on the back of her neck.

"Keep your arm tight against your body," he instructed, throwing the sling on the bed.

For an instant their eyes met before he moved his hands to the top of her blouse and began to unbutton it. Her heart raced as she remembered the way he'd done that the night before.

When he slipped the blouse off her shoulders, his gaze dropped from her eyes to her shoulders to her breasts before he reached behind and unhooked her bra.

The smoldering flame she saw in his eyes startled her, but as quickly as it appeared, it was gone. Gently, he guided her injured arm into the sleeve of the sweatshirt. When he had it completely on, he pulled the sling over her head and adjusted her arm in it.

"Does that feel right?" His gaze was as soft as a caress.

"Colt," she started.

He leaned in and silenced her with his lips, brushing against hers softly at first, then more demanding. When he withdrew, leaving her mouth burning for more, he reached for her waistband and unzipped her slacks.

This time his eyes stayed on hers. "I imagined the worst when I saw you walk up the steps and heard the explosion."

A tear trickled down her cheek. "I know." She reached over and ran her thumb across his lips. "But nothing happened. I'm okay."

Without another word, he pushed her slacks down around her ankles and eased her onto the edge of the bed. Bending over, he untied her shoes and removed them, then pulled her slacks off before swinging her legs onto the bed.

"Get some sleep, Lainey. Tomorrow, we've got to figure out how to keep you safe."

He turned and walked out of the room, leaving her alone with an intense ache that had nothing to do with her shoulder.

You still love him, don't you?

Lainey opened her eyes to see Tessa standing over her bed.

"It would never work. He only sees me as your little sister."

Tessa laughed. *I guarantee that was no little sister kiss I just saw.*

"I would always be thinking about the two of you together," Lainey said with a sigh. "It would ruin it."

Tessa pulled back the covers and slid in beside Lainey. *Move over. I have something to tell you.*

TWENTY-THREE

*I never had sex **with Colt.***

"What?" Lainey turned sharply, paying the price when a searing pain shot up her arm to her neck. "You never slept with Colt?"

Who said anything about not sleeping with him?

"Quit playing games, Tessa. You can't blurt out something like that, then act coy."

We slept together, but we didn't have sex.

Lainey tossed that around in her head. "You're lying. How else could you have convinced Colt he was Gracie's father?"

Tessa blew out a loud breath. ***I'd been home from school about a month, and I hadn't told anyone I'd flunked out. Mom didn't even know. She thought I was exhausted from all the schoolwork and was just taking a long semester break.***

"Did Colt know?"

Not at first. I only told him I wasn't sure if I was going back. Tessa rose up on one elbow and glanced toward Lainey. ***Colt and I always had this great friendship. Hell, I'm the one who talked***

him into going out with Carrie in the first place. She paused. *Anyway, I was pissed off at David for some stupid reason I can't even remember, and Colt was not real happy about being stuck in Vineyard.*

"I've heard this story before," Lainey interrupted. "You both got drunk and ended up in bed."

That's right. We did. We thought it would be fun to drink our troubles away all night, so we emptied our pockets and came up with just enough for a bottle of cheap whiskey and one night at the Shady City.

Both of them jumped when Colt knocked lightly on the bedroom door. "Is everything okay in there?"

Lainey covered her mouth to stifle a giggle. He'd think she really did have a head injury from the explosion or she was just plain loony if she told him she was talking to a ghost. "I'm fine, Colt. I'll turn down the TV. Sorry to bother you."

She turned to Tessa and both of them cracked up.

When she was sure Colt was back in his room, her gaze settled on her sister, her eyebrows raised in question. "So, I'm confused. Did you sleep with him or not?"

Technically, I did. We started drinking then decided to play Strip Poker. Remember how good I was at that? When Lainey nodded, she continued. *I had him down to his skivvies in no time. Of course, he was so far gone by then, he fell asleep. That's when I hatched the plan.*

"What plan?"

I got naked and climbed in beside him. The next morning he was mortified when he thought we'd done the horizontal boogie. He kept saying David would kill him.

"Then you told him you were pregnant several weeks later," Lainey said, shaking her head as she finished the story for her sister.

I'd already fessed up to Mom about school. I couldn't bear to see the disappointment in her face again if I told her I'd gotten pregnant by a guy I only knew as Bubba. Since I hadn't seen David since the semester started in September, I knew I couldn't pass him off as the father.

Lainey leaned back into the pillow. "Even for you, this is a new low, Tessa. Do you realize how your lie changed Colt's life?" She didn't wait for her sister to answer. "He went from dreaming about being a vet to giving up college altogether to be a husband and father. You already knew how he felt about staying in Vineyard." She shook her head in disgust. "How could you do that to him?"

He's not the victim you make him out to be, Lainey. He loves his job as sheriff, and he idolizes Gracie.

"That's just great. You screw up his life, then justify it because he's got Gracie. Well, guess what, Tessa? That's not good enough. You have to tell him."

I can't do that. He's the only person in this world who ever saw the good in me.

"That's exactly my point. You owe him the truth now." Lainey paused, thinking about Colt asleep in the next bedroom and the precious little girl whose life revolved around him.

No, Tessa shouted. *I don't want anyone to know.*

"Then you shouldn't have told me," Lainey responded. "I would never be able to live with myself if I allowed him to go on believing there's a chance he's really Gracie's father."

266

Tessa laughed again. ***Good luck convincing him I told you about that night, Lainey. He'll think you've been smoking some of that wacky tobaccy.***

Lainey twisted to face her sister, but Tessa had already disappeared like she always did when the going got tough.

For a long time afterward, Lainey lay awake, rehashing her sister's story. Tessa was right about one thing. Nobody would believe her except her other siblings, and they might already know the story.

She had to find a way to fix this before she left Vineyard. She owed it to Colt.

"Are they all here?"

Danny nodded. "Even yours, like you instructed."

Colt stared at the phone records of his employees. It would take most of the day to get through them by himself, but he couldn't risk any of his men getting wind of what was going on. If there really was a bad cop out there—and he prayed to God he was wrong—he didn't want to tip him off, not just yet.

"Go back to your desk and act normal, Danny. I'll call you if I find anything."

As soon as he was alone, Colt picked up the first record and scanned it. Other than calls to and from the station, Jeff Flanagan only used his cell phone to call his kids and occasionally, his mother. Like Colt, Jeff had been divorced several years, but unlike him, his wife had custody of his kids. Jeff only got them every other weekend.

Thank God he had Gracie.

At the thought of his daughter, a cold knot formed in Colt's stomach. Ever since Tessa had implied he wasn't her father, he'd been terrified someone would find out. Sooner or later, he'd have to deal with that, but for now, he pushed it to the back of his mind.

No matter what it took, he wouldn't let anyone separate him and Gracie. Tessa's death had been hard enough on the child. She couldn't lose her father, too.

Colt grinned, remembering the way Gracie had become attached to Lainey after the first day they'd spent together. She'd bolted right past him this morning after his mother dropped her off and headed straight for Lainey when she'd noticed the sling.

So much for him being the most important thing in his daughter's life!

Thinking of Lainey brought another smile to his face. He'd all but guilted her into wearing the damn sling the first day after the explosion. He finally dropped the argument this morning, knowing she'd do what she wanted anyway, like always. As scary as the explosion had been, at least now she might leave the police work to him. But nearly getting killed was no guarantee, given the woman's stubborn streak. It drove him up a wall.

As suspected, the fire was the result of a massive gas leak. Unfortunately, the fire marshal couldn't say if it was deliberate or not. Colt didn't need anyone to answer that. Dogs don't lock themselves in the barn.

The dark spot on the door latch turned out to be dried blood. He'd meant to replace it several months ago because the edge had snapped in two. For once his procrastination might pay off if the DNA from the sample the CSI guys were able to lift pointed to the killer.

There was always the possibility Ted McDougal had scratched himself when he tended to Colt's horses, or quite possibly the blood belonged to Gracie. Hoping whoever had sabotaged the guest house had left a little DNA on the latch was a long shot, but so far, he didn't have much else.

He picked up the next record on the stack, glancing out at the squad room as Landers looked up. Colt shook his head. If he found the prepaid phone number on any of the records, the plan was for Danny to run out to Shakerville with a picture to see if the owner could make a positive ID.

But an hour later, just when he'd started thinking the clerk had been mistaken about a Vineyard police officer buying the phone, he found it. The muscles in his neck which had finally started to relax tensed up again as he stared at the number on the record in his hand.

Eight different entries, all made after midnight over a period of two weeks.

His stomach churned, the contents threatening to come back up as he stared at possible proof of a bad cop in his own house. He reread the report, hoping he'd made a mistake, hoping it was as simple as the number being off a digit.

But it wasn't.

Although Colt racked his brain to come up with a logical reason why one of his guys would be communicating with a possible killer on eight separate occasions, he came up short of any explanation.

A wave of apprehension swept through him as he walked to the cabinet and pulled a file. Staring at the picture of the man who'd been on the force longer than he had, he wondered what made a good cop go bad. Their lives were all about protecting. What could have happened for a man to turn rogue?

Even as the question formed in his brain, Colt already knew the answer.

The God Almighty dollar!

With a heavy heart, he dialed Danny's cell phone. "Come to the office."

When Danny walked in, his eyes were nearly as sorrowful as Colt felt. "Who is it?"

"Romano," Colt said, his voice resigned as he shoved the file across his desk.

"Ohmygod! I had dinner with him and his family last weekend. Played basketball with him and his kid."

Colt didn't want to hear any of that. They had a job to do, friend or no friend. "Run a copy of his picture and head out to Shaker-ville."

Danny picked up the file. "I know it can't be him, boss. There must be some other explanation."

"The sooner you get there, the faster we'll know for sure," Colt said. "And run silent. We want as little attention as possible on this."

For several minutes after Danny left, Colt scanned the remaining phone records to make sure he didn't have a bigger problem than one cop on the take. Other than finding out Tom Rogers probably had a girlfriend on the side, there was nothing. He glanced out the window to the squad room, wondering what other secrets he didn't know about his men.

His eyes settled on Phil Romano's empty desk. Earlier when Colt passed him on the way to the coffee pot, Phil mentioned he was working a drunk and disorderly from the night before. When Colt thought he looked a little peaked and asked if he felt all right, Phil said he hadn't slept well. Something about greasy food from Ruby's. Maybe he'd taken his suggestion and gone home to catch up since things were slow at the station.

Colt continued to stare out the window, hoping Phil had a believable explanation, that the man he considered a good friend hadn't sunk so low he'd resorted to collusion or worse, accessory to murder. But his instincts told him that was not the way this would turn out. He remembered Phil complaining just the other night about how much it cost keeping three kids in clothes. How he never had enough money for anything lately and never got to see his kids because he worked so many extra hours.

The signs were all there, but Colt was not ready to jump to that conclusion. He owed his friend the benefit of the doubt.

The door to his office flew open, interrupting his thoughts as it banged against the wall. Maddy burst into the room, visibly upset, tears in her eyes.

"Roxy Moretti just called. Jerry's dead."

———

Lieutenant Phil Romano sensed something was wrong the minute he walked past Danny Landers. The kid had scooped up the papers scattered across his desk and quickly pushed them under a stack of files. Despite his best efforts to get a look at what was so important, he wasn't able to. He was contemplating how he could get Danny away from his desk when the younger cop's cell phone rang. After only a minute or two, Danny gathered up the papers and headed to Colt's office.

Is it possible they're on to me?

His stomach felt like it was on fire, and he popped two antacids into his mouth.

No way could they have traced that phone back to him that quickly. When the man had called wanting an untraceable phone in a hurry, he'd made it a point to drive to the far side of Shakerville to find one. Even found an ID to use that seemed untraceable. When they'd discovered the number on Thornton's phone, he still hadn't panicked, since only the neighboring cities had been included in the search area.

Get a grip, man. The paranoia's freaking you out.

How could they have discovered the convenience store over fifty miles away? Even if they did, there was no way the clerk could identify him. He'd worn his hoodie and his sunglasses and kept his face away from the security camera.

But his cop instincts were telling him otherwise, and he popped two more antacids into his mouth and quickly chewed them. He knew the sausage and gravy biscuits from yesterday would come back to haunt him. He'd been miserable half the night, and now the indigestion was back with a vengeance.

He watched anxiously through the slats in the blinds of Colt's office, trying not to make it too obvious. When Danny emerged about fifteen minutes later carrying a folder, the fire in Phil's stomach flamed again, burning all the way up his chest as he sucked in his breath.

Since Colt only kept employee files in his office, it didn't take a rocket scientist to figure out they were getting too close for comfort. He had to find out exactly how close they were.

Watching Danny shut the door to the copy room set off more warning bells in Phil's head and more heat in his gut, especially when the kid walked past his desk without making eye contact.

Danny was like a younger brother to him and always joked around. Plus nobody ever made their own copies. That's what Maddy was for.

Something was definitely up.

Romano breathed deeply, wondering what his next move should be. He hadn't given much thought to "what if," confident he'd covered all the bases. He hadn't counted on that weasel Thornton getting himself killed.

He glanced up as Danny returned to his desk and fished in the drawer for his car keys before exiting the station with a large envelope in his hand. Phil waited several minutes, then grabbed his own keys and followed Danny out. Before he jumped to any conclusions, he had to find out where the kid was headed.

Halfway to Shakerville, Phil's heart began to pound. He was definitely busted.

Keeping a safe distance behind Danny's cruiser, his breathing picked up a notch. By the time they were in the city limits of the small Texas suburb, a band of sweat had broken out across his forehead.

When Danny pulled into the convenience store and walked in with the envelope, Phil was perspiring so heavily he switched to air conditioning despite the temperature being in the low sixties.

Parking his own cruiser far enough away so Danny wouldn't spot him, he debated whether to risk calling the number again. He decided it didn't make much difference. If Danny was here in Shakerville flashing his picture around, the likely scenario was they'd already discovered the other calls.

With shaking fingers he dialed the number.

"What now?" the gruff voice asked.

"They're on to me."

There was silence on the other end.

"Did you hear me?"

The man cleared his throat. "You sure?"

"I'm sitting outside the place where I bought your phone. If my guess is right, one of my coworkers is in there right now trying to get a positive ID from the clerk."

"Shit! How could you be so stupid?"

Romano's anger flared. "You didn't give me time to come up with much of a plan," he shouted before he took a calming breath. "I thought there was no way they'd look in Shakerville."

"Christ, Romano, I'm paying you because you're supposed to be a veteran cop. Even a rookie has better sense than that. You should have driven to Fort Worth when I asked you to pick me up a phone." Another pregnant pause. "Can they trace it to me?"

"No, it's registered to a dead guy out of state."

"At least you were smart enough to do that. So, what now?"

"I need to disappear. I'll call in with some excuse about my mother in Oklahoma. Winslow knows she's been under the weather. That will give me some time to figure out how I can explain the phone."

"It's your word against theirs."

"That's true, but I still think I should get out of town for a while," Romano said. "To date, I haven't seen a penny of my cut. I can't wait any longer for it."

"You'll get it when the deal is made, and I get mine. Don't go running scared on me. Not when we're so close to the big payoff."

The sweat was pouring down Phil's cheeks now. He jacked up the cool air and positioned the blowers directly onto his face. "I can't promise how long I'll last if Winslow interrogates me. He knows me too well. That's why I need to leave now."

Romano knew he was playing with fire. By all accounts, the man on the other end had killed Thornton. The Waco man had probably put pressure on him exactly the way Phil was doing now.

But he wasn't afraid. He knew how to watch his own back. No matter what happened, he needed cash now. His wife had already left him once, taking the kids to her sister's after one of their many screaming sessions over money. He hadn't meant to hit her, but when she accused him of not being a man because he couldn't support his own family, he'd lost it.

What did the woman want from him? He was already working two jobs. He'd even stopped taking the expensive blood pressure pills the doctor had given him when the samples ran out. How much more could he do? She needed to quit buying shit on the Internet.

"Meet me at that old abandoned warehouse out by Vineyard Medical Center," the man instructed. "Stay calm and we'll figure this out."

"Only if you bring my money."

"I can't get that much together right now, but I'll give you what I can. The rest will be waiting when you get back into town."

Romano hung up just as Landers pulled away from the convenience store. He rolled down the car window and stuck his head out. When the cold air hit him he breathed deeply, unbuttoning the top two buttons of his uniform. Thinking he might be coming down with something, he popped a couple more antacids before easing into traffic several cars behind Danny.

It probably didn't matter if Danny saw him or not.

His entire body jerked when his cell phone rang. He pulled it out of his pocket and laid it on the passenger seat. He already knew why Colt was calling. He was in way over his head.

He touched his revolver still in the holster, hoping he didn't have to use it, but willing to do that if it become necessary. When he came to the outskirts of Vineyard, he turned off and headed toward the south end of town and the empty warehouse.

Suddenly, his chest felt like a brick building had fallen on him, and he twisted the front of his shirt in his fist. The police cruiser veered off the double lane highway and plunged into a culvert, sending his cell phone crashing to the floor out of reach. The last thought in Phil Romano's mind before his world went black was how badly he'd fucked up his life.

———

Colt arrived at the Moretti house just as Flanagan and Rogers drove up and parked beside him. All three rushed into the lavish house that once belonged to Jerry's grandfather. A quick glance toward the living room showed nothing out of the ordinary except someone had eaten popcorn, probably watching TV.

"Back here," Roxy's high-pitched scream summoned them. "Hurry."

When they walked into the master suite, Roxy Moretti was crouched in the corner, her eyes wide with terror. She pointed to the bed.

As Colt approached, he saw Jerry Moretti on his back, his mouth open, his eyes staring grotesquely. He slipped on the gloves he kept in his pocket and felt Jerry's neck for a pulse he knew he wouldn't find. The body was already cold, although for a moment, Colt wondered if he'd missed the pulse. Jerry's skin wasn't the bluish color of a dead man.

"What happened?"

"I don't know," Roxy said, her voice without emotion. "I woke up this morning, and he was dead."

Colt glanced at the nightstand and reached for the prescription bottle. "Did he take one of these last night?"

"I think so," she mumbled.

"You think so?" Colt arched his eyebrows. "Seems like your husband taking his little blue pill would be something you were aware of."

Roxy stood and walked to the side of the bed, keeping her eyes on Colt. "He got home late last night. He may have taken one then."

"Where had he been?"

Roxy shook her head. "I don't know that, either. He said he had a business meeting. Left around nine. When he got home, I could tell he'd had a lot to drink." She turned and walked to the chair on the other side of the room and sat down. "Liquor always makes him horny. Unfortunately, it also makes him—not always ready, you know?"

The last thing Colt wanted to discuss was Jerry's inability to get it up. "So, he took a pill. Then what?"

"I pretended to be asleep. I can't stand him crawling all over me with his beer breath."

Colt couldn't stop from thinking her past profession should have prepared her for anything, but he kept that thought to himself. "Did you have sex?"

Again, Roxy shook her head. "Usually, it takes about forty minutes for Jerry to get a hard—to get ready," she said. "I had a busy day yesterday and came home exhausted. I must have fallen asleep. When I woke up this morning, I knew something was wrong. Jerry never misses an opportunity." She lowered her eyes but there were no tears. "He looks so gross."

Colt focused on Moretti, spotting a large bruise on his right forearm. Bending down for a better look, he noticed the faint but distinct odor of almonds radiating from the body. He straightened and made eye contact with Roxy. He could have sworn her lips tipped in a smile. Before he could pursue that further, Mark Lowell and the CSI team filed into the bedroom.

"We really do have to stop meeting like this, Winslow," Mark Lowell said as he donned his gloves and opened the three-way bag carrying his equipment. A minute later, he glanced at Colt. "You thinking the same thing I am?"

Colt nodded, then turned and strode out of the room to the living area where Flanagan and Rogers were already checking things out. "Call Maddy and have her get a search warrant," he ordered Flanagan. "Then you and Rogers tear this house apart again."

"What are we looking for, boss?"

"Cyanide."

TWENTY-FOUR

COLT TRIED ROMANO'S NUMBER again. Since Danny had called with news that the convenience store owner had positively identified Phil as the one who'd purchased the prepaid phone, he'd tried to reach him several times with no answer.

The intercom buzzed.

"Lab needs to talk to you, Colt. Said you've been waiting on them."

"Thanks, Maddy." He picked up the phone and clicked the blinking light. "Winslow."

"You were right about blood on the latch from your horse stable, Sheriff. We had enough to run a DNA."

Colt's breathing quickened as he anticipated hearing who had blown up his guest house. "Were you able to get a hit when you ran it through the data base?"

"Unfortunately, no match. The only thing I can tell you is that it's female DNA."

"Shit!" That probably meant Gracie had scratched herself opening the door.

Another dead end.

"Thanks, Pete. Let me know if you get anything from the other samples."

Colt stared at the phone a full minute after he disconnected. This presented the perfect opportunity to get a cheek sample from Gracie without anyone wondering why. He could say he wanted to verify the dried blood was hers.

He twisted his head from side to side to massage the knot on the back of his neck that had popped up when he got back from Moretti's. The niggling thought wouldn't go away that, with Gracie's DNA in hand, he could run over to Fort Worth and run his own sample to compare with hers. Whether he was her biological father or not would no longer be driving him crazy.

He chased that thought from his head. He didn't need some damn blood test to prove he was her father. He'd been the one who had sat up all night with her when she was so sick with the flu she could barely stand to throw up. He'd attended all her school activities, all her soccer games just like the other parents. He'd even started researching to prepare for her sex questions, which he knew were right around the corner.

Gracie was his, pure and simple.

Maddy's voice on the intercom jarred him from his thoughts. "Jeff Flanagan needs to talk to you."

Colt picked up the phone. "Find anything?"

"Oh, yeah!" The cop chuckled. "Lowell said he was pretty sure the pills were laced with cyanide. Something about a faded color and an almond smell. He won't know for sure for a few more days, but we found a small bottle of the poison."

Colt sat upright in his chair. "Where?"

"Tucked behind some cans in the pantry. Unfortunately, CSI couldn't lift any prints. The bottle was clean."

"Did you confront Roxy with it?"

"She denied ever seeing it before. We Mirandized her, and we're on our way in now."

"You and Tom did a great job, Jeff. I'll see you when you get here."

"There's something else, Colt."

"What's that?"

"We found a key to a hidden safe in the bedroom."

"Tell me you found the prepaid phone with Moretti's prints all over it."

"No, but there was a sealed copy of his will and a bunch of financial papers."

"What's so unusual about that?"

"Apparently, Moretti never bothered to change his will when he married Roxy." Flanagan cleared his throat. "He left everything to your ex-wife."

———

David Rivera drove down Teasdale toward Shakerville Medical Center, unsure what his next move should be. About two miles before the turnoff, he saw flashing lights ahead and slowed. As he approached, he could make out two ambulances and a fire truck on the side of the road. When he got close enough, he saw a Vineyard police cruiser wedged between the culvert and the cement barrier.

He rolled down the window. "Somebody get hurt?"

The fireman directing traffic walked over to the car, apparently noticing the city emblem on the side. "A police officer went off the road and hit the culvert. He took a pretty good hit to his head, but we think he may have had a heart attack before he went off the road. They're working on him now."

"Do you know the officer's identity?" David held his breath as he flashed his city hall ID.

The young man handed it back to him. "Lieutenant Phillip Romano, according to his driver's license."

David reacted quickly to keep the smile off his face. "Is he dead?"

"Not yet, but it doesn't look good. The paramedics are giving him CPR now."

Rivera lifted his foot off the brake and glided forward. "I'll say a prayer for the guy," he said. "Y'all are doing a great job out here."

He drove about a mile down the road before making a U-turn and heading back to town. When he passed the accident scene again, two paramedics were lifting the stretcher into the ambulance.

Although he couldn't see Romano's face clearly, it was obvious the sheet was not pulled over his head.

Damn it!

He watched for a few seconds as the EMTs continued working on the cop. Unfortunately, the hospital was only two minutes away. He could only hope the fat prick kicked the bucket before he made it there.

Rivera reached into his jacket pocket, removed the gun, and placed it back into the glove compartment.

He wouldn't need it after all.

Colt stood outside the emergency room cradling Denise Romano in his arms. The doctor had just recited the usual rhetoric—the old "despite their best efforts to revive him, Phil hadn't made it." Probable cause of death was either a heart attack or a stroke, but the doctor wasn't ready to declare either one without an autopsy.

Denise trembled in Colt's arm at the mention of a post mortem, and he pulled her closer to his chest.

"I kept warning Phil he needed to start taking better care of his body, especially after the doctor told him his blood pressure was dangerously high."

Colt stiffened. This was the first he'd heard about Phil having a medical problem. He couldn't help wondering if the added stress of the other things he was just now learning about his long-time friend hadn't somehow contributed to his death as well.

Colt wasn't ready to say for sure that Phil had been involved in the murders despite the eyewitness identification. There could be a perfectly plausible reason why Romano would purchase a prepaid phone, if he was the one who actually bought it. Eyewitnesses were known to finger the wrong guy.

"Sheriff?"

Colt glanced up at one of the paramedics who'd worked so hard to keep Phil alive.

"Can I talk to you in private?"

Colt loosened his grip on Denise and brushed away a tear sliding down her cheek. "Do you want me to get someone to drive you home? We can swing by the house with the car later."

She shook her head. "I need to pick the kids up from school. They…" The tears rushed down her face. "I don't know how I'm going to tell them their father is never coming home."

Colt brushed her forehead with his lips. "Why don't you let me speak to this gentleman for a minute, then I'll send Maddy with you? She's good with kids."

After Denise nodded, Colt turned and walked to the other end of the long hallway, away from the noise and constant flurry of activity. When he stopped by the large window overlooking the small pond in front of the hospital, he faced the paramedic. "What'd you want to talk to me about?"

"I'm not sure if this means anything or not, but when we arrived on the scene, Lieutenant Romano was still alive." He stopped to glance up the hall as if to make sure the widow couldn't hear.

"I know you guys did everything you could to save him," Colt said.

"He kept muttering something. His eyes were almost in a panic as he repeated it over and over."

Colt inhaled sharply. "Were you able to figure out what he was trying to tell you?"

The young EMT shook his head. "It didn't make sense to us. It sounded like he was saying 'river'. At one point he grabbed my shirt sleeve and pulled me closer. Then he convulsed and went into cardiac arrest. He never regained consciousness."

River? What the hell did that mean? Vineyard didn't even have a creek, let alone a river.

"I appreciate you hanging around to tell me this," Colt said. "Maybe after I think about it for a while, I can make sense of it."

"Or maybe he was already delirious from the bump on his head from when his car hit the concrete embankment."

Colt nodded. "That's a possibility." He patted the young man on the back. "Thanks again." Then he walked back to Denise Romano to make sure she didn't need anything else before he headed back to the station.

After he called and worked it out so Maddy could be with Denise when she told her kids, Colt thought back on Phil's last words.

Was the dead man trying to tell them something, or was it simply the head injury talking?

———

"They've arrested Roxy Moretti," Maddy said as soon as Lainey answered.

"Do they think she's the one who blew up the guest house?"

"I don't know about that, but she killed Jerry."

"What?"

"So far, they don't really have any evidence except a bottle of cyanide they found at her house," Maddy said. "She swears she's never seen it before."

"Do they think she killed Tessa, too?"

"That will be hard to prove. There are no prints on anything."

"What does Colt say?"

"I'm not sure. There's so much going on down here right now it's hard to know what he's thinking." Maddy paused. "Do you remember Phil Romano? He was a couple years older than me, married Josie Caruso's younger sister."

"Kinda, why?"

"He works here, next in line under Colt. Anyway, he had a heart attack and wrecked his car."

"Dear Lord, what else can happen? Is he okay?"

Maddy's voice softened. "He died about a half hour ago. Colt's there now with Phil's widow. I'm on my way over there to be with her when she tells her kids." She sighed. "Phil was a good man."

"I'll talk to you later."

"Sounds good, Lainey. I gotta run. Someone's hollering for me."

Lainey disconnected but held the phone in her hand, trying to get used to the idea that Roxy Moretti had killed her sister. Was it the money or was she afraid Jerry was still in love with Tessa? Neither would surprise her.

She turned on the TV and tried to get interested in Dr. Phil ripping apart some guy who was a habitual cheater. The guy was a jerk, smiling like he thought he was a rock star. She flipped it off and walked into the kitchen for a snack, even though she wasn't the least bit hungry. After staring at the inside of the refrigerator, she slammed the door shut and grabbed her purse and car keys.

The rental company had towed the old car after the explosion and delivered a brand new one this morning. Lainey climbed into the driver's side and tugged at her sling until it was over her head. She threw it into the passenger seat and switched on the ignition. At the gate, she turned down the road that would take her into town.

———

Roxy stumbled as the two cops led her into the police station.

"Come on, Jeff. Are these really necessary?" A woman she recognized as one of Tessa's sisters leaped from her chair to grab Roxy's shoulders and keep her from falling.

Roxy attempted a smile as the bigger of the two cops, the one the other lady had called Jeff, removed the handcuffs. She wiggled her fingers trying to get feeling back into them, skeptical that one of the Garcia women would act like anything other than a bitch. She hadn't met the doctor and the other sister, but if Lainey and Tessa were any indication, those two would be high and mighty, also.

Since the first time Jerry had introduced Roxy to Tessa, the woman had acted like she needed a gas mask to stay in the same room, like she was some kind of lowlife.

What was the difference between having sex in front of the camera and screwing around with everything that walked?

She would never understand what Jerry had seen in that whore.

"Sit down, Mrs. Moretti," the shorter cop instructed. "Colt's on his way from the hospital now."

"Is Jerry there?"

He glanced up at his partner. "He went straight to the morgue."

She waited for him to explain further, but he apparently wasn't about to enlighten her.

"I need to call a lawyer."

"Nobody's asked you any questions yet."

"I still want my call."

"Tom, let her use your cell phone," Jeff said. "I'm waiting on a call back."

Roxy dialed the number she thought she would never have to use again. She cringed as soon as she heard her former producer's voice. When she married Jerry, she thought she'd never have to deal with the filthy leach again.

"Monty, this is Roxy Moretti. Roxy Delight," she corrected, wishing she could wipe the smirk off the short cop's face. "Do you still have that friend in Dallas who does all your legal work?"

"Yep. What kind of trouble have you gone and gotten into now, sweet cheeks?"

Roxy hesitated, not really wanting to give any details, then deciding she had no choice. "They think I killed my husband."

Monty laughed, infuriating her. "So now, after all these months when you wouldn't return my calls, I'm supposed to jump in and rescue you?" He paused. "How about I do that and in return, you take a look at this new script that just came across my desk this week. Your fans are still clamoring for more Roxy."

Damn him! He could make you feel dirty right out of the shower.

"I know you'll love it. It's got a great plot."

Great plot, my ass! There was never any plot—girl meets boy, girl fucks boy, girl fucks another girl, both girls go down on boy.

She truly believed she'd never have to stoop that low again.

"I'm waiting, doll face. You say the word, and I'm on the phone to my guy. I don't care if you did off your old man, he'll have you back in your own bed for a before-dinner nap."

Roxy bit her lower lip. God, she did not want to do this, especially now that the entire vineyard and winery was about to be hers—at least half of it.

She smiled to herself. Getting Lainey's half wouldn't be too hard. She already had a plan in motion.

"Okay," she agreed, thinking she could back out after this mess was behind her. "I'm at the Vineyard Police Station. Tell him to hurry."

She handed the phone back to Rogers. "I've got a lawyer on the way," she said just as Colt Winslow walked into the room.

Now there's a man I wouldn't kick out of bed.

"Too bad about the lawyer, Roxy. All I wanted to do was have a little talk about Jerry. I realize you don't even have a motive since he left his half of Spirits of Texas to Tessa and her heirs," Colt said.

Roxy shot straight out of the chair, and all three cops reached for her. She shrugged off the tall cop's hand on her shoulder, but eased back down in the chair. "You're lying."

Colt smiled as he shook his head and threw a legal document in front of her. "See for yourself. Seems you'll be lucky to get the house and the cars."

"God damn that prick!"

She didn't realize she was squeezing her fists so tightly until the pain from her fingernails digging into her palms shot up both arms. "He promised I'd get the vineyard," she said, unclenching her hands.

"Apparently, he lied," Colt sat down opposite her and leaned across the table. "Did you kill your husband, Roxy?"

"How stupid do you think I am, Sheriff? Even if I did, would I really make it this easy for you?"

"Things would go a lot smoother if you did," he said. "The DA is always looking to cut a deal and save the taxpayers some money."

"You can kiss my ass," she said, glaring at him.

"I've seen a lot of guys do that already," the taller cop said, his smile irritating the hell out of her.

Colt shot him a look, and the smile disappeared.

"We're waiting on a call from the lab right now. My guess is, we're gonna find out Jerry's little blue pills were covered with cyanide. Not too many people had access to those."

"Why would I kill him in my own bed?" She tsked. "Really, Colt, you don't give me nearly enough credit."

"Should I?"

"Jerry had his prescription refilled the other day. Maybe you should be checking out the people at the pharmacy."

"Why would anyone at the pharmacy want him dead?" Rogers asked, bending over the table toward her, close enough she could tell he'd had tuna for lunch.

"Oh, I don't know. Maybe because he was a jerk to everyone in this town."

Colt stood as his cell phone rang, turning his back as he talked. When he faced her again, he smiled. "That was your lawyer. He's driving up from Dallas. Doesn't want us talking to you until he gets here. I guess we'll have to wait to finish this conversation."

She couldn't keep from smiling. Watching the disappointment on their faces, especially the one who'd make the catty remark earlier, was worth the price she'd have to pay. Even the god-awful blow jobs Monty would squeeze out of her before it was all over couldn't compare.

She folded her arms across her chest and leaned back in the chair, sliding two fingers over her lips to imitate a zipper. All three cops glared before they made their exit.

When she was alone, her smile faded as she thought about what Colt had said. How could that SOB leave everything to his bitch of an ex-wife?

Roxy had known all along Jerry was still in love with Tessa, even suspected he might be doing her on the side.

But to leave the whole damn fortune to her?

Burn in hell, you slimy bastard. You got just what you deserved.

TWENTY-FIVE

LAINEY LEFT VINEYARD MALL with several bags draped over her good arm. She still needed a few personal items, but a trip to Target would fix that.

She glanced at her watch. Target would have to wait another day. It was after six, and she was exhausted. Since she couldn't use her left arm, she'd already made several trips to and from the car with the stuff she bought to replace everything lost in the explosion.

Thinking about her narrow escape, Lainey remembered her promise to her sisters at lunch today. With the news of Jerry Moretti's death and Roxy's arrest, Tessa's killer, or killers if it turned out the two of them had been in cahoots, was no longer a threat to her. Maybe now Tessa could get the peace she deserved.

A gush of sadness washed over her as she thought about the wasted years between her and Tessa. Hearing her sister's story had cleared up a lot of questions. All this time, she'd believed Tessa had seduced Colt to spite her, only to discover she'd been wrong.

Her older sister had been a humiliated, frightened young girl who thought sex was the only way she would be noticed. When she found herself with no way out, she turned to the only person she trusted—Colt.

Hell yes, what she did to him was absolutely unconscionable, but as Tessa had argued, his life hadn't exactly been horrible because of it. He loved being a cop and lived for his baby girl.

That was another thing on Lainey's mind. Should she tell Colt what Tessa had confided the other night, or should she keep it close to the vest? And could she live with herself if she did?

She was still agonizing over what to do when her cell phone rang just as she turned onto the road to Colt's house.

"Hey, Henry, what's up?" She knew why her agent was calling. She'd been avoiding him all week after missing the interview in Florida a second time.

"What's the story, Lainey? I got a call from the station manager in Tampa a few minutes ago. They can't hold that job forever."

She pursed her lips. She'd given this a lot of thought since Dan went back to Savannah. For the first time in her life, she wanted something for herself, not something everyone else wanted for her.

"I've decided to stay in Dallas." She held her breath waiting for his disapproval.

"You're kidding, right?"

"No," she answered quickly. "I've been away from my family for too long."

She heard papers shuffling on the other end before her agent got back on the phone. "Somewhere on this desk is a memo I got this week with available anchor slots around the country. There may be an opening in Dallas."

"I don't want to anchor."

"Why the hell not? That's always been your dream."

She heard the catch in his voice. He'd been her agent since she graduated from college. "Sometimes dreams change," she said, hoping he didn't pick up on the uncertainty in hers. "I've decided to get involved with the winery, at least part time. My sister loved this place. I want to find out why."

"You love being in front of a camera. You can't just walk away because of someone else's dream. You'd be bored in no time."

Perhaps Henry was right, but she had to give it a try. She owed it to Tessa for trusting her, to Gracie who had already lost so much when her mother died. "You're probably right, but it's something I have to find out for myself."

"I can't change your mind?"

She smiled, knowing she was making the right decision. Having her sisters ten minutes away whenever she needed them was worth more than any high-profile job in a city where she didn't know a soul. "Sorry, Henry. I appreciate everything you've done, every extra dollar you've squeezed out of KSAV for me, but it's time to go in another direction."

"Hold on now. Don't go thinking about breaking our contract. What about if I put out some feelers to see if any of the morning shows in Dallas are in the market for a host? Maybe even a co-host?"

She hadn't thought about that possibility. She could spend a few hours every morning in Dallas, then come back to Vineyard and take care of the winery in the afternoons.

"Can I take your silence as a yes? A maybe?"

She laughed. "You can talk an Eskimo into buying air conditioning." She paused, trying to decide. "I think I might like that. Go ahead and check it out."

"Fantastic! I'll get back with you after I investigate the market."

After she hung up, Lainey had the unmistakable feeling she was finally coming home. Now that she'd reached a decision, there was so much to do, so much to learn. The first thing she needed to do was figure out how she would run the winery with Jerry dead and Roxy in jail. She hoped Carrie would stay on. With her wealth of knowledge of the winemaking business, she'd be invaluable.

Lainey made a quick U-turn and headed back the other way. It was already dark, but she wanted to swing by Spirits of Texas and see if she could take home the books to get a feel for the financial end of it. It would be like homework and fill up the days until she found a permanent place to live.

She couldn't stay at Colt's much longer, not if she truly wanted to move on. Being so close to him, knowing he could never love her the way she wanted was way too hard. It was time to make a clean break.

As she pulled into the parking lot at the winery office, she noticed both Jerry's and Carrie's cars still there. They'd probably have to have his car towed to his house.

She called Colt's cell phone and left a message that she was staying in town a few more hours at the office. Now that she was living in his house, she didn't want him to worry if she got home late.

She exited the car gingerly, careful not to bump her left arm which still hurt like hell when she moved it the wrong way. Opening the door, she heard Carrie and Roxy in Jerry's office screaming at each other.

What the hell is Roxy doing out of jail?

Both women turned when she entered his office. It was only then that Lainey noticed the biggest gun she'd ever seen in Roxy's hand pointed directly at Carrie.

———

The investigation was driving Colt nuts. Every time he thought he was on to something, someone died. He was losing prime suspects left and right. Maybe it was time to call in the Feds, but then he'd have to reveal Phil Romano's involvement. He wasn't ready to do that yet.

First off, they had no real proof Phil was involved, and it made no sense to hold up his death benefits while they investigated. Denise and the kids had enough on their plate already without a delay in the insurance money. If they discovered definitive evidence proving Romano was dirty, then he'd call IAB.

The loud growl in his stomach reminded Colt he'd skipped lunch. After finishing the paperwork from Romano's death, he'd gotten so absorbed in searching for a link to connect the murders, he'd forgotten to eat, and it was already after six.

He'd dropped Gracie off at the skating rink for a birthday party. He had no doubt she'd pig out on pizza and cake and wouldn't be hungry when she got home. Thinking ahead, he decided he'd pick up a couple of steaks to grill for him and Lainey. Maybe he'd add a loaded baked potato and a couple ears of sweet corn.

He smiled, knowing Lainey would complain the whole time about all the calories while devouring every bite. She was the only woman he knew who could eat like a lumberjack and still look amazing in tight-fitting jeans.

He'd noticed how his pulse quickened when he thought about her, which seemed to be constantly since they'd spent the night together. When he'd undressed her the night of the explosion, it had taken every bit of his self-control to keep from ravaging her again.

If he didn't stop thinking about that, he wouldn't be able to walk out the door without embarrassing himself.

Lainey was off limits for several reasons—the most important being she was probably involved with another man. He still hadn't asked about Dan, knowing he wouldn't like the answer.

Throw in the fact she was Gracie's aunt, and all kinds of warning bells went off.

Still, when he'd held her in his arms, it had felt right.

He squirmed in the chair as his lower anatomy responded to his musings, and he smiled to himself. Maybe he should bring home some dessert, too. That way, they'd both be so full, sex would be the last thing on their minds.

Did he just think about another go-round with Lainey?

Jeez, Winslow. What the hell's the matter with you?

The dessert idea was probably the way to go, he thought as he pulled out his phone to call and make sure she hadn't already eaten. Noticing a voice message, he wondered why he hadn't heard it ring, then remembered he'd been on the phone with Mark Lowell about the lab results and had ignored the incoming call. He'd used Mark as his sounding board on most of his cases, but this time, the CSI boss was as clueless as he was.

He dialed voice mail and smiled as he heard Lainey's voice. When she said she was at the office and reminded him not to wait up for her, the smile vanished.

So much for steak and baked potatoes.

———

"Don't come any closer," Roxy said, waving the gun to direct Lainey to Carrie's side.

"What are you doing, Roxy?" Lainey asked, baffled. "Why aren't you in jail?"

Roxy laughed, one of those sarcastic laughs having nothing to do with humor. "It pays to know people." She jerked the gun toward Carrie when the woman moved slightly. "I said don't move, bitch, or I'll blow your lying head off."

Lainey reached deep into her interviewing bag of tricks for something to calm Roxy down. The rage in Jerry's wife was unmistakable, not to mention the gun in her hand, which was terrifying.

"Can't we talk about whatever it is that's got you so upset?"

Roxy turned sharply, swinging the gun toward Lainey. "Don't try your psychobabble on me. I wasn't born yesterday." She nailed Carrie with a look that was almost venomous. "This bitch ruined everything for me."

"I know you're upset because Jerry's dead." Lainey tried again to diffuse her. "But Carrie had nothing to do with that. Someone with access to his pills put the cyanide on them." She clamped her lips shut before mentioning that someone was probably Roxy. "Maybe someone at the pharmacy screwed up," she suggested.

Okay, that was a stretch, but Lainey's cache of investigative maneuvers was just as empty as her interviewing one. She had to find a way to calm this mad woman down before her shaking fingers pulled the trigger and someone got hurt or worse.

"She killed him," Roxy screamed, raising the gun level with Carrie's head. "The bitch killed your sister, too. Did you know that?"

Lainey's mouth flew open before she realized how absurd that was.

"I already told you I had nothing to do with either murder," Carrie said, her voice catching slightly. "Tessa was my best friend, and Jerry was my bread and butter."

"Shut up!"

Carrie's body jerked back, her face unable to hide the fear.

Lainey had to do something to keep Roxy talking. "Why would you think that? Carrie had nothing to gain."

"I haven't figured that part out yet. All I know is those hours alone in the police interrogation room got me thinking. Who else had access to Tessa's computer and credit card? I know I didn't order the cyanide. For a while I believed it might be Jerry."

"It was Jerry," Carrie said, a hint of hope returning to her voice. "He was working a deal that would have put several million dollars in his bank account, and Tessa got in the way."

"Right." Roxy huffed. "And I suppose Jerry poisoned himself for the same reason?" She forced a laugh. "How stupid do you think I am?"

"Everybody in this room knows you're not stupid, Roxy," Lainey said, "But think about it. Carrie didn't have access to Jerry's pills."

Roxy's face hardened. "That's where you're wrong. Jerry didn't want anyone to know he couldn't get it up. She usually picked up his prescription." Roxy used the gun to point to Carrie. "I know she killed him."

Just then Lainey's cell phone rang, startling Roxy. In that split second, Lainey lunged for her and knocked the gun out of her hand, sending it skittering across the floor. As she fought with Roxy, the gun went off and Roxy's body went limp in her arms.

Sliding her to the floor, Lainey bent down to check her pulse.

"Get up, Lainey."

Lainey whirled around to see Carrie standing over her holding the gun.

"We need to call an ambulance fast. She has a pulse but she's barely breathing." Lainey stood and reached for the phone on Jerry's desk.

Carrie stepped in front of her, blocking the way, hatred in her eyes. "I said let her die."

"Carrie," Lainey started. "You don't want to do this. I know you're pissed because she accused you, but let Colt handle it." Lainey glanced down at Roxy, noticing the stream of blood now flowing from the right side of her head. "We have to hurry, or it will be too late."

Carrie laughed out loud. "Tessa always said you were the smart one. I'd say she grossly overrated you."

Confused, Lainey made a second attempt to reach for the phone. This time Carrie smacked the back of her hand with the butt of the gun. The sharp pain made Lainey scream.

"You don't get it, do you? You're as dumb as your slutty sister."

I came back as soon as I figured out Carrie had something to do with my murder. I hope I'm not too late to prevent yours.

TWENTY-SIX

Lainey's head snapped back when she heard her sister's voice. Tessa was standing near Carrie, glaring at the woman she thought had been her best friend.

Ask her why she killed me.

Unsure that was the right strategy to get out of this room alive, Lainey's eyes narrowed. "Are you sure you want me to do that?"

"Who are you talking to?" Carrie took a step closer. "Give me your cell phone."

Lainey reached into her jacket pocket and handed the phone to Carrie.

Tell her I'm here, Tessa instructed.

"She won't believe me."

"God damn it, Lainey, quit talking." Carrie's eyes had changed from half-crazed to totally deranged.

"Tessa wants to know why you killed her?" Lainey held her breath, expecting to hear the gun go off, waiting to fall to the floor beside Roxy's now-dead body.

"Ha! Good try, Lainey. I happen to know you haven't spoken to Tessa in years."

"She's right beside me," Lainey said, trying to remember the words of the Act of Contrition.

Dammit! Why had she drifted so far away from her childhood religion?

"Another good one. You're stalling, and it's pissing me off."

"I know you plan to kill me, too, but at least tell me why you killed my sister."

"Tessa was a whore, just like you. If I hadn't screwed up, you'd be dead, too."

"You were the one who set off the explosion?" Lainey asked, incredulous.

Jesus! She's wacko. We gotta get you out of here.

Carrie's smile was evil. "Roxy said you spent the night with Colt, then jumped right into the arms of another man. You're just like your sister, always trying to steal what isn't yours."

Lainey scrunched her face, confused. "What are you talking about?"

"I know you had your eye on David."

"What? The only time I've seen that man was at my sister's funeral."

"Quit lying. David tells me everything."

Lainey took a step toward Carrie. "I swear I had no contact with him," she argued, but Carrie wasn't listening. She watched in horror as the woman threw back her head and laughed, an evil, spine-chilling sound that left no doubt she was mentally unstable.

"The night Tessa died, I snuck in and put the poison in the wine while she showered. Then I stayed on the patio to watch her suffer. It was sweet revenge." The smile faded and her face grew hardened with rage. "It wasn't enough your sister stole Colt from me and totally humiliated me. She had to go after David, too. Both of you are conniving whores." Carrie shook her head. "I couldn't let her do that to me again."

Lainey glanced to her left. "Did you make a play for David?"

Not no, but hell no. I have no idea why she would think that.

"Tessa says she never had a thing going with David."

"You are a Looney Tune if you expect me to buy into the talking to Tessa thing." Carrie paused, moving toward Lainey. "David admitted she called him one night when I was out of town, and they met for dinner. He said Tessa confessed she'd never stopped loving him and wanted to pick up where they'd left off a long time ago."

That's a goddamn lie!

"Tessa says that isn't true."

"Yeah, well, I know for a fact she met him on several occasions. I started getting suspicious after I couldn't reach him whenever I was out of town. When I confronted him with a receipt from the downtown Sheraton, he came clean about Tessa. He said he wasn't sure how he felt about her and needed time by himself to think."

"Is that why you killed her?"

Carrie's face flamed. "How would you feel if you discovered your best friend had screwed you over not once but twice?" She stopped to swipe at her tears. "I followed him one night when he thought I was on a business trip. My heart broke when I saw him and your sister at an intimate bar laughing like they were lovers."

"Tessa?" Lainey waited for an explanation.

It's true. I did meet him for drinks one night, and dinner another time.

Lainey tried to hide her disgusted look, but Tessa noticed.

It isn't what you think. I found out Jerry was talking to a real estate company from New Jersey behind my back about selling the vineyard to a bunch of foreigners. My source said the new company was planning on ripping up all my vines and replacing them with tall buildings and concrete. I couldn't let that happen, so I called David to see if he'd help me prevent it.

"Why David?" Lainey asked.

He'd worked so hard to have Spirits of Texas proclaimed a historical landmark, I thought he'd be as upset as I was when I told him what they planned to do with it.

"Was he?"

Tessa nodded. *He said he would put an end to that nonsense immediately. I trusted him.*

Lainey took a deep breath before repeating her sister's words. "Tessa only met with David to ask for his help when she found out Jerry was wheeling and dealing behind her back to sell the vineyard."

Lainey watched Carrie's face as she absorbed this information. "A likely excuse. That doesn't explain why she slept with him."

After turning to see Tessa shaking her head, Lainey said. "There was no sex."

"You must really take me for an idiot, Lainey. Anyone who knew your sister was aware of the way she used sex as a weapon, as a bribe. Hell, as everything. She was hell-bent on getting what she wanted even if it meant destroying me in the process. I—"

"Tessa swears it never happened."

Carrie turned her head for a moment then met Lainey's eyes in a cold stare. "Seriously, do you think I'm buying any of your bullshit? Come on, who believes in ghosts anyway?"

Tell her you know about the time her dad raped her so violently she couldn't go to school for several days. Remind her how I played hooky with her, and we both got in trouble. Spent three weeks in detention.

"I didn't know your father abused you, Carrie. That must still be painful to think about."

"Nobody knows about that," Carrie shouted, waving the gun at Lainey. "Nobody but Tessa." Suddenly, her eyes darted around the room as if the realization Lainey might be telling the truth finally hit home. "Tell me how you knew about my dad, and I might let you live."

Lainey stared at the gun, praying she could keep Carrie talking. "Tessa appeared to me at the funeral home and has been showing up ever since."

"Are you saying she's here now?" Carrie made another scan of the room. "Not that I believe any of this," she added, the crack in her voice saying otherwise.

"She's right beside me, saddened that you turned on her." Lainey didn't know why, but it was working. Carrie had calmed down somewhat, although she was still pointing the gun.

"Me turn on her?" Carrie's voice escalated as her face turned the color of her bright red lips. "I told you that bitch was about to humiliate me a second time. You know that old saying—trick me once, shame on you. Trick me twice, shame on me."

Ask her about Jerry.

"Why'd you kill Jerry?"

"That ass! Somehow he figured out I was the one who ordered the cyanide. He threatened to go to the police unless I talked David into working a deal with him and splitting the money from the real estate guy."

"David? What does he have to do with this?"

"Absolutely nothing."

All three turned toward the door as David Rivera walked through.

"What's going on here, Carrie?" he asked as he stepped over Roxy's body.

"Thank God, you're here," Lainey said, letting out a sigh of relief. "Maybe you can talk some sense into her."

Colt turned down Main Street to pick up something quick from Taco Grande. If he couldn't have a good juicy steak, Mexican food was the next best thing.

Waiting in the drive-through lane for his order, his mind returned to Phil Romano and his last words. Why would Phil talk about a river? It made no sense.

Before he'd left the office, Colt had taken a second look at all the employee's phone records hoping to find something he may have missed. He'd even pulled the records for the police station and scanned the hundreds of calls that had come in that week.

Still nothing except several calls from City Hall over those seven days. Probably the DA trying to rush them on a case. But other than the unsolved murders, they weren't working on anything for the prosecutors. So why all the calls from City Hall?

Colt paid for the burritos and headed home, resigned to the fact no one would be there to greet him except the dogs. When he passed Spirits of Texas he noticed four cars out front and wondered what was going on so late. He recognized Jerry's car and Tessa's old Jaguar, and a city-issued vehicle. The fourth was probably Lainey's new rental car.

Roxy must have driven straight to the winery when they'd released her earlier, Colt thought. He'd known there was no real evidence to hold her, but he'd wanted to find out what she'd say after the lawyer arrived.

Talk about a sleaze bag! The man looked like he'd stepped right out of an Al Capone movie. The way he undressed Roxy with his eyes had even made Colt uncomfortable. But he had to give it to the guy. He had her out of there in under three hours.

The city car most likely belonged to David Rivera, probably picking up Carrie for dinner. He was reminded once again of his own solo dinner in the bag next to him.

At the corner of Main and Highway 114, a huge light bulb exploded in his head as sudden awareness stopped him cold. He slammed on the brakes, pissing off the guy behind him who laid on his horn after nearly rear-ending Colt's car.

"Shit," he said aloud as he connected the calls from city hall and Phil's last words.

He jerked the car across the lane and headed back in the other direction, his siren blaring.

He'd always known it was probably so obvious it would bite him in the ass.

As he pulled into the parking lot, he called for backup.

"Carrie, give me the gun." David demanded, inching toward her. "You don't want to hurt anyone else."

I have a bad feeling about this, Tessa said.

"She knows I killed Tessa and Jerry," the distraught woman replied, turning back to Lainey. "I can't let her tell Colt. It will ruin all our plans."

"She won't, will you, honey?" He smiled at Lainey. "Not after our long talk last night."

Lainey watched in horror as tears streamed down Carrie's face. Why was David pretending he had an intimate relationship with her? Carrie was already beyond a basket case. This wasn't the way to calm her down.

"Give me the gun, Carrie, then we can go home and Daddy will love you the way you want to be loved. She doesn't mean anything to me anymore."

Oh, Christ! This is big trouble.

"No!" Carrie screamed. "She'll try to take you away from me again."

He was almost next to her now. "She won't, Carrie. I'm only in love with you."

Carrie was sobbing now, her shoulders heaving as she stared into David's eyes, pleading. It was pathetic watching her beg for any scrap of love he'd give her.

David closed the gap between them and took her into his arms. Both Lainey and Tessa breathed a sigh of relief.

Then the gun went off and Carrie's eyes widened in surprise before she went limp.

Oh my God, Lainey. He's the one, Tessa screamed. *David's the killer. You gotta get away from him now.*

David lowered his fiancée's body to the floor then turned to Lainey, his face void of all emotion. "Now that was one stupid bitch."

He moved closer and Lainey's entire body tensed and she closed her eyes, waiting for the next bullet. When she felt his breath on her cheek, she opened them.

David had stopped directly in front of her, sliding the gun from the top of her chest to her cleavage. "Too bad I don't have time to show you the right way to get fucked. You'd find out in a hurry Winslow is merely a novice in that department."

"David," Lainey started.

"Shh." He ran the gun over her lips. "When will you women realize you should be seen and not heard? Let me enjoy the moment."

Lainey, you have to get out of there. He's gone over the edge.

Lainey's heart was racing, her mind in overdrive searching for a way to distract him. She forced a smile as she reached with her good arm and slowly began to unbutton her blouse.

"I like the way you think," she said, trying to sound seductive while controlling her shaking hands.

He met her gaze and smiled. "You are just like your sister." With one hand on the edge of her blouse, he yanked, sending the buttons across the room, exposing her breasts brimming over the top of Kate's one size too small lacy black bra.

"You even dress the part." David rubbed one hand over the swell of her breast. The distinct wail of an approaching siren caused him to flinch, and he turned to look out the window.

In that moment, Lainey brought her knee up hard between his legs, doubling him over. It gave her just enough time to sprint from Jerry's office to the front door.

Her panic mounted when she realized David had dead-bolted the door when he arrived. She switched directions and headed for Tessa's tiny apartment in the back, knocking over a flower arrangement in the front office when she rushed by.

She heard him swear and knew he was close behind. Racing for the vineyard, she quickly unlocked the back door. When a final glance behind revealed David coming into the room, his face a portrait of homicidal rage, she screamed.

The bullet barely missed her head as she ran into the vineyard, lit only by the faint glow of the mercury lights placed about every twenty rows. She prayed it was dark enough to protect her until help arrived, if help was really on the way.

Crouched behind a row of vines, Lainey concentrated on slowing her breathing so David wouldn't be able to pinpoint her location.

A terrifying thought smacked her in the face, and she bit her lip to keep from crying out.

David Rivera was going to kill her unless she outsmarted him.

This way. Tessa appeared again, pointing. *You can circle back to the front. When he comes looking for you, dart into the house and out the front door.*

Lainey hesitated.

Hurry! Tessa commanded. *He's fucking crazy.*

Lainey followed her sister's ghost and they snaked their way toward the front. The overwhelming feeling she was walking right into David's trap wouldn't leave her.

"Lainey," he called. "Come on out so we can talk about this like two reasonable people."

Like we're believing this asshole is reasonable!

"Come on, Lainey," he coaxed. "We'll tell Colt I had to shoot Carrie before she killed you. We can split the three million when we make the deal." He paused. "Think what you could do with that kind of money. Hell, you could buy your very own television station."

Cover your mouth. You're breathing too loud, Tessa cautioned.

Lainey clamped her hand over her mouth as Tessa said and concentrated on breathing out of her nose. When she did, her eyes widened in terror. She was breathing more than air.

God damn him! He set my vineyard on fire.

———

Colt jumped from the car, debating whether to wait on backup. The distinct sound of a gunshot made the decision for him, and he bolted toward the front door.

Lainey's in there, he thought, praying he wasn't too late. Drawing his weapon, he pushed the door, but it was locked. He raised his leg and kicked as hard as he could, but the door wouldn't budge. Running to the window outside Jerry's office, he paused for a second to look in. When he saw two people lying on the floor, his heart sank.

Shattering the window with the butt of his gun, he kicked the glass in with his boot. Fortunately, the window was low enough for him to climb through.

"Shit!" His hand shot up to his face as a shard of glass pierced his cheek. His fingers were already sticky with blood when he pulled his hand away, but he couldn't waste time to see how bad it was.

He said a quick thank you to the powers above when he realized the two bodies on the floor were Roxy and Carrie. One glance told him there was nothing he could do for either of them.

He called Lainey's name, searching the office. When he walked into Tessa's apartment, the first thing he noticed was the blast of cold air coming from the wide-open back door. Halfway there he smelled the unmistakable odor of burning leaves.

When he saw the vineyard, his hopes spiraled downward. The entire front half was in flames. With the swirling wind and dried leaves, it wouldn't take long for the fire to consume the rest of it.

Just as he covered his mouth to keep out the noxious smoke, he saw David Rivera step out from a row of vines about thirty feet in front of him, a gun in his hand.

Colt raised his own weapon and shouted. "Drop the gun, David."

David coughed as the smoke circled around him. "I can't find Lainey."

A sudden lump formed in Colt's throat, and he swallowed hard. "Where is she?"

"She killed Carrie and Roxy. Did you know that?" David choked out as he raised the gun.

Colt fired a warning shot at his feet. "I don't want to hurt you, David. Drop the gun and we'll talk. Right now, I need to find Lainey."

David threw back his head and laughed. "You never give up, do you, Winslow? You couldn't have Tessa, so now you're hot after her sister."

"Lainey," Colt shouted again, ignoring David. He pulled the front of his shirt over his nose and mouth as the black smoke increased. His collar was already soaked in blood from the gash on his cheek.

"I'm here."

Both Colt and Rivera turned as Lainey stumbled out of the thick smoke, coughing uncontrollably before she bent over and gagged. When David pointed the gun at her, Colt shot him in the back, not caring that he fell right into the burning vines.

He rushed to Lainey's side, pulling her close to his body to protect her from the shooting flames. When she winced, he repositioned his arms away from her shoulder and led her toward the building just as Flanagan and Rogers burst through the back door.

"The fire department's on the way," Flanagan said. "They're sending an ambulance, but it's too late for the two inside. How bad is Lainey hurt?"

"She's got a lot of smoke in her lungs. I hope to hell they hurry." Colt released her long enough to take his jacket off and drape it over her shoulders.

When the emergency vehicles arrived, the paramedics insisted Lainey lie down on the stretcher in the truck while they administered oxygen.

Noticing the cut on Colt's cheek, one of the paramedics tried to talk him into letting him take a look at it, but Colt refused. There was no way he was leaving Lainey's side.

He'd even delegated Flanagan as the lead in the investigation. He'd never done that before, not in his six-year career, but he had to make sure Lainey was no longer in danger. His track record for keeping her safe pretty much sucked so far, and he vowed to make sure that changed.

As he pushed back a stray lock of her hair stuck in the oxygen mask, he knew he was in love for the first time in his life. It didn't matter that Lainey might already be in love with another man or that she would most likely be out of his life soon. Admitting that he loved her was a huge step for him. He never thought there'd be room in his heart for anyone but Gracie.

When he glanced down at Lainey, she tried to smile to reassure him, but the mask covered most of her face.

It was in that moment he made a promise to himself.

No matter what it took, he would find a way to make this woman stay in Vineyard.

TWENTY-SEVEN

LAINEY GLANCED AT HER family sitting around the table, and her heart melted. She'd missed this all those years because of a stupid rift between her and Tessa. She wondered how her sisters would react when she told them she wasn't going back to Savannah, wondered if Colt would care.

"Want me to top that off?"

She glanced up at Colt standing beside her holding the coffee pot. Since last night, he'd hovered over her like a rescue helicopter, waiting to swoop down and whisk her away from some unknown danger.

"Yes or no?" He pointed to the coffee pot when she glanced up.

She shook her head. "No thanks. After Deena's lasagna and Maddy's chocolate cake, I'm ready to pop."

"You can't kid a kidder, Lainey. I know how you like to eat. You're dying for another piece of cake," Colt teased.

"Holy crap! This guy's got your number already," Kate said with a chuckle. "Live a little, sis. You had one helluva scare last night."

Lainey pursed her lips then held out her dessert plate. "Just a sliver, Maddy."

"If you bring her just a sliver, she'll slit your throat," Colt said, causing more chuckles around the table.

When the light moment ended, all sat in silence. They hadn't really discussed what happened last night. Since Colt got back from the station a few hours ago, perhaps it seemed like if they ignored it, it hadn't really happened.

"Did they ever find David's body?" Deena asked, finally breaking the ice.

Colt sat down and sipped his coffee. "Yeah. It wasn't a pretty sight."

"What happened to David, Colt?" Kate asked. "Everyone thought he was headed for the mayor's office."

"I know." Colt's voice held a hint of regret. "I guess all that money was too hard to resist. I never realized how much David hated Tessa and me until Lainey told me what Carrie said."

"You never told us any of this, Lainey. What'd she say?"

Lainey shivered remembering how manipulative David had been, remembering the way he'd trailed the gun down her chest. "David knew Carrie had been jealous of Tessa all her life. He used that to make her think they were having an affair."

"Is that why she killed Tessa?"

"Yes, but I still can't figure out why he wanted her dead after all these years," Colt said. "It doesn't make sense for him to risk everything for revenge."

"It wasn't revenge," Lainey said.

Colt turned to her. "Did he tell you that?"

She blew out a breath. "Tessa went to him about a month before she was killed. Jerry was going behind her back to sell the winery to some real estate company out of New Jersey. They were trying to broker the deal for some foreign investors who planned to turn it into a concrete jungle of some kind. She thought David would align with her to stop him."

"How do you know that?" Colt asked. "Did Prescott talk to you about it?"

"What did Tessa's lawyer have to do with it?" Lainey asked, confused.

"When I pulled him into the office and questioned him about his connection to Jerry, he confessed he was also looking to score the finder's fee if Jerry sold."

That double-dealing piece of shit!

Lainey didn't even flinch when she glanced sideways to find Tessa standing behind Kate's chair.

"Now I get it," Colt said. "The last thing David wanted was for someone to put the skids on the deal. Knowing how forceful Tessa could be, he tricked Carrie into thinking he was still in love with her. Then when you inherited Tessa's share, he pretended you and he had a thing." He shook his head.

Jackass! I feel so stupid for going to him.

"Hello, Tessa," Lainey said, finally acknowledging her. "I knew this family was missing something. Now, it's complete."

Lainey watched as Tessa's eyes opened wide in surprise before filling with tears.

"What are you talking about, Lainey?" Colt demanded. "You didn't hit your head last night, did you?"

Maddy laughed. "Brace yourself, Colt. We have something to tell you."

Lainey grabbed his hands. "Before you start thinking I'm seeing ghosts, let me put your mind at ease." She giggled. "I am seeing ghosts."

He jumped from his chair. "That's not funny, Lainey."

Au, contraire! My sister's finally developed a sense of humor. She gave Lainey a thumbs up. *Good one.*

"Tessa's spirit showed up at the funeral home," Deena explained. "Only Lainey can see her."

Colt's eyes moved from sister to sister, clearly searching for a sane one in the bunch.

"How do you think we knew stuff about the night she was murdered before you even got lab results?" Kate asked. "I didn't believe it myself, at first."

"She led me away from David last night." Lainey turned to Tessa. "I owe you my life."

I'll be glad to trade with you anytime, Tessa deadpanned before she got serious again. *Guess you could say that was payback.*

Lainey nodded, her eyes brimming with tears.

"You don't have to do this to prove how much you loved your sister." The concern in Colt's eyes was apparent.

"She asked us to find her killer. That's why I couldn't quit, even when I made you so angry you threatened to throw me in jail." Lainey playfully bopped him on the head.

"I can't believe you threatened my sister with jail, Colton Winslow!" Maddy exclaimed.

Colt smiled. "I did, and I would have followed through if that's what it took to save her pretty ass."

There's that pretty ass thing again.

"Let's talk about something else," Colt suggested. "All this ghost stuff is freaking me out."

Ask him about the real reason he stayed in Vineyard after his dad was killed.

Lainey tilted his chin toward her. "Tessa wants you to tell me why you never went back to A & M after your dad died."

He stared at her for a moment then jerked his head out of her hand. "Everyone knows it's because my mom fell and broke her hip."

Not everyone knows she fell because she was groggy from an overdose of sleeping pills. Or that you called your friend, Phil Romano, who was a rookie officer at the time, to cover it up so no one would find out how depressed she was.

The tears slid down Lainey's cheeks. Even though Colt might believe her if she repeated what Tessa had said, she couldn't bring herself to do it. The pain on his face at just the mention of that awful time in his life was hard enough to witness.

"You know, don't you?" he said, almost inaudibly.

Lainey nodded.

"If you're really talking to your dead sister, ask her about the e-mail she sent me a few weeks ago."

"I don't need to ask. I already know."

He choked back a sob.

Tell him, Lainey. I can't bear to see him in that much pain.

Lainey turned to her sisters. "Dinner was great, and I love you guys, but now I need time alone with Colt."

The love shining back at Lainey from all three of them gave her the courage to do what had to be done. After they gathered their dishes and Maddy lifted her sleeping daughter out of Gracie's bed, they left.

For several minutes, Colt stared at the table, his face unreadable.

Lainey walked behind him and put her hand on his shoulders. "I have to tell you something about Gracie."

He twisted around to face her. "I already know I'm not her father, if that's what you mean."

"There's more."

As Lainey repeated Tessa's story, she watched Colt swallowing in rapid succession to keep from breaking down. She wanted to stop, to put her arms around him, to reassure him everything would be all right, but she couldn't.

When she finished, he sniffed, then put his head in his hands. "She really isn't mine?"

When Lainey shook her head, he continued. "I'd held out the hope this was only Tessa's way of getting back at me for not agreeing to joint custody." He forced a laugh. "So, I'm the only guy in town who never slept with your sister?"

At another time, this would be funny, but she had to keep going to make him understand. "You were the only real friend Tessa had when she found herself in trouble. She knew the best thing she could ever do for her unborn child was to make you a part of its life." She massaged his shoulders. "You were the only person she trusted."

"Stop," he commanded. "I don't want to hear any more of her bullshit reasons."

Lainey couldn't watch him hurt like this. "You're the only solid thing in Gracie's life. You are her father and always have been. As angry as you are right now at my sister, think about it this way. She gave you the most precious thing in your life. She gave you Gracie, knowing you were far better at parenting than she could ever hope to be."

"God damn it, Tessa, I don't need you to tell me I'm not Gracie's dad. I know I am. I learned a long time ago that sperm doesn't make you a father, but dammit, I trusted you."

Tessa hung her head. *I know.* Then she looked back up. *I would do it again in a heartbeat.*

"She said—"

"I heard her." Colt shook his heard. "Honest to God, I heard her, but I can't see her."

Lainey turned to her sister when she noticed her walking toward the door. "I love you, Tessa," she called out.

Tessa turned, the smile breaking through her tears. *Me too, little sister.*

For a while, neither Lainey or Colt spoke. A lot had happened in the past week. A lot had happened tonight, and it would take a lot more time for it to sink in.

Lainey stood and walked to the sink to start the dishwasher, suddenly exhausted.

"Lainey?"

She whirled around to face Colt who had come up behind her. Without a word, he kissed her—not the I-want-to-rip-your-clothes-off kind of kiss, but a gentle sensuous one that carried no less of a punch.

When he pulled his lips from hers, he held her at arm's length. "I know you're leaving for Georgia soon, but I can't let you go without telling you I've fallen in love with you."

"You what?"

His eyes darkened with dashed hopes. "I don't expect you to do anything with that, but I couldn't let you leave without admitting it."

"You love me?"

He smiled. "Why's that so hard to believe?"

She pulled his face to hers and smothered him with tiny kisses all over. "Colton Winslow, I've been in love with you since I was fifteen. I've been waiting all my life for you to notice."

He cocked one eyebrow. "Seriously?"

She laughed. "There were times I thought if only you could see into my heart, you'd know, even though I knew you could never love me back. I figured I would always be Tessa's little sister to you."

He picked her up and swung her around. "You didn't look like Tessa's little sister in that hot outfit the night you tried to seduce Porter," he teased.

"I did not try to seduce that man," she protested, laughing. "So you noticed me that night?"

He huffed. "Everyone noticed you that night. Your legs looked like they went all the way up to your neck."

He put her back on level ground, the smile fading. "So what now? I'm not sure how a long-distance relationship works."

She giggled. "Good thing you won't have to find out." When he looked dejected, she added. "I'm staying in Vineyard."

If she wasn't sure before, the joy in his eyes told her she had made the right decision. It would take several years for the replanted vines to bear fruit, but she was positive she wanted to be the one to see her sister's dream continue.

"What about Tessa?"

"What about her?" Lainey repeated.

"Will she always show up and talk to you?"

Lainey thought about that. "I'm not sure, but somehow I think her work here is done. She can go off and enjoy eternal peace or whatever."

"Until a Garcia girl gets into trouble again, I'll bet."

Lainey smiled at the thought of her and her sisters having their own guardian angel. Then she laughed. Did she really just think angel?

She and Tessa had come a long way in their relationship, and Lainey no longer thought of her sister as the spawn of the devil, but come on. Angel?

Not in this lifetime!

She looked up and winked. *Goodbye, Tessa.*

THE END

Nicole Bushland

ABOUT THE AUTHOR

Lizbeth Lipperman (Dallas, TX) is the author of the Clueless Cook mystery series (Berkley Prime Crime). She worked as a registered nurse before becoming a writer.